FECKLESS

Tales of
Supernatural,
Paranormal,
and Downright
Presumptuous Ilk

multi-author anthology edited by

ellen c. maze

LRP

ISBN-13: 978-0692229231
ISBN-10: 069222923X
Also in eBook

2020 EDITION
Little Roni Publishers LLC
Clanton AL
www.littleronipublishers.com

Tales of Supernatural, Paranormal, and Downright Presumptuous Ilk

Cover Design: Elizabeth E Little, Hyliian Graphics
Cover art: Licensed ©depositiphotos/liqwer.20.gmail.com
Interior Design: TAM Graphics

PUBLISHED IN THE UNITED STATES OF AMERICA

The Storytellers

▶ Angela Dolbear

▶ Kat Heckenbach

▶ Krisi Keley

▶ Elizabeth E. Little

▶ Stu Loudon

▶ Ellen C. Maze

▶ Kevin R. Maze

▶ Pete Turner

The Stories

Pink-slip..1

Vegas 4

Comeback 11

Victory...20

Delete..36

dtour..50

Gloves..56

Lab-Rat 71

Tzadik 76

Regeneration..89

Shocked 94

Thirst 99

Runaway 107

Friends 114

Quack..127

Canaan 140

88 147

Valéry 154

Bully 171

Excursion...179

Magier 187

Hunk 208

The Feckless Authors 222

Pink-slip

by Elizabeth E. Little

From the desk of James Vaughn
Executive Producer, *Survive-Alive*

Victor Klaw
666 Bitewood Lane
Las Vegas, NV

Dear Mr. Klaw (A.K.A. Wolf-Man),

I regret to inform you that your services on "Survive-Alive" are no longer needed. I've received numerous complaints from your co-workers regarding your once-a-month "mood changes," and while I sympathize with your affliction, mauling and devouring the other actors is simply unacceptable.

The others collectively agree that in addition to Lycanthropy making you a menace with whom to work; it has also given you an unfair advantage on-set in regards to physical strength and, well, "survivability."

In particular, one actor (who prefers to remain anonymous) complained about February 14th of this year regarding your Valentine's Day present of returning the liver you had previously stolen from a M. Hebert. Not only is stealing a man's liver illegal, returning it the following week to his widow is simply wrong.

2

I decided to mail your termination notice rather than deliver it in person because I am fresh out of silver bullets.

Just kidding.

But seriously, the others and I have filed a restraining order against you. "It was a full moon" is not a valid excuse. See you in court.

Yours Truly,

James Vaughn

James Vaughn, Producer

Vegas

By Ellen C. Maze

IT SEEMED LIKE A GOOD IDEA AT THE TIME.

In hindsight, Rafa and I were three sheets to the wind, which may have contributed to our faulty reasoning. See, I thought I was a vampire, so naturally, I asked Rafa to bury me up to the neck in the sand. This way, if I turned out to be cursed for all eternity, I'd be immobile and unable to escape.

So there I was, kneeling in a hole being filled by my friend Rafael Santos, the best salesman in our division, with only my head left poking out like a giant golf ball. Did I feel claustrophobic? Sure. Did the sand in my shorts cause a hellish irritation that I couldn't scratch? Certainly. Was I happy to sacrifice my life if only to assure that I didn't spend my nights sucking the life out of people? Absolutely.

If only the vampire who attacked me had been as considerate.

Ten hours ago, following the conference, Rafa and I took the company car down to the Strip to play. Three hours and four casinos later, we'd won enough money between us to stay through the weekend. I phoned my wife and explained the situation in a way she'd understand (the boss needed us to visit clients the next morning in town). Rafa called his mother and told her the truth (such a good kid). We had the concierge direct us to the wildest party in town and we set our faces to the adventures ahead.

It was midnight when we arrived at the converted warehouse that pulsed with fevered life. I'd never seen so many beautiful people at one time in one place, and Rafa was convinced we'd entered the Twilight Zone. I, too, was suspicious of why we'd been admitted. I mean, Rafa looked okay, but I'm fifty pounds overweight, mostly bald, with a face pock-scarred by a decade of adolescent stress. Why did they pick Rafa and me out of the queue and usher us in like VIPs? Was it our company logo? Everybody likes IKEA, right? Or maybe, the concierge called ahead and got us in, hoping for a big tip.

Either way, before two hours had passed, I'd danced with seven Miss Americas and eight Playboy Bunnies while consuming enough alcohol to cripple Secretariat. By 2 a.m., I'd forgotten I was married and proposed to the baby Calvin Klein model who was busy giving me the biggest hickey ever. It was around then that I had a moment of clarity through the fog of intoxication. Across the room, appearing and disappearing through gyrating dancing bodies, I caught a glimpse of a vampire.

I'm a sane person; I rationalized the situation, but when Calvin's sexy daughter bit my neck and began sucking my blood, I sprang into action.

She was a hundred pounds at most, but strong as an ox. I used every bit of my underused muscle to push her away, wishing, when she didn't let up, that I'd bought Tony Horton's P90-X off the television infomercial last week. When I sensed my head swimming from blood loss, I did the only thing I could—I body-slammed the kid into the nearest wall with every last ounce of my two-hundred and seventy pound 6'4" frame. She popped off me like a bottle cap and I scrambled for the door as fast as I could.

Dancing with a Native American beauty near the exit, Rafa caught my eye as I stumbled past. He grabbed my arm, his eyes widening as he read the panic in my face.

"What's up, 'migo? You're white as a sheet."

I showed him my bite mark and pulled him toward the door. "I got bit, man! Here there be vampires!" My voice had taken on a melodramatic, theatrical tone.

Rafa's response was to beat me to the door, barking in an accent exaggerated by panic. "*El vampiro? Vamos aqui!*"

I recalled enough of my high school Spanish to agree and chase him to the sidewalk outside. Rafa must have been drunker than I was because he didn't go through the normal stages of monster denial. He beat me to the car and slipped into the passenger side. Only when the Lincoln reached the main drag, did he finally find his voice.

"Are you okay? How do you feel?"

I shrugged and slammed the brakes as another car cut me off. It was 2:30 a.m. and the city was wide awake.

I considered my body. I felt good. I felt fine. My throat ached a little, but no more than you'd expect after being bitten by a mythical monster. Maybe I felt fine because I was one of them now. I looked at Rafa. Did he look tasty?

"You might have to kill me. I might be a vampire," I said and turned off the Strip. Rafa ran his hands over his face and huffed.

"No way, man, you can't know for sure," Rafa replied and winced dramatically as if he'd bitten his tongue. The guy was beside himself. He looked at my profile. "How do you know how the vampire-thing works? In every single movie, it works a different way."

He never said, *how do you know it was a real vampire.* This guy was a superstitious son-of-a-gun, but he had a point. Maybe I was immune to the vampire venom, if that's what it was. My whole life, I'd baffled the doctors with my amazing resistance. I'd never had a virus or any hint of systemic illness because of the supernatural might of my white-blood cells. Maybe I was vampire-proof. I didn't want to die if I didn't have to.

"Okay, how can we be sure?" I asked Rafa as I drove further away from the lights of Las Vegas. On either side, the desert spread out like a dark blue blanket and I had an idea. I shared it with my friend and we put the plan into motion.

By the time we'd headed back for shovels and bottled water, and returned to the desert, it was nearly 3:30 a.m. I parked the car by the side of the road and we started walking.

"We'll walk an hour, dig a hole, bury me up to the neck, and wait for the sunrise. If I'm still a man, you get me out of there and we'll go home. If I'm a vampire, well, then, it's *sayonara, amigo.*"

He gave me a half-hearted smile, and stuck his finger in his mouth, feeling his tongue. I didn't mention it since it was my fault he bit it in the first place.

We walked without speaking, both of us sobering quickly. I walked a straight line; maybe the vampire's curse had already cleaned my blood. Maybe I'd want to bite Rafa on the neck soon.

I looked over at him, both of us carrying newly-purchased shovels from the all-night hardware store. He was a handsome fella, tall and strong, with a thick neck. What would it be like to bite him there?

Frowning Rafa caught my eye and showed me the business end of his shovel. "You better stop looking at me that way or I'll bash in your *cabeza* just to be sure."

I laughed because he was right; it wasn't polite to ponder killing your friend.

"I'm drunk. Sorry, dude," I offered and was quiet until we reached a place to start digging. Forty-five minutes later, I folded myself into the hole and helped Rafa bring the sand back around me. When it was half-full, he insisted I sit on my hands and allow him to fill in the rest; his reasoning being that I'd be less likely to get free if my hands were pinned by my body as well as two hundred pounds of packed sand. About 5:15, I was buried and Rafa gave me a sip of water.

"I hope you're not a vampire, *'migo.* That would suck."

I laughed at his joke, still in a pretty good mood. If it turned out that I wasn't a vampire, we were going to have a great story for the guys back at the office on Monday.

"What happens in Vegas, stays in Vegas," I said as a cool breeze whipped between us. Rafa sat cross-legged facing me, his expression grim.

"What happens in Vegas can kill you," he said, not at all happy at the admission. "So how'd it happen, man?" he asked, taking a swig from his own bottle, still guarding his injured tongue.

"This chick bit my neck and started sucking my blood. It was crazy. I got out of there as fast I could."

"She just bit you, man?"

Rafa didn't seem surprised that there were vampires in Vegas. I nodded my head as well as I could, my chin bumping the cool sand.

"Maybe it takes three bites like in Dracula."

"I hope so," I said, thinking about all of the vampire movies I'd seen in my life.

Melanie loved those *Twilight* movies. If I came home sporting fangs and an appetite for fresh blood, she'd probably put on that slinky negligee and try to seduce me. When was the last time she wore anything from her lingerie drawer? When was the last time she tried to get me in the sack? I'd been working a lot lately, trying to make my quota so the boss wouldn't lay me off. The economy was killing the middle man and I'd been in the middle my entire life. If I'm not a vampire, I'm going to take Melanie out for a steak and romance her as if we were teenagers.

I looked at Rafa's profile and felt the chilly air touch a tear on my cheek. Forgetting my hands were pinned, I tried in vain to wipe my face.

"You cryin,' man?" Rafa asked, turning to look at me in the odd purple light of dawn.

"I hope I'm not a vampire," I sniffled. Melanie and I had no children; my kids couldn't swim. If I died in the Vegas desert, she'd be all alone, and it'd be my fault. I should've flown home like I was supposed to.

Rafa put his hand on my bald spot. "I hope not, too, 'migo. Look, it's almost dawn."

He pointed eastward and by careful planning, that's the way I was facing. The orange glow that lay on the horizon brightened by the moment in an amazing kaleidoscope of majesty. I was waxing poetic, and beginning to think about something greater than myself.

"Rafa, do you believe in God?" I asked him, still watching the show.

"*Absolutamente, mi amigo*. No doubt. He's up there. If you're going to die, He'll catch ya."

I wasn't so sure. I'd grown up in a nice little country church. I'd said prayers to Jesus. Was that enough? I sniffled again and Rafa rubbed my head.

"You're fine. Just believe."

Rafa removed his hand and pulled out his wallet to show me a photograph. It was a mass-produced tiny print portrait of Mary and baby Jesus.

"You might want to apologize for smooching those girls at the party before you go, though. God doesn't go for infidelity, man."

Rafa was right; I was a cad. I closed my eyes and told the Lord I was sorry. I also told Him that I didn't want to die, and that I hoped Melanie was having a good morning back home.

"*Madre de dios*, pray for me," Rafa was mumbling, "forgive me for my behavior at the party tonight. I shouldn't have let my body do my thinking for me, and I'm really sorry about slugging Maria Tina across her pretty *boca*."

"What? You hit a woman? When was this?" I was completely taken aback. Rafa revered women to the extent that we teased him about it back home. When had he punched a woman in the mouth?

"I met her tonight at that party," Rafa whispered as if ashamed to hear the words. His eyes were on the lower sky. "I didn't know it at first, but she was a *prostituta*. I shouldn't have gone into the back room with her. I'm ashamed."

I had stopped watching the horizon and looked to see Rafa's face. The sun broke free of the earth and lit up his profile—the big man was crying. In the back of my mind, I tried to take note if the UV rays bothered my exposed skin, but I also wanted to comfort the friendly bear beside me.

"Look, man, you repented. It's all good now, right? God forgives you. It's going to be okay," I promised as my left cheek reacted pleasantly to the sun's kiss. "You're a good man, you helped me. God will reward you for protecting the world from a killer. There has to be a reward for that—a big one."

"Yeah, I guess so," Rafa agreed, and leaned back on his hands. "Well, there she is. Are you burning up yet?"

My face was warm, but not painful. "So far so good," I replied and glanced his way. Rafa's silhouette was steaming. "What's that?" I asked him and he looked at me sideways.

"Que?"

"That," I pointed with my nose as best I could. A misty, white plume was erupting from his collar. "It looks like smoke."

Rafa looked around and then stood to his feet and turned a circle. I couldn't tell if he saw it or not. He reached around to the back of his neck.

"Yee-ouch!" he yelped and began slapping his head, hopping on one foot. It looked like he was doing an Indian dance, but then smoke began to pour out of his sleeves. *"Estar ardiendo!* I'm on fire! Help!"

Rafa danced a little more, patting his arms and neck, as if it would put out the flames neither of us could see. My mind raced.

"Why did you hit that girl at the party?" I screamed.

"Because she bit my tongue! Ouch, you gotta help me!" He fell to his knees, clawing at the dirt that entombed me.

"She bit your tongue? Man, Rafa! She turned you into a vampire! Run for cover! You're going to burn up!" I was hysterical; all this time and Rafa was the one who should have been buried in the sand.

"No! I don't believe it!" he barked, still whapping the crap out of himself.

Again, I yelled at him to run, but he collapsed, writhing in pain, and screaming at the brightening sky. He flipped and flopped a dozen times as the plumes of gray smoke filled the clearing, smelling like a Hawaiian bar-b-que. Then, *poof!* He turned to ash before my eyes.

Rafa was a vampire. Go figure.

Currently, the sun is up, the scorpions and black birds are starting to think my pink golf ball-head looks like breakfast, and I'm *not* a vampire.

The chances of being rescued are slim, so maybe I'll just take a little nap. I'll send a shout-out to Rafa's God and fall asleep. Maybe I'll wake up, maybe not, but either way, I hope Melanie isn't too lonely. I should've just gone home.

Man, I sure hate Vegas.

Comeback

by Ellen C. Maze,
Based upon an idea by Kevin R. Maze

THE APTLY-NAMED "GREASY SPOON" SAT PRECISELY thirty miles out of town off Interstate 101, forming the heel of an aged and dying Camarillo neighborhood. Offering "down-home" Southern fare to wayward California travelers, the Spoon did good business while making the regulars fat. I sat alone at the long, faux-marble counter and three other patrons filled the booths behind me. The air was thick with the aroma of seared meat, and I ordered up two hamburgers with sweet-potato fries and iced tea.

I'd just been let out of my contract on a new series starring Corey Feldman. Unfortunately for me, it never made it past the pilot stage. I had been cast to play the guy's gay dad—what the hell? A gig was a gig, and a thousand bucks a day was better than the nothing I'd been collecting since *Survive-Alive* killed my character. I loved that show. What happened?

I hit my marks without fail, showed up ten minutes before call, and stayed five minutes after in case of reshoots. I memorized and delivered my lines like the professional actor that I am, and I never once took issue with the director's vision. So why aren't I still cashing checks?

Worse, why is Sterling Hawkins on the screen in my place?

The snot-nosed brown-noser whose name is now on my trailer and whose character is romancing my on-screen woman doesn't have the talent of a flea, much less a TV star. How in the world did this happen?

"If we don't get to the shore before sundown, we're sunk," the dashing blond-haired, blue-eyed Hawkins said on the TV in the corner above me. I rolled my eyes and glanced at the waitress for some support. No use; she was absorbed in the program, obviously a fan. Had she noticed *me*, yet? I continued to stare at the back of her head until she rotated her face enough to meet my eye.

"Wait a minute," she mumbled around cracked lipstick. "Wait one second," she said a little louder. "Are you? Are you?"

I didn't help her; make her work for it, I say.

"You look just like Bob Piney—the guy this new hottie accidentally dropped off a cliff a while back. Is that you?" the waitress asked and ambled closer, genuinely interested. I paused a second and then decided to throw her a bone. Maybe she *was* a fan. *My* fan.

"I'm Phil Meddle," I said, using a decibel or two of my TV voice, "I played Bob Piney on *Survive-Alive.*"

"Oh, my God!" she exclaimed and put both palms to her cheeks. "Kelly! Get over here!"

She gestured violently for the only other waitress in the joint, a younger version of herself, with half her weight and twice the applied cosmetics. I sat up a little straighter and sampled a side-ways grin, the one Bob Piney used with the ladies on the show. By the time Kelly made it over, Opal, the first waitress, had pulled out a slip of paper and pen presumably for me to sign.

"Mr. Piney, I mean, Mr. Meddle, I hate to ask this but…" she said and hesitated. I gave her an understanding nod and reached for the pen. Emboldened by my actions, she looked at Kelly, gathered her nerve, and set the paper down before me, next to my beer. "Please jot down Sterling Hawkins' address. I promise I won't do nothing weird. I just wanna send him a note and tell him how wonderful he is. Can ya do that? Will ya? Huh?"

"Yeah, please?" Kelly offered up standing beside her tubby older twin. I surprised myself with my reaction. Calmly and with very little spittle, I politely refused and pushed the paper away. I may have taken it too far when I tossed Opal's pen over the counter to the floor at her feet, but I still think I handled it well. At any rate, both women got my meaning and moved away. Opal turned up the TV and Kelly disappeared into the kitchen.

"Sterling Hawkins, where have you been all my life?" Opal said under her breath, probably so I'd hear.

Stupid woman. They all adored him. The viewing public loved him so much that I heard the execs at the studio had promised him a *Truman*-like reality show called *Sterling Shines,* where they'd follow him around all day with a camera and show the best of each day in a late-night slot. Presumably, they were already in production. He'd be competing with Leno and Letterman, but it wouldn't surprise me if he did okay. The viewing morons *loved* him. It was crazy.

Above my head, Hawkins delivered another ridiculous line, but unlike me, he wasn't able to pull it off. *Survive-Alive* started out as an experimental marriage of a *Survivor*-type reality show with a *Lost*-like episodic drama. The cast played big business board members who are forced to do a roughing-it reality TV show. Our dialogue was scripted, the stunts performed mostly by able-bodied doubles, and usually, our audience chose to forget we were pretending. When my character slipped off a cliff, people thought I was Bob Piney and that I was actually dead. We were *that good* at acting as if we'd been abandoned in the Mojave Desert with only a spoon, a blanket, and a box of condoms.

Anyway, I'd been top-dog on that show for three seasons. When they started out, they trailed every other similar show by a dozen points.

When they gave my character a boost to tribal leader in the third shoot, suddenly, the ratings zoomed straight up and the little-show-that-could was on the map. I brought in corporate money—real green—that the higher-ups turned into better sets, better writers, and much better production value. By the time *Survive-Alive* had been running two seasons, it was writing its own ticket. *Damn*, I was on fire! Everything was fine and dandy until Vaughn, the executive producer, decided to put newbie Sterling Hawkins in for one of the guys killed off at the end of season two. As soon as that no-talent jerk hit the soundstage, the quality of the entire show began to suffer.

I'm no prima-donna; I took my concerns to the director, his assistant, the writers, and finally to James Vaughn, himself, but no one saw what I did: that Sterling Hawkins was turning our scripted reality show into a side-show farce. His acting was stiff and he refused to emulate me—a known positive commodity—in an effort to improve. Thankfully, we didn't have any scenes together since they wrote his character into a parallel story-line, but when I watched the dailies, I'd fume at his performances.

How did he convince them to push me out? This is what I just can't figure. My agent fed me a load of B.S. when they didn't kiss my feet at re-up. My co-stars stopped taking my phone calls. Even Phoebe, my on-screen paramour, returned the roses I'd sent her with a note that said, "Buzz off." Not understanding what happened is what bothers me the most.

"Stop pining for Bob! He's gone, Isabel, get over it!" Hawkins as CEO Brent Wilson said, shaking my former Phoebe by the upper arms, as the cabin of their boat swayed to the rhythm of crashing waves outside. I looked at the TV. The lines were familiar—hadn't I said those same words to her my last full season when her brother and sister were mauled to death by a bear?

"But I saw you…you…YOU DROPPED HIM OFF THE CLIFF!" Phoebe yelled and tried to turn away from Brent's blazing eyes.

I sneered; the jerk looked good, all his parts were in the right place and in the right order, but his eyes were those of a child. Who'd believe he was the head of a giant multi-billion-dollar corporation? Not me. I sipped my beer and looked at Opal. She wiped down the counter with a brown rag in her right hand, her left hand clutching her lapel as she stared at the TV screen. Oh, geesh, I thought I might throw-up.

I want to kill that guy so bad.

I blinked and set down my beer. That sentiment made sense, but

I'd never consciously *thought* it before. That time, I'd heard it in my ear, as if I'd spoken aloud. But I hadn't; I was just really, really, really sick of Sterling Hawkins.

I could kill him so easily.

There it went again. I ordered another beer and Opal handed one over without looking my way. I knew how to handle a gun, I knew a little karate, I could wield a sword. An actor had many talents, and I am the best actor I know. As I mentally pictured Hawkins lying dead at my feet, the tinkle of bells behind distracted me from my fantasy.

I didn't turn to see who'd entered, and the new guy flanked me at the bar and sat one stool down. Without turning, Opal set the newcomer up with flatware and a menu, her eyes glued to the screen. Brent Wilson had taken Phoebe into his beefy arms and was forcing a kiss on her rigid mouth. Was she repulsed or had Harvey directed her that way? I sipped my new beer and the fellow next to me touched my elbow.

"Phil? Phil Meddle?" a soft, friendly male voice asked. "It's me, Sterling."

Of all the gin joints in all the world... I met his eye, forced a believable grin, and shook his outstretched paw. "Oh? Yeah, right," I said, incredibly smooth, "Hey, Sters, what's up? What are you doing this far north of Stage 15?"

Sterling smiled as big as Texas and pumped my hand too many times. "I've been looking for you, man! Didn't you get my messages? I've been trying to get you on my new show. Where have you been?"

Was he serious? I maintained my grin and nodded. "I was on set with Corey Feldman a while, but I'm free again. What about your new show? Is this the day-in-the-life show I heard about?"

Sterling nodded with enthusiasm. "Yeah, awesome, isn't it?"

"OH-MY-GOD!" Opal woke up at the counter and rushed toward us. I was thankful the Formica top separated us by four feet. "STERLING HAWKINS! RIGHT HERE IN MY PLACE!"

I watched to see how the kid handled the woman, expected a giggle, but nothing fun happened. Sterling took both of her hands in his, leaned forward and pecked her glistening cheek, and whispered in her ear. I wish I knew what he said, because she promptly left the counter and began ushering the other patrons out of the diner. I looked back at them, disgruntled and oblivious to the fact that a pseudo TV star and a washed-up has-been were hamming it up at the counter. Sterling looked over the menu and hummed quietly, as if waiting for

15

the place to empty. When Opal returned to the counter, she took Sterling's order fairly calmly, blushed like a teenager, and disappeared into the kitchen. I looked at him and awaited an explanation.

"Oh, that?" he chuckled.

I despised the friendliness in his tone. Did this guy think we were pals?

"I wanted a little privacy. That's all." Sterling set his menu aside and turned three-quarters to face me. For the first time, I noticed that he was wearing a pin on his jacket with my face on it. Beneath my smiling "Bob Piney" mug were the words, *"What about Bob?"*

One thing I knew for sure, I wasn't being paid for them to plaster my face anywhere they damn well pleased. I gestured toward the pin. "Tell me about that?"

He puffed his chest out a few inches so I could better see my likeness. It wasn't necessary; I looked away.

"You are my muse, Phil. We didn't get to interact much on the set, but I wanted to," he said and held up his hand when he saw me about to disagree. "Oh, my agent and the execs, all those guys, they tried to create this tension between us, for the good of the show, for the good of the finale, but you and me? We can be friends."

I didn't allow my emotions to show, but I wanted to shout to the heavens, *"NO WAY, YOU CRAZY BACK-STABBING JERK, WOULD I EVER BE FRIENDS WITH YOU!"* Cuss word, cuss word, cuss word, inserted for good measure.

But I was quiet.

Sterling inclined his head. "On *Sterling Shines*, I spend the first two weeks looking for you and trying to get you to guest on my show. It's like a comeback campaign I'm starting up, you know, on Facebook and Twitter. To get the fans involved." He pulled an iPhone from his pocket and touched the screen a few times. "You should follow me, look, I tweeted about you this morning."

I didn't own a computer and my Blackberry kept me up on my email. The idea that Sterling Hawkins was concerned about my potential comeback almost rang true, but I caught myself before I fell for his bull. Morbidly curious, I leaned over to read the display. The bubble on the screen read, *"Yo! Dude's harder to find than a chastity belt at Madonna's house! Pozzie up, folks!"*

"Pozzie up?" I asked, and then realized that I just reinforced the guy's impression of my lack of hip.

"*Positive*, pozzie, get it? I want my fans to be glass-half-full-types,

16

you know? Pozzie up. It's my thing. I am going to start some new jargon with this show."

I decided to ignore my other inane questions; I truly wasn't interested in the answers. The smug face looming so close to mine wanted badly to be punched. My fists clenched, but thankfully remained on the counter top.

"So, what do you say? Will you come on the show?" he asked, maintaining his sideways stance, and tapping the fork Opal left him. "What else do you have to do?"

Kill you, maybe?

I smiled and nodded my head the tiniest bit. He'd interpret that to mean I might be interested. It was our lingo, our special actor's code. Then, a brilliant flash wakened my mind. I was two miles from Jones' Lake. I'd once taken a lady to an abandoned cabin on Jones' Lake and it was very secluded. If I could get Wonder Boy, here, down to that cabin, alone, without Opal or Kelly knowing where I went…I could put his lights out. Oh, how I wanted to do that.

My face must have looked different because Sterling turned toward me all the way and set his feet to the ground. "What's up? You get an idea for the show?"

I glanced at the ridiculous Bob Piney button and smiled. "Yeah, Sters, yeah." I stood up and dropped a ten-spot on the counter. "Will you step out to the parking lot with me a second? I want to ask you something in private." I eyed the kitchen and Sterling got my drift.

"Of course, man. Lead the way." And he followed me to the exit.

This is so easy, I thought, and I led him to my beat-up Camaro.

"Okay, Sters, I want to introduce you to some of Corey's people." I held up my hand as if he were about to protest, but he didn't. "I know the guy hasn't been much in the spot light, but he has connections. We all need connections, right?" Sterling nodded, interested enough to be quiet. "Okay, look. Corey's people invited me to a party at his cabin. I'm headed there now. You wanna come? I'll introduce you to his producers. They have some really good ideas, and I think they're casting a movie, and looking for a guy like you."

"You kidding! Of course, I want to come!" Sterling reached into his pants pocket and retrieved his keys.

"Ride with me, man. We can pick up your car after."

Sterling nodded, smiling. "Yeah, my guys will come pick it up for me later. No biggie. So let's go!" he said, fairly cheerful. I slid into the driver's seat and he folded his tall frame in beside me.

The ride to the cabin was mercifully short. Mercifully so, because Sterling did not quit talking the whole way. It was almost as if he were on camera with all the yammering he was doing. I pulled up as far as the overgrown brush would allow and applied the parking brake. Sterling barely stopped describing everything he saw when I got out of the car and opened the hatch.

"Phil, where's the party, man?" Sterling said, climbing out of the low car. He put his hands on the roof and scanned the woods on all sides. "Did you get lost?" he chuckled and finally looked over to see what I was up to. "What'cha got there, Phil? I think you're up to something, you rascal!"

Sterling wasn't alarmed in the least. Maybe I should have noticed that, or maybe I should have cared, but I blithely removed a short-handled spade from the back of the car. I'd stuffed it back there a month ago when a neighbor returned the borrowed tool to me late one afternoon. I'd never put it back in the garage, and look! Now it was in my hands! Wow. How handy.

"Phil, what do you have in mind? You're always looking for new ways to make a better show. What's that for?" Sterling asked, fearless.

He walked around the car and faced me head on, the ridiculous "Bob Piney" button staring me down like a second pair of eyes. I studied the wooden handle long enough to decide where to place my hands for the blow. I lined up his head and the shiny end of the spade and made ready to swing. Sterling laughed.

"Oh! This is good! Yeah!" he said, giggling, and then he held both hands out in surrender as his eyes continued to laugh. "Wait, I need to beg for my life. Hang on—" he said, and dropped to his knees.

Waving his arms about wildly and manifesting a terrified moan, he began to implore me to drop my weapon. I began to think he'd lost his mind. Didn't he know I was about to bash his brains in? Why didn't he take me seriously? Oh, well, not my problem. Taking one last mental measurement from forehead to blade, I exhaled and swung the tool down with all of the gusto I could manage. Every scene I'd never be in, every set I'd never walk on, every director I'd never work with, every costume I'd never wear—they all paraded past me as I took my best shot at the one who stole my life.

Milliseconds before my weapon of choice made contact with his temple, Sterling said the strangest thing.

I wasn't sure, but I thought I heard him say, "Are you getting this, Tim?"

Are you getting this, Tim? Who is he talking to? Too late, my $14.99 Wal-Mart spade slammed into Sterling Hawkin's brow and the guy's body arched away from me and landed hard on its back. I stood over him, shovel in hand, staring down on his blank—now dead—face, and I stared into my face on his button. Bob Piney dressed in his tuxedo, the one he wore to the executive ball on the show about his promotion. An expensive Italian-made suit, complete with cuff links, and a jewel in the authentic bowtie.

A jewel in the neck? Bob Piney would never wear such a thing. What was that?

Are you getting this, Tim?

And what about those dumb last words?

The jewel was large—too large and too stupid to be put on there by costume. Someone put it in post-production. I leaned in, curious now at the sparkle emanating from the diamond-like bump.

Are you getting this, Tim?

Behind me a good fifty yards, the sound of a truck motor approached and switched off. It didn't distract me and I reached out for the Bob Piney button. I was so handsome in that role; they were such fools to replace me with the Wonder Kid.

Are you getting this, Tim?

Who was Tim, anyway?

Once I had the three-inch metal and plastic button in my fingers, I gave it a pull to bring it close. It was wired to Sterling's chest.

"What the—?" I hissed, yanking the thing loose and holding it up to the red glow of my rear lights. Several bodies crashed through the crackling woods on all sides. I turned toward the sound, Bob Piney's face pinched between my finger and thumb, and a man with a microphone burst into the clearing.

"We're still rolling, people!" a disembodied voice called, fast closing in on our position. "Tim dialed 911 already, frame his face, Howie—frame his face!"

Stunned and confused, I looked down at the Piney button again. That jewel—a camera? *Sterling Shines*, already in production? Phil Meddle, guest star of the first installment?

Are you getting this, Tim?

Sterling's last words.

The first five words of my autobiography; the one I'll write from prison.

Some comeback.

Victory

by Ellen C. Maze

BILL'S BEHAVIOR WAS PRETTY LOOPY, BUT TWO HUNDRED milligrams of Ketamine will do that to you. Even if you're a vampire.

It was his way of relaxing, of knocking the edge off his hunger—his disappointment. He and Bill were operating under new self-imposed parameters and tonight was an off-night. They'd have to go without; it was for the best.

Carey watched him set up for the next game, rounding up the multi-colored balls using a combination of the pyramid and telekinesis. It didn't really matter; the guys in the billiard room were plastered. If one of them thought he saw a ball rolling by itself toward his tall black friend, he'd probably think he was hallucinating. Just then, as if to make his point, a loud peal of laughter followed by a crash of furniture boomed to Carey's far right. He gauged the seriousness of the incident, and then shook his head. Mortals were especially interesting when drunk.

Bill stood up, raised his arms high above his head, and cracked his back with a toothy grin. He was feeling fine. Carey couldn't help but smile. The six-foot-six ebony colossus had been his partner for twenty-five years and their personalities were well-matched. Bill laughed and smiled with ease while Carey planned and pondered the crap out of everything. The dichotomy worked.

"Your shot, Tree," Bill cooed, now twisting his spine both directions, pushing one arm behind him with the other. Carey heard his vertebrae crackle like green wood on a campfire.

Bill was the only person in the world that called him "Tree" and the nickname had no real origin. When asked why, Bill gave different answers on different occasions. He called him Tree because, unlike Bill who was tall and slender, Carey was shorter and wide, muscled like an NFL tight end. Or, he called him Tree because when they first met, Bill asked him how old he was and he said "tree-hundred and four" (which was not what he said, but Bill was on Quaaludes back then and had more than a few screws loose). Or perhaps it was because Carey made Bill feel safe and above—like a cat on a high tree branch. *"Putty-tat runs up there when he's scared,"* Bill had said, *"but from that limb, he sees everything and feels powerful."*

Carey chuckled at the memory. Now and then, Bill definitely waxed poetic.

Now focusing on the green field, Carey chose his target—stripes this time—and lined up a shot sure to drop three balls into the cup. He cocked back his elbow and glanced up at his pal, but Bill was looking over his shoulder toward the entrance. No matter. Carey took one last measure with his eye and poked the cue into the white ball. Three thunks and his turn continued.

Bill whistled under his breath. "It's an off night, right? How strict is this new rule of yours?"

Bill was still watching the door. Carey didn't turn, but maneuvered to the left flank for his next shot.

"It's our rule, not my rule. And yes, hands off." Carey spoke with humor as he picked a delicious shot sure to sink at least three more balls.

"Let's start tomorrow night, Tree," Bill said in a monotone, still looking away.

Carey cocked back his stick and took the shot. Milliseconds before the chalked tip met the cue ball, it hopped to the left, the shot ruined. Carey growled and glared at his partner whose eyes were still focused behind him.

"Bill, I'm not playing with you if you mess with my balls," Carey huffed and Bill looked at him finally.

"Oh, that's hilarious. Please, say that again," he laughed and leaned backward onto the edge of the pool table behind him. Two men playing there stopped their game to glare at the intruder. Bill paid them no mind, his smiling eyes deep into Carey's.

Carey absorbed the icy stares of the offended a moment before coming around the table to take Bill's bicep.

"Okay, what are you going on about?" He successfully pulled his friend off the other table and back to their own. Apparently oblivious to the fact that he'd just been rescued from inadvertently initiating a barroom brawl, Bill leaned his palms on their table and flicked his gaze toward the bar. Carey followed his line of sight and then shook his head.

Sitting on a bar stool, facing the room was a thin brunette. She wore a pastel-yellow summer dress, too low up top and too long below. Seconds into his observation, Carey knew more about her than he wanted to know. She was single, twenty-seven, a breast cancer survivor, a Pisces, and a borderline manic-depressive personality. It was his talent as a vampire that told him all that and even though Bill was quite a bit younger, he would have discerned nearly as much.

"Don't make eye contact, Billy," Carey mumbled and made a grab for the cue ball.

"Not her, Tree. Her friend. She just went into the ladies'. Wait for it…" Bill's voice had taken on a soft tone Carey didn't often hear.

"It doesn't matter, Bill," Carey whispered and repositioned the white ball. "We came here because women don't."

"Oh. Oh. There," Bill said, barely audible. Moved by irrepressible curiosity, Carey rose up from the shot and looked back to the bar. Bill was on to something.

"Oh," Carey said softly, his voice mimicking the wonder in his pal's. "I see."

The friend walked toward the brunette, straightened her black knee-length pencil skirt, and poked around in her purse. She had wavy waist-length hair the color of winter wheat. Carey was a sucker for blondes; thought they complimented his own looks. And she was the right height; petite enough to stand at his chin as he was barely six feet tall in dress shoes. Bill didn't favor any type that he knew of, but this woman exuded a non-physical quality that, no doubt, most attracted his friend.

"Okay. Sorry about the pit stop. Let's go. We can still make the party."

Although the women were fifty feet away and whispering, he and Bill heard every word. The brunette covered her mouth and replied even softer.

"Those guys at the pool table are really checking us out. Maybe we can party right here. Can you shoot pool?"

Carey told himself to look away, but he could not. The blonde glanced their way and then shyly averted her eyes. Beside him, Bill's respiration increased.

"Monica, please. Let's just go."

"Don't be such a bore, Anna. The big one is mine."

Out of the corner of his eye, Carey saw Bill make a tiny nod toward the women.

"Set up the balls for a new game, Tree. We got company," Bill said giddily as he watched the brunette approach. Her friend, Anna, hung at the bar, still making up her mind.

"It's still an off-night, Billy. I'm serious," Carey whispered as Monica came within earshot and stood ten feet away, hands on her hips.

"Good evenin,' fellas. Can girls play this game or is it boy's night out?" She spoke with a Virginia accent and Carey pegged her as a miner's daughter who barely escaped the life.

"Two on two?" Bill asked, his voice rumbling with testosterone now that the blood-game was afoot. He glanced behind her and she turned to see her friend still at the bar.

"Yeah, two on two. Set 'em up." Monica stepped into their space and put out a manicured hand toward Bill. "Monica Spills. Nice to meet you."

Bill chuckled at her name and straightened up again. "I'm Bill, this is Tree."

"Monica," Carey said with a nod as he poked the balls into the triangle.

"Your friend comin'?" Bill asked and Monica set her knock-off Coach purse on the wide edge of the table.

"Give her a minute. She's not from around here. Kinda uptight, you know the type." Monica leaned over the table threatening to spill her breasts from her scooped top. Carey sighed and reminded himself of cold showers.

By the time Monica had selected a pool cue, Carey heard soft steps that sounded like a woman of Anna's weight heading reluctantly their way. He kept his eyes down and instead watched her sandaled feet. She had cute toes.

"Hi, I'm Anna."

Her voice was lower than he expected and Carey guessed she was nervous. He subconsciously scanned her circumstances, as he'd done with her friend, but when nothing came up, he recognized the rarity. So, she was hard to read; did that have anything to do with her anxious countenance? Carey considered her heart rate. It was only slightly elevated. Yet the other signs were there; increased perspiration, a tapping foot, and a boost in her breath-rate. What was she afraid of? He and Bill looked like any other couple of dudes letting off steam after a hard day's work. They didn't sparkle, neither of them was particularly attractive, and they always dressed down in worn jeans and out-of-fashion plaid flannels. "Don't attract attention" was Carey's earliest lesson as a hunter living among his prey. The vampire's creed, his maker called it. So why was this visitor from out of town whiffing danger?

Bill clapped his shoulder, introducing himself to the blonde and once again he called Carey, "Tree."

Carey looked up and met Anna's eye, her pulse quickening further. His stomach grumbled. "It's Carey, actually. Nice to meet you, Anna."

Anna touched his outstretched hand briefly, but didn't shake. Something wasn't right. Carey's instincts grew needles and he looked at Bill; it was time to leave. Bill's lips parted as he worked up his response to the sudden frigid air between the blonde and the vampires, but there was movement now from Anna. She backed three steps, rear-ended the next billiard table, and turned away. Monica made a noise of irritation and slammed down her cue.

"Be right back," she hissed and followed her friend across the room. Carey and Bill watched as the blonde made straight for the exit and continued on through, her brown-headed friend cursing loudly behind her.

"Weird," Bill said.

Carey agreed with a grunt. Oh, how he hoped she didn't come back in.

"Let's go after them," Bill mumbled as he laid his pool cue across the table top. "We can start our new plan tomorrow night."

Carey sucked his teeth a few nanoseconds to avoid speaking too harshly. Bill had been with him almost three decades, but hadn't learned the self-control Carey had. When ready, he looked up and met Bill's eye. "She's untouchable. Let it alone."

Bill's mouth opened as he pondered Carey's words.

"You remember the Untouchables, right Billy?" Carey whispered, leaning in to speak in his partner's ear. "Seattle, 1986? The man with the leopard-spotted tie?" Carey waited for Bill to give a sign that he remembered, but his eye was far away. "The guy who almost took your head off with an axe? That guy?" Carey hissed and finally Bill leaned back and met his gaze.

"The *blonde?* An Untouchable? Nah." Bill shook his head, his face a question mark. "You can't know that. What makes you say that? Come on, Tree."

Carey hung his cue on the wall rack and yanked his coat off the chair. "Let's go home."

Bill copied his move and followed him toward the door. "How can you tell? I didn't see anything. Was it her touch? Was it electric or something?" He asked his questions with respect and by the time they reached the deserted parking lot, Carey thought it secluded enough to answer.

"It was a lot of things, but mostly it was experience, Billy." Carey faced his friend and placed his right hand over his middle. "I feel it here. You will too, eventually, if you're willing to learn how."

"Geesh, Tree, I can taste her blood, man. I just don't think you're reading her right." Bill ran his palm over his shaved head. "Look. They're still here. Goodie." He pointed across the lot where two females were having an animated discussion inside a brown Honda.

Carey sighed angrily and took Bill's arm. "Get in the truck."

Bill walked to the Chevy, but when he opened the door, he turned once again to the women a dozen cars away. "They're talking about you. Listen."

"No, Monica! I know what I saw and that blond guy is a cold-blooded killer."

"You are such a drama queen! You're not psychic! You're just cold. Cold and rude and selfish!"

"I don't have to be psychic to know when I'm in danger. I'm sorry, but I am not going back into that bar. Ever!"

"I wish I hadn't brought you along tonight. I'd be better off alone." Monica hit the steering wheel. *"I'm going back in, and I have the keys. Find your own way home, Sandra Dee!"*

As they watched, Monica slammed the driver's side door and stomped off toward the bar. Anna remained in the car a full minute before getting out and leaning back on the hood. She fished out her cell phone and looked around the dark lot. On the second scan, she spotted Carey and Bill on either side of their Tahoe.

"Tree—let's give her a ride. Oh, god, my head's spinning. Look at her. Untouchable or not, let's give her a go."

Bill's voice was pained and Carey understood his discomfort. He felt the same visceral draw for the woman, but it was impossible. Neither of them would ever be able to take her blood. Bill was his best friend, but he was also a naïve fool.

"She'd never take a ride from us, Bill. And you can't coerce an Untouchable," Carey said and watched Anna speak into her phone. She was calling a taxi and her eyes flitted back and forth between them and the bar.

"How do you think she knew you were a killer?" Bill asked, his voice dreamy.

"Untouchables can *see*. That's what makes them different from the rest. If she'd looked at you up close, she'd have seen it in you, too. I'm sorry I haven't taught you all this. I just see them so rarely. I keep wishing they'd die out."

"Is she like a witch or something?"

"Kind of," Carey said quietly. He'd watched her so long by now, he was fully mesmerized. She seemed to move in slow motion, her lips incredibly sensuous as she gave the cabbie her location at half-speed. Her hand came up languidly and brushed back a lazy curl that was blown free by the wind. The world was coming to a halt around them and Carey was defenseless to stop it.

No, he could stop it if he wanted to. But why should he?

He began to feel sleepy and he heard Bill call his name as if from the next county.

"*Tree?*"

Bill was calling him through a tunnel now, the word echoing off the sides.

"*Tree?*"

The Untouchable closed her phone and dropped it into her purse. She was several car-lengths away and she met Carey's eye more boldly now. She smiled very slightly, but her eyes remained round and worried. Did she know he was a vampire or was she too green to discern her intuition?

An explosion of light and pain wracked his head and Carey was shaken awake.

"Carey!" Bill shouted and balled his fist for another swing. Carey caught his hand seconds before it made contact with his temple and he reflexively shoved him to the ground.

"Don't be sore at me, man. You were gone. Gone and gone. Don't ever do that again. You hear?" Bill sat on his rump in the red clay of the lot. He put out his hand and Carey pulled him up.

"Gone? What are you talking about? I'm right here!" Carey replied, forgetting to keep his voice down.

Bill dusted off the seat of his jeans. "You split on me, man. You're body was here, but your mind—" Bill cursed. "I didn't like it. I was *alone*, Tree. Don't do that again. I was *alone*."

Carey inhaled and prepared to berate his friend for his weakness, but Bill's eyes watered; he'd been truly terrified. What exactly happened? Did the Untouchable just try to suck him out of his body? Could they do that? Whatever happened, the towering monster who feared no man, was about to cry and fall into Carey's arms. Carey motioned for the truck.

"Okay. Okay. Get in. Let's go home."

"Tree, I don't want that woman anymore. Let's stay clear of the pool room for a while."

Carey climbed into the cab of the truck. "Agreed, my friend."

"I hope some maniac slips in here and kills her while she waits for that taxi."

"If only we'd be so lucky," Carey agreed, but inside, he was miserable. They were going to run into her again. And again. And again. It was the way of the Untouched. They were tenacious, and in the end, one of them would be dead—either the vampires or the woman.

Carey wasn't ready to die just yet.

◆

"Why do you think Hollywood vampires are all sexified and wimpy?" Bill asked, walking alongside Carey as they exited the movie theatre. Carey smirked.

"Darren said Hollywood is the best thing that ever happened to us. Just think about it. Who in their right mind would believe in vampires? Nobody. Only crazies and religious nuts. When we slip up and leave a drained body somewhere, they never look around and think, 'we've got a vampire on our hands, boys.' Hollywood's done that for us. As for me, I hope they keep it up."

"These vampires are all moody and depressed, not to mention horny. What vampire ever had what it took to have sex—and why would he want to? Have you ever known a vampire that could get it up?" Carey shook his head, still smiling. Bill was agitated and not amused. "It doesn't bother you that we're being misrepresented?"

"What?" Carey glanced at him to see if he was joking. "I don't want to be represented at all. Neither do you, dummy. You eat them—" Carey whispered, pointing to the heads on all sides as the flow of foot-traffic left the building. "You want to be invisible. There are no such things as vampires. Keep telling yourself that, Bill. You'll live longer."

"I guess," Bill mumbled and fell silent. Carey shook his head. Bill was very young and had no idea how he became a vampire. He was asleep when it happened, and he never met his maker. Carey, on the other hand, chose his path, knew exactly what he was getting, and he served under his heartless creator for a full century before being set free.

Just then, a million needles pricked his consciousness as Carey sensed the Untouchable before seeing her. His hair stood on end and a nauseating rumble roiled in his gut. He made an abrupt right turn, away from their truck, forcing Bill to jog up when he noticed the change.

"It's her, isn't it?" Bill looked warily around at the men and women filing toward their vehicles on all sides.

Since the run-in at the pool room, Carey did his best to explain to Bill the dangers of such a woman. Carey met his first Untouchable in the late '50s. He'd been seeking shelter in an abandoned building in the forgotten parts of New York when he was discovered by an elderly man seeking food. The grey-haired gentleman stumbled through the cement edifice that Carey staked as home base, digging through tossed paper bags and flipping over cans. Carey watched him from the shadows, not really hungry, but not sure he wanted to let a free meal pass him by. As he considered an attack on the guy, the man stopped walking, stood up straight, and searched the room with an eagle eye. Carey had never seen such behavior and he remained stock still to see if he'd be discovered. The man scanned the room three times, relaxed his shoulders only a fraction, and reached into his pocket.

"I know you," the old man said, his voice a near-whisper. He was turned forty-five degrees away, and brandished a six-inch knife he'd withdrawn from his pants. "I can't let you live..."

Bill bumped Carey's arm and shook him back to the present. "Tree—is it her?"

"Yeah, she's here somewhere," Carey hissed and ducked into an opening in the garage wall behind the elevators. Bill followed suit and they stood side-by-side in the close space barely breathing.

Do you think she knows what she is? Bill whispered telepathically.

Carey pondered the question. He'd been wondering the same thing and hadn't decided. She didn't seem to know what was happening between them back at the pool room. But then, there was that mysterious smile as she hung up the call.

"You said they don't usually attack in public," Bill stated in an undertone, glancing left to see Carey's reaction.

"Bill, I told you, I've only met three in my whole life. One attacked me alone, one attacked you in a parking lot, and the third we avoided at Smitty's Billiards last week."

Carey leaned out of the cubby and checked the area; no gorgeous blondes within view.

"How do we fight them? The Untouchables? Will our strength and speed be enough?" Bill's voice wavered and Carey wished he'd shut up. His friend's fear did nothing for his own anxiety.

I killed the first one with my bare hands, Carey whispered telepathically, still sniffing for the woman. *I killed yours with his own axe. This one...it's tricky. She has something the other's didn't... I can't put my finger on it.*

"Do you see her?" Bill said softly.

"Shut up!" Carey hissed and put a hand to Bill's mouth without looking at him. The roiling in his gut had passed and his headache eased. The woman was gone; it was a near miss. Carey sighed and left the cement nook, and Bill followed without another word.

Emergency averted, for now.

♦

Bill begged off Carey's latest trip to the cemetery, but he didn't mind. Once a month, he liked to change the flowers on Yoni's grave as a way to honor her memory. Bill had never met her and usually picked that night to sleep in or watch TV, so Carey walked alone to the graveside across the dark rows of headstones. Once he reached Yoni's grave, he put the roses into her vase and stooped down. She'd died centuries ago, when he was a very young new creature. Whenever his travels brought him to the area, he'd honor her grave. It was therapeutic, more than anything. Yoni had been mortal and he'd never tasted her blood. If he had, her memory would be much less lofty. Happiness was *not* murdering your best girl and letting her die at a healthy old age. Carey blew her a kiss as he turned from the grave.

Trudging back toward the car, Carey glanced at odd tombstones along the way, wondering at their occupants' lives, and their deaths. Half-way to the car, he caught a whiff of perfume; a soft, subtle aroma that at first smelled of flowers, but then more like fruit. It was remarkably similar to the blonde Untouchable's scent. Then he heard a whimper.

To his right a dozen yards, a figure moved low to the ground, and as he watched, it sat up and tried to stand. Carey took a step toward it, his instinct being to pick off a straggler that had wandered too far from the protection of the herd. It wobbled, leaned on a nearby concrete bench, and then fell to the grass, still.

Carey checked the area for other heartbeats and heard none, so he jogged for the fallen figure. He was four feet away when he saw her face. It was Anna, the blonde Untouchable from the pool hall, and she'd been attacked. Blood seeped into her hair at the base of her skull and grass stained her khaki pants from hip to knee, as if she'd been dragged. Maybe she'd fought back.

Carey nibbled his lip and looked both ways. She was defenseless, completely at his mercy, and such an opportunity would never present itself again. In two seconds, maybe sooner, he could snap her neck and chalk up another point for his team. Carey knelt to her side, the wet ground moistening his knees through his slacks. Anna mumbled then, groaned once, and fell silent. He sensed she was coming around and he had less than a minute to finish her off.

Reaching down, Carey thought to grasp her throat, but instead, he put one hand under her shoulders and the other behind her knees.

What was he doing?

He lifted her off the ground. Where was he going? Carey began to walk toward the parking lot. One other car sat a few yards down from his, a blue Escort; it must be hers. He started for it and the woman stirred in his arms. He didn't know what to say to her, if he said anything at all. *I want to kill you, ma'am, but for some reason, I'm helping you instead. No, ma'am, I have no idea why. Maybe I've lost my mind.* Et cetera.

Carey smiled to himself as he reached the lighted parking lot. Under the first sodium lamp he glanced down at the woman's face. She was looking dead at him.

"You're Carey, from the bar," she said matter-of-factly. When he said nothing in reply, she tapped his arm. "You can set me down. I think I can walk."

Carey stopped walking and carefully dropped her feet to the ground. She held onto his arm with both hands and tested her balance. Carey held her firmly until she was steady.

"Somebody hit me from behind." Anna looked at her wrist, no watch. "What time is it?"

Carey looked up to the starless sky. "'Bout ten."

Anna followed his line of sight. "You know that by looking at the sky?"

"The moon," Carey said, still supporting most of her weight on his right arm.

"I had a watch on," Anna mumbled after a second, and then she looked around. "I also had a purse. I think I was mugged."

It occurred to Carey that somehow, she didn't suspect him. Why was that? Did she simply *know?*

"When did you get here?" Carey asked, still not meeting her eyes.

"Oh, I came right after work. So, about six." Anna tried to take a step by herself. She stumbled and Carey caught her reflexively. "My head feels horrible. I think somebody hit me in the back of the head." She felt in her hair and Carey averted his eyes.

"Your head's bleeding. You should get that looked at." He spoke in a monotone and she tried once more to stand on her own. It was no good.

"Yeah, they say concussions can kill you if you don't respect them," Anna said, leaning on Carey again for support. Carey helped her hobble to her car and she leaned back on the hood. "You have family buried here?"

Carey glanced at the dark cemetery behind him, and then met her eyes. He'd resisted because he didn't want her to see what she'd seen before: that he was a cold-blooded killer. In the generous light of the parking lot, her face was illuminated so he knew his was, too. She held his gaze, unblinking, and waited for his answer. Carey cleared his throat.

"Uh, yes, my wife, Yoni." Carey pointed in the general direction of her grave. He'd exaggerated their relationship, but Yoni would have married him if he hadn't been killed and remade in his maker's likeness.

"Oh, I'm sorry," Anna said with sincerity and then had a pertinent question. "Do you have a cell? I need to call the police and maybe an ambulance."

"The police, yes," Carey said and backed a step away from her car. "No, I don't have a cell phone, but let's see…" His mind racing, Carey took in the perimeter of the lot and then the pavilion attached to the dark mausoleum. Not a pay phone in sight. He sighed and Anna walked around her car, leaning on its skin, and tried the door.

"Locked. And my keys are in my missing purse."

She didn't sound upset or unnerved, just irritated. Carey swallowed, unwilling to offer her a ride. He was immensely grateful that Bill wasn't with him.

"Hey, Carey, what's your last name?" Anna asked, now leaning against her door, one hand to her forehead.

"I go by Carey Pullman." *I go by…?* Carey kicked himself. He was acting as if she knew he was a vampire—but she didn't, right? The other two Untouchables he'd encountered knew him by sight, but then, they knew their condition as well. Carey played it cool and waited for her to do the talking.

"Carey Pullman. Okay," Anna smiled a small smile and touched her head wound again. "Ouch. I feel dizzy. Am I safe with you, Carey Pullman?"

"What?" he asked, taken off guard. He frankly didn't know the answer to her question. Inside, he still knew he needed to kill her before she killed him.

"I-I," Anna stuttered, and then her eyes rolled. "I'm passing out—" Carey reached out and caught her before she hit the ground. She was out cold.

Undecided on when and how to dispose of her, Carey carried her to his Volvo and carefully lay her across the back seat. Her head brushed his jacket as he stood to close the door and a swath of dark red blood stained the brushed leather. Slamming the door, Carey brought the spot to his face as he opened his door.

The blood of the Untouchables—when he killed the guy with the spotted tie, he and Bill both drained him dry. Carey's maker, Darren, had told him that in general, the Untouchables should never be drained; that their blood would sicken or weaken a vampire, perhaps even kill him. But they'd been so angry that night, the dark evening in November when a crazed Untouchable attacked Bill with an axe before pulling a gun on him. Carey had arrived home in time to end the guy, but it had been too close for comfort. Bill was a newbie then, barely ten years into his new life, and had only been with Carey a few months. What a horrible night that was.

Carey started the car and pulled away from the lot and toward the exit. He sniffed his sleeve again, putting his tongue to the leather. Nothing weird happened.

On the main thoroughfare now, Carey humphed and reached to the back seat with his right arm. He had to stretch, but he was able to tug the woman's shoulder enough that his fingers brushed her wound. It was tacky, closed, probably going to be fine. Before returning his right hand to the wheel, he quickly tasted the clotted blood on his fingertips. Nothing untoward happened to him. Was Darren funning him back then with all of the hocus-pocus regarding the Untouchables? Would he do that? Or did their blood gain potency over time, or under certain circumstances? What were the rules?

Carey smiled ruefully, wishing that Darren had been more forthcoming. His maker had been a cruel one, with man and vampire alike. Carey's stomach grumbled and he checked Anna's position in the rearview mirror. Her sleeping countenance was angelic and the tiny sample of her in his gut ramped up his hunger. Without expressly planning to, he sent out a mental beacon to his partner.

"You home, Bill?"

Immediately, the reply came back in the affirmative.

"You eaten yet?"

This time, his friend sent back a woeful, *"That's a big negatory, Tree."*

His face lax, and not sure why felt such trepidation for what his mind planned of its own accord, he answered his friend with three simple words: *"Dinner's on me."*

The woman in the backseat groaned and he noted motion in his peripheral vision. Was she coming to? Carey sped up, taking the interstate off-ramp faster than he should. Anna's body slid against the back of the seat and she groaned again.

"You awake, Anna?" Carey said, hoping she'd say yes while

wishing she'd remain unconscious until he got her home. Silence from the back so he sped on.

He and Bill shared a small ranch house on the outskirts of town. It sat on eleven acres and was fenced with post-and-rail. In past lives, he'd kept horses and sheep there as blood substitutes, but when Bill joined him, he pretty much stopped feeding off animals. Between the two of them, they'd developed a system of killing that rarely attracted the attention of the authorities.

Around the bend in the road, the streetlight that delineated his drive came into view. Impatient to get inside, he forced the iron gate open with telekinesis and zoomed through. Bill stood in the open front door and he screeched to a halt at the wrap-around porch.

"You haven't brought anyone home like this in forever, Tree," Bill said as he joined him at the car. "You okay?"

"I'm fine. Just bring her inside," Carey replied and turned for the house. Behind him, Bill opened the back door and whistled. Carey got indoors and called to his friend, "Hurry."

He didn't want to develop a conscience before the deed was done. Already, he was second-guessing himself, looking for alternatives, thinking about how to explain to his giant friend that he'd changed his mind and decided to let the woman go unharmed. Carey shook himself and standing in the living room entrance, he turned and faced the door. Bill came in, the woman cradled in his arms.

"This is for me?" he asked, rightfully incredulous. Carey nodded. "So, it's okay, then?"

Carey nodded again, hoping his friend would hurry. He was losing his nerve. The woman moaned and her eyelashes fluttered then were still. Carey gestured for Bill to close the door and he did so with his heel.

Why hadn't he made his move? Carey pressed his lips together and glared at his friend. The big oaf knew what he was waiting for—why didn't he go for it? Carey didn't want to have to speak. If he did, he might say, "let her go" or some other such nonsense.

Bill remained where he was, trying to read his partner's eyes. "What about you?"

Anger and frustration built exponentially inside Carey's heart. He swallowed and focused one last thought toward his friend, hoping there'd be no further discussion.

"Kill her, Bill," he sent over and clenched his fists. Bill didn't need much more encouragement. With an easy movement of lifting his arms,

the girl rose until Bill's face disappeared in the hollow of her neck. Carey's stomach roiled. Within moments, the scent of fresh blood hit the air and Bill was at it.

Carey sighed and released the pent-up breath. Now, it would be over soon, the Untouchable would be dead and he and Bill would be safe. A normal, run-of-the-mill mortal posed them no danger. Both vampires could out-maneuver the strongest and most clever man or woman who might accost them. But the Untouchables were the only ones who saw them for what they were, and they alone knew their weaknesses.

Carey was facing Bill, listening to his noises of satisfaction, heeding the advice in his mind to stay put until the woman's heart stopped, when she opened her eyes and looked right into him. Carey hardened his heart and stared back.

She shouldn't have trusted him.

Carey waited for her eyes to dilate and finally close. Bill sunk to the floor and grinned. Carey lowered his eyes.

They would live because she died.

An empty victory was still a win.

As before, after saving Bill from the axe-man, Carey covered his face and hid his tears from his friend.

Delete

By Kat Heckenbach

THE NAME APPEARED IN MY EMAIL INBOX LIKE A phantom. Derrick Raines. Years ago, those two words raked my back like claws. Now, they summoned little more than a tic at the corner of my eye. I rubbed my temple to stop the twitching and clicked the mouse button. My heart froze as I read the message.

I died that night. Because of you. Now it's your turn.

Every muscle in my back tightened and I sucked in a deep breath. I needed to relax. It was just an email. No reason to panic—the solution was simple.

Click, *delete*. Click, *block sender*. Problem solved.

Before I could release my breath, a new line appeared in my inbox. *Derrick Raines, (no subject).*

A window popped up without me opening the email. At first, the message was empty, but letter by letter, words formed before my eyes.

Nice try. You can't delete me. Not again. I told you, I died. You can't kill someone twice.

I jumped up from my chair and checked the windows. No one on the street, no cars on the road. The neighborhood looked exactly as it did every day at this time. He couldn't possibly see me. How did he know I deleted the message? Returning to my desk, I looked at the screen again. Letters flashed as a whole sentence appeared at once.

I'm not out there…I'm in here.

And then I held my breath as scratchy lines began to etch the gray screen with black. Tiny strokes joined together to form the shape of a face. Like ants, they crept inward, molding the features from inky pixels. The style was distinctive, like Derrick's old sketches. The face that emerged was all too familiar, but the eyes were sunken, the cheeks hollow. I forced myself to breathe. Trembling, I sank back into my chair. A tear coursed down my cheek, and my tongue adhered to the roof of my mouth.

The picture began to move, the eyes rotating, as if taking in the surrounding room, before settling on me. A smile crept across the face.

Then it spoke, in Derrick's voice.

"Nice place. The kind of place we could have had together. If you hadn't run away."

I shoved my chair back and the wheel caught on the carpet. I tumbled to the floor, but my eyes remained glued to the screen. I gagged as bile surged to my throat. My instinct was to flee, but something held me in place; I couldn't summon the strength to struggle.

The face on the monitor laughed and my back burned from the

37

stroke of imaginary claws.

"Why don't you speak?" he asked angrily. "I came all this way to see you! I just want back what you stole from me."

The words slipped through against my will. "Wh-what did I steal from you?"

"My happiness." The lined eyes glared.

Arms straining, I scooted until I was sitting upright. My hand wandered to the collar of my shirt. I squeezed the fabric and felt the poke of silver charm underneath; the panic began to subside. It was true, I'd run away before, but it had been the only way to end things. The only way to get out of a parasitic relationship. Things were different now, and I wasn't going to run away again. I didn't have to this time.

"Your happiness," I mumbled, "is what I was trying to give you when I left."

"You thought taking away the only thing I ever loved would make me happy?" His words tore across the room, distorted by the tiny speakers on my laptop. I cringed.

The phrase echoed in my head...*the only thing I ever loved...the only thing...*

That's what I had been to him. A thing. A possession. He'd wanted to own me, and thought that would make him happy. I realized then that I'd left for more than one reason.

"Derrick, I did love you. I wanted you to love me, too. But I wanted to be some*one* you loved, not some*thing*."

The eyes narrowed. "You never loved me. You walked away and let me *die*."

No, I didn't. He was alive. On some computer somewhere, hacked into my inbox. I didn't know if that was even possible, but it was the only explanation. Derrick hadn't died. If he had, I wouldn't have been afraid all these years that he'd find me.

"You didn't die that night. You got married, years later. This isn't funny. Whatever you're doing to my computer, you need to stop, or I'm calling the police."

He laughed again. Ice traveled down my spine.

"My body didn't die. But my body isn't me."

I began to tremble. The panic was gone, but it had been replaced by a different kind of fear. Fear that ran deeper. Derrick wasn't in the room—it was only his face on a screen. His voice coming from the speakers. But he was somewhere. How far from here, I had no idea, but if he'd found my computer, he'd find *me*.

I dropped my hand to the floor to support myself, and felt the bump of a cable under my palm: the cord to the laptop power supply. I had plugged it in moments before checking my email because the battery had run down to almost nothing. A bad habit that was about to pay off. I yanked the cord with all my strength. The plug pulled free from the outlet in the wall and the laptop slid backward. But the desk had a hutch, and the laptop caught.

The eyes widened and a scream nearly shattered my eardrums. I cringed as the squeally distortion ripped from the speakers like a howl from another world. A hiss sliced through and silence followed. As I watched, the face disappeared, line-by-line, until all that remained were those computer-ink eyes. And then they disappeared with a pop.

My heart pounded hard and fast, and I breathed in pants to slow it down. Releasing my grip on the power cord, I dragged myself to my feet and stumbled out of the room.

◆

"Dana, why is your laptop dead?" Nathan called from the top of the stairs.

It had been two days, and I still hadn't plugged the computer back in. I slouched down farther on the couch, gripping my coffee with both hands to keep it from sloshing. *Why did he have to use the word 'dead'?*

Nathan appeared at the bottom of the stairs. "I plugged your laptop in. You really shouldn't let it die like that."

I shivered, and coffee splashed onto my hands.

Nathan furrowed his brow and stepped toward me. "Are you OK?"

"Just really tired."

"Anything I can do?"

I shook my head.

"Well, get some rest then. I'll be in the garage." He turned and headed out of the room.

◆

I'd managed to avoid turning the computer on for a whole week. Nathan asked me about it only one more time. I told him I needed a break, the emails could wait.

"What about your writing?" he asked.

"I'm in the brainstorm mode right now," I said, pointing to the spiral notebook on the coffee table. "It's been good for me. I've come up with a lot of ideas. Things I probably wouldn't have thought of cooped up in my office." *Oh, if he had any idea of the thoughts that notebook contained…*

He shrugged, and dropped the subject. What could he say? He was a stereotypical, left-brained accountant and knew nothing of the creative process of writing. I relaxed a little, knowing he wouldn't keep pressuring me, and decided to go shopping. My first time leaving the house in a week.

I had just turned onto Main Street when my phone rang. Nathan must have forgotten to put something on the list he'd given me. I groped the passenger seat with my right hand as I steered with my left. When I felt the phone in my palm, I grabbed it and hit *talk* without even looking.

"Hello?"

"You can't avoid me by ignoring your email."

The car swerved and I jerked it back, my hand gripping the wheel hard enough to pop my knuckles. The phone slid from my hand and fell between the seat and console. I grabbed the steering wheel with my other hand and drove stiffly to the next side street, where I turned and pulled into the nearest parking lot.

Shoving the car in park, I grabbed the wheel with both hands and peered between the seats. I could just see the light from my cell phone in the crack, but my hand refused to reach for it. I breathed. Swallowed.

Just get out of the car.

I loosened my grip enough to slide my hand down to the key in the ignition. Before I could turn it, a voice rang out from my car speakers.

"Uh-uh-uh. Oh, no. You shut this car off and you won't make it back home."

My hand froze. I breathed. Swallowed again.

"Why, Derrick? Why are you doing this?" I wanted to know *how* as well, but I didn't think my brain could wrap around whatever answer he gave.

"I told you, Dana. Come on, you're not stupid. Don't play games. You left me. I needed you and you left me. I had *no one*, Dana, and you knew that. I had nothing to keep me going but you. You promised to love me.…you promised we'd be together forever, and you lied. Just like everyone I've ever cared about."

I couldn't take the blame for that; I had tried, for two years. I knew his past, the abuse he'd received from his family, the desperate need he had for love. And I tried so hard to provide that. Too hard. I'd almost succeeded. But there was no succeeding with Derrick. Kindness only ignited the flame of need in him. I could never spend enough time with him. Giving him love only made him want more, demand more. It was too much for one person to provide.

"Derrick, I would've kept my promise if you had kept yours. The day you hit me—"

"That wasn't me! I wasn't myself that day…I lost control, just that once—"

"That's exactly it!" My heart raced with anger. I released the steering wheel and pointed at the stereo. "You see—it wasn't *you*. So I didn't leave *you*, I left the Derrick that hits. And the reason it only happened once is because I left."

Realizing how strange I'd look if someone were to walk by, I ran my hands through my hair and took a deep breath. I then peeked out the windows; no one was around.

Thank God.

Then I realized how ridiculous it was to be scared of a voice in a car stereo. Derrick wasn't here, and when he was, I'd fought him off just fine. What could he do from inside a speaker?

Inside a speaker, how absurd. He'd called me on my cell phone. He was probably following me, saw me drop the phone, saw me pull over. Since he was really into gadgets when we were together, he could have used something to hijack the frequency on my stereo. He was close, but not close enough.

I snapped off the stereo.

Silence.

I fished out my cell phone; a text message awaited me.

"You left the car on, so I'll let you go home. But I'll be waiting for you."

I deleted the message. *See, the little coward. He's just trying to scare me. It's not going to work.* I called home, and Nathan answered.

"Honey," my voice cracked and I cleared my throat. "Would you mind meeting me outside when I get home? I should be there in about ten minutes."

"Anything wrong?"

I let my hand wander to my necklace and grip the cool metal.

"No, it's just the car making some noise and I want to know if you hear it when I pull in."

♦

Nathan actually did hear something when I pulled in, which prompted a complete over-haul on my car. Fine, that was perfect. He'd be occupied in the garage all weekend, and I'd have loads of time to read. I could get lost in another world just by opening a book, and I reveled in that now. I fled to other worlds where ex-boyfriends didn't show up in people's computers and cell phones.

"Are you ever going to check your email?"

Nathan's voice shattered the illusionary world created by the book in my hand, and I peeked over the top of the page.

"How do you know I haven't?" I cocked my eyebrow at him.

His gaze shifted to the side. "I checked. You have a hundred and eighty-seven emails." He coughed. "Well, you *had* that many. I deleted all the junk for you."

"You did *what?*" I slammed my book closed.

"I didn't read anything!" His cheeks flushed.

Of course he didn't. I knew he'd never do that. I trusted Nathan. But he knew nothing about Derrick, and I wanted it to stay that way.

"I'm sorry," I said. "I know you meant well. I just have a system for sorting everything out."

"Well, you should read your email. Maybe you got an acceptance letter for that last story you wrote. And I saw Trish's name in there a lot. You know she'll get worried if she doesn't hear from you."

"I'll call her then."

He nodded, seeming satisfied, and left the room.

I picked up the cordless and dialed Trish's number. Voice mail. I left a message. The second I hung up, the phone rang. It was Trish. *She must have been on the other line.*

"Hello?"

"Expecting a call?"

My blood froze. I double-checked the caller ID: Trish's number.

I gripped the phone, trying to calm the shaking in my hands. "I'm calling the police. This is stalking. If you're at Trish's—"

"I'm not at Trish's. I'm not anywhere, Dana. I told you that. I died." He laughed, cold, metallic. "My body isn't even at Trish's, it's still back home…living its little life…with its little wife."

His sing-song tone invoked images of a jack-in-the-box; a creepy, springy clown, ready to pounce.

Pop goes the weasel…

"My body doesn't even realize it has a new inhabitant," he said.

What was that supposed to mean?

"I'm calling the police and sending someone to Trish's!" I slammed down the phone.

It rang again, Trish's number. I let the machine answer as I rummaged through my purse looking for my cell phone. *Damn! It's still in the car.*

The voice in the machine really was Trish. I snagged the phone.

"Trish?"

"Hey, girl! It's been so long. Why aren't you answering—"

"Trish, is somebody there? In your house? Has anyone been in there, broken in?"

"What? Dana, what are you talking about? I've been here alone all day. I didn't answer before because I was on the phone with Josh. No one's here. Are you OK?"

"Yeah, yeah. Just a little stressed. I'm trying to take a break from things. Have some 'me' time, you know. I was just afraid you'd worry if you didn't hear from me."

"Well, I was a little worried, but I know how you get when you're in the throes of writing," she said and laughed. My heart finally began to settle down. "So, what's this about someone breaking in?"

"Oh, that!" I laughed, hoping it didn't sound too fake. "I heard on the news there's been some break-ins around your area."

"Really, I hadn't heard that."

"Well, maybe I heard wrong. I'll hope that's the case. Anyway, I should go, get dinner ready. I'll talk to you later."

I hit *end,* and had to squeeze the phone to keep from dropping it.

He wasn't at Trish's. He was in *the phone…*

No, that was preposterous.

In the phone.

I laughed out loud. Derrick was messing with me. He'd hacked into my computer, gotten my phone numbers, hijacked the stereo frequency with…what? Didn't know, didn't care. But Derrick knew. He was a gadget geek, and obviously still into his toys. Never grew up. Never let go of things.

Never let go.

He'd never let go of me.

The phone hit the floor.

♦

I had Nathan drop me off at the library the next day. He left me at the bottom of the steps as he headed to the auto parts store for…something…something that was going to take a while to replace. Good. I'd told him to pick me up when he was done working, that I wanted to look up some books, but I headed for the computers.

Sitting at the first one I came to, I skimmed the sites as quickly as possible. The library limited you to an hour online. I didn't think it would take that long, but who knows.

I Googled "Derrick Raines," and a lot of links popped up—Facebook, Linkedin, Classmates.com; all the places that want to help you connect with loved ones, old friends, whatever. Derrick fit into none of the categories. There wasn't a service to help track down psycho ex-boyfriends whose souls have died, but bodies are still running around.

…back home… living its little life…with its little wife…

…pop goes the weasel.

He'd lost it. I was sure of that.

And then, there it was. The link was titled "Derrick Raines, Inventor." I clicked and an article and photo appeared. It was Derrick, all right. A little older, a little thinner, but definitely him. Standing next to some ridiculous contraption at a competition somewhere. A pretty thirty-something stood next to him. She smiled. He smiled.

Nothing like any smile I'd ever seen on his face before.

I checked the date of the article. Six months ago. In a town just miles from here.

♦

"This must be some workshop. You're shaking."

I looked down at my hands. Nathan was right.

I'd told him I was going to a writer's workshop in a neighboring town. A whole day of classes to keep me gone for hours. I hated lying to him, but I needed this over with. It had been a week since discovering how close Derrick lived. The longest week of my life.

Nathan kissed me good-bye, and I wanted to cling to him, beg him to not let me go. Beg him to just move away. To Alaska, or anywhere we couldn't be found. But if what Derrick said was true, we could move to Siberia and he'd find me.

I turned and walked to the car.

The hour drive stretched across eternity. I refused to turn on the stereo and I left my cell phone on silent. Derrick wasn't going to call anyway; he knew I was coming. I had no idea how, but I was sure of it. Maybe he'd been lurking in the library computer and spied on my searches. He would never have shown his face, though. That wasn't his style. Never a public display. Save it for the private times.

My grip on the steering wheel tightened when I realized how close I was. The map I'd printed showed his house just a mile away. Two more turns. One more.

There.

His driveway. I pulled to a stop in front of the house three lots down.

He stepped out the front door as I shut off the engine. Kissed his wife. Brushed her hair behind her ears. So loving. So gentle.

So not Derrick.

Oh, he'd been that way at first, but not at the end. Caressing my hair turned to grabbing my neck. Holding hands turned to squeezing my wrist. I tolerated it all, because I knew it came from a need to hold on to who he loved. *What* he loved. Until he hit me; that was the line I swore I'd never let him cross.

He waved to her as he ducked into his car. Much too casual for Derrick. When he pulled out of the driveway, I followed; staying close enough to see where he was going, but far enough back to make sure he wouldn't suspect me. Isn't that how they do it in the movies? I didn't have to keep it up for long. He pulled into the parking lot of a warehouse.

Yes, this must be where he did his "inventing."

I parked across the street and crept over as soon as he stepped inside. We had to be some place private, or he'd never talk to me. Keep it private.

The door was shut, but not locked. I slipped inside and entered a room full of electronic equipment. I snapped a picture with my cell and then tucked it back into my pocket. I had 911 on speed-dial; one number to push and send. It was the best I could do. To calm myself, I closed my eyes and took a deep breath.

"Hey! What are you doing in here?"

My eyes popped open. Derrick was striding toward me, scowling.

"You can't come in here," he said, "some of this stuff is dangerous." He didn't sound angry, just concerned. His face softened. "Sorry. I must have really startled you. I didn't mean to. How did you get in here?"

"Th-the door."

Did he recognize me?

"That door is supposed to lock automatically." He stepped over and inspected the lock, and then turned back to me. "It was unlocked?"

"Yes."

"Ma'am, I'm really sorry to have scared you."

He was staring at me. I must have looked terrified. I tried to smile. A whimper slipped out instead.

"Are you OK?"

He reached out to touch my arm. The moment his skin met mine I knew; this was Derrick's body, but this wasn't Derrick.

"Is your name Derrick Raines?" I asked, barely a whisper.

"Yes."

He really doesn't recognize me.

"I…I saw your picture in the paper."

"And you followed me?" Now the angry face returned. "Do you work for Randall Davis? Are you spying on me?" he asked and grabbed my wrist.

My heart rate shot up even higher and sweat trickled down my back. The picture I'd just taken with my cell phone would not help my case. I needed to convince him of who I was.

"No, no of course not!" I forced myself to smile. "I just, we went to high school together. Dana Thomas." My maiden name. It should have triggered a reaction. A big one. But Derrick just stared at me.

"I don't remember you." He scrunched his brow. "You went to high school in Montana?"

Montana? Where had that come from? Derrick and I had met in Austin, where we'd both grown up. And now we were in North Carolina. But he seemed so sincere. He gave every indication that he truly didn't recognize me. We were completely isolated—if this were really Derrick, my Derrick, my *ex*-Derrick, he'd be reacting. I started to laugh. *It must be me. I'm the crazy one. Not him.*

Derrick took a step back. "Can I…can I call someone for you?"

Oh, yes, this was rich. Derrick grew up to be perfectly sane, and I'm the one who lost it. I just never knew. I laughed harder, until my eyes began to water.

"No," I gasped when the laughing subsided. "I'll leave now. You're not who I thought you were. It's just such a funny coincidence. You look exactly like a Derrick Raines I once knew. But, I guess you're not him."

Then the laughing started again, harder as I walked through the door, leaving Derrick staring after me.

"And I'm not me."

♦

I turned the ignition, and the engine roared. Then, the stereo clicked on.

"Believe me now?"

My laughter stopped dead. Tears burned my eyes, and then dripped over my lids, trailing down my cheeks.

"No, I don't. Because you're not you and I'm not me. Leave me alone." I reached over to snap off the stereo, but the knob was already turned to that position. It took everything I had not to scream. "How are you doing this?"

"That's not important, Dana. What's important is that you know this is only temporary. This…place I'm inhabiting." He laughed. "And speaking of inhabiting…did you like the new Derrick? The one who took my body? He's a nice guy, I have to admit. Has no idea, either."

…back home…living its little life…with its little wife…

…pop goes the weasel.

"But you, Dana, *you* are going to know what it's like to have your soul transferred."

My breathing stopped and my hand fumbled at my neck as if it had a mind of its own. It wrapped around the cool metal of the charm. I exhaled.

"When?" I asked.

"Now, Dana. I'm tired of waiting."

The gearshift moved into drive.

"Press the gas, Dana."

I pressed the gas and pulled out of the parking lot.

"See you when you get home," Derrick said, and then the stereo knob turned. The Cure's "Love Song" drifted softly from the speakers. The tears that streamed down my cheeks dripped onto my shirt.

♦

Nathan was gone when I got home.

Thank you, God.

He had nothing to do with this, but would be the one who suffered the most if I refused. Once Derrick had what he wanted he would leave—I was sure of that—and Nathan would never know. But, if he *didn't* get what he wanted…

I climbed the stairs to my office. It had to end there; where Derrick first contacted me. My muscles ached with each step. Was I climbing to my death? The door creaked as I pushed it open. How appropriate. Dark, lonely house, creaky door leading to a room I had avoided for weeks—it almost felt staged.

Derrick, everything has to be a drama with you.

My laptop buzzed and began to boot up before I even made it to the desk. Yes, Derrick had planned it this way. But why? To suck out my soul. That didn't make sense. To kill my soul and leave my body?

That was it. I had to leave my body, so Derrick could take it. Inhabit it. Own it. Own me. But, like he said, *my body isn't me.* Fine, I lose my body, but keep my soul.

Where?

Wherever he was now. That temporary place he'd found to store himself until he found me, and took what he thought belonged to him in a way that it could never be taken again.

The screen flickered and went gray. As before, the inky lines scrawled into shape. Derrick's sunken eyes stared at me.

"Good girl, Dana. Good girl."

What now? I couldn't speak. I couldn't scream. I allowed the tears to flow and wrapped my hand around the charm on my necklace. It was cool against my skin. I was burning up.

"Now come closer."

"Are you…are you in there?" I asked. I had a right to know. If that was where he was sending me, I wanted to know. He only stared. I spoke louder. "Are you *inside* my computer?"

"Yes."

"Is that where you're putting my…my soul?"

Those inky eyes leered. "Yes."

I squeezed the charm tighter. "And I'll be able to move around, from there, like you do?"

He frowned, glaring at my hand wrapped around my charm. "No."

What was that in his eyes? Jealousy? I opened my hand and looked down at the charm. The silver cross Nathan had given me for my birthday five years ago. Did he know this was a gift?

This was insane. Derrick had somehow made a digital imprint of his soul. Should I have just run away? Moved to Amish country—no computers, no cell phones—would he have been able to follow me then? I had a feeling he could take things much farther. The digital soul was just the beginning. And if he could take my body, he could take someone else's. A body he would use to track me down.

I refused to spend the rest of my life running; I refused to make Nathan do the same.

"OK, then," I said, stepping toward the laptop that held the ink-sketched face. My dried tears bound my cheeks as I tried to smile. "You want me, take me. But do it now. Quickly."

The inky lines resumed their ant-like crawl. Derrick's face distorted with a wicked grin and the lines merged into a pixilated blob.

Which began to glow.

An orb of ghostly light floated out of the computer screen and headed directly toward my chest. My hand dropped from my necklace and mirrored my other hand, palm-back, as I backed toward the wall.

The heat from the orb swelled toward me, warming the skin on my chest. My breath caught, and then released with a jerk, as my necklace seemed to absorb the heat—my skin cooled except for the cross that lay against my breastbone. The cross burned like fired steel, but my hands refused to lift it from my skin. I stood paralyzed, breathing in spasms, as the metal of my charm boiled and the glowing orb began to shrink.

I braced myself against the wall. Why wasn't I feeling anything besides the heat of the metal? Shouldn't I have sensed Derrick's presence as he entered my body? Shouldn't I be feeling my soul ripped out of me?

And then the heat disappeared, and the necklace slinked from my neck. The thump of it hitting the floor barely met my ears. The invisible bonds that had held me against the wall disappeared and I slumped to the floor. The necklace lay in front of me on the carpet. The chain had broken where the charm had hung; the link had melted, as had the charm. The metal of the cross had spread and hardened in the shape of an elongated heart. I touched it with the tip of my finger. Still warm, but no longer burning hot. Picking it up, I cradled it in my hand.

What happened to Derrick?

The question had popped into my head, but I knew the answer. A tear slid from the end of my nose and landed on the charm. Lifting my head, I peered at my laptop. The screen had returned to normal. I slipped the melted cross into my pocket and walked over to my desk.

I pulled up my email and scanned the list of messages: Two hundred and seventy-four unread. Easy enough to solve that.

Click, *select all.*

Click, *delete.*

dtour

By Kevin R. Maze

Sarah 08:37: wut cha doin?
Justin 08:38: nothin
Sarah 08:38: where r u
Justin 08:39: micky d's
Sarah 08:39: get me a big mac lol
Justin 08:40: lol where u at
Sarah 08:40: beach bound baby!
Justin 08:41: take bikini pics ;)
Sarah 08:41: :)

▪▪▪

Sarah 10:06: ugh dtour
Justin 10:07: wuts up?
Sarah 10:08: road closed. Gotta dtour
Justin 10:08: you shouldn't txt n drive
Sarah 10:09: inorite
Sarah 10:09: nobody out here. Dark. Nothing's out here!!!
Justin 10:09: call me

▪▪▪

Sarah 10:11: no signa
Justin 10:12: no signa?
Sarah 10:12: signal
Justin 10:12: oh
Sarah 10:14: there is NTOHING out here!!
Justin 10:15: ntohing?? rofl
Sarah 10:16: cant spell lol
Justin 10:17: miss you
Sarah 10:18: u 2

▪▪▪

Sarah 10:44: car smoking!!! hissing!!
Justin 10:44: huh?! u ok??
Sarah 10:45: hot water stuff on windshield. cant see gonna blow
                up!!
Justin 10:45: what?!
Sarah 10:46: omg its cold and scary out here
Justin 10:46: where r u

Sarah 10:46: idk
Justin 10:47: in the car?
Sarah 10:47: no it looks like its gonna blow up. Something leaking bad under car
Justin 10:47: call 911
Sarah 10:47: signal week
Justin 10:47: ?
Sarah 10:47: txt, no talk help!
Justin 10:48: oh
Sarah 10:48: Help!!
Justin 10:48: do you know where u r?
Sarah 10:48: no
Justin 10:49: wut city?
Sarah 10:49: IDK!!!
Justin 10:50: ur only hour or 2 away. im coming
Sarah 10:51: theres a house w/light on. maybe see if someones home
Justin 10:51: no wait by car
Sarah 10:51: car could blow up! its cold n scary!!! I hear dogs
Justin 10:52: bad idea be careful

▪▪

Sarah 11:11: old woman gives me the creeps. where r u??
Justin 11:12: left 30 minutes ago. im coming. Wut old woman?
Sarah 11:12: old woman lives here. Looks like granny from
Justin 11:13: from where?
Justin 11:14: hey

▪▪

Sarah 11:23: sorry didn't wanna b rude. Granny got me hot tea. Don't think she's seen a cell phone b4.
Justin 11:23: don't drink 2 much tea. Ill b looking 4 dtour sign.
Sarah 11:24: hour away tho right?
Justin 11:24: hang on
Justin 11:25: u there?
Sarah 11:25: omg screaming in basement!! get here now!!!
Justin 11:26: u kidding me??
Justin 11:26: hey
Justin 11:26: sarah?

Sarah 11:27: said its her sick son. 40 but brain like baby.
Justin 11:27: in the basement?
Justin 11:28: hey

■■

Sarah 11:34: im back
Justin 11:35: where u been?! i was scared
Sarah 11:35: I had 2 w8 til bathroom. granny said I was being rude
             texting. dont want 2 make her mad. shes kinda scary.
Justin 11:36: what about basement boy?
Sarah 11:36: he was hungry. I told her I had 2 use bathroom n she
             went 2 basement.
Justin 11:37: how r u doing
Sarah 11:37: creeped out. get here soon! this place smells funny
Justin 11:38: Im going as fast as I can
Sarah 11:38: go faster

■■

Sarah 11:42: help 9111
Justin 11:42: what is it?!
Sarah 11:42: hes after me
Justin 11:43: Who?
Sarah 11:43: get here noWKLSZN 8OHS
Justin 11:43: hey
Justin 11:44: sarah
Justin 11:44: r u ok
Sarah 11:46: SHE MINE
Justin 11:46: who is this??
Sarah 11:48: FREND
Justin 11:49: dont touch her
Justin 11:49: let her go
Justin 11:50: Im calling police
Sarah 11:52: HAHA
Justin 11:52: u r in trouble
Sarah 11:53: WAYTNG FOR YU

■■

Justin 12:37: i know ur in there. open the door. i saw her car. this is the house. open door or i'll bust in down.

Sarah 12:38: BUST DOR I BUST HER HED

Justin 12:39: Open the door

Sarah 12:40: NO

■■

Sarah 12:44: BACK DOR LOCKD HA HA

Sarah 12:44: YES I SEE YU

Sarah 12:45: DONT GO TRY CELLR DOR

■■

Sarah 12:50: DONT WAKE THE BABY

Justin 12:50: where is she

Sarah 12:51: STOP YLLING OR SHE DIE

Justin 12:51: where is she? where are you

Sarah 12:51: LOOK BEHIND YU

Justin 12:52: where?

Sarah 12:53: HAHAHA

Justin 12:53: lol very funny. enough. where is she?

Sarah 12:55: LETS PLAY A GAME

Justin 12:55: no games. Release her

Sarah 12:56: GAME HAS ALREDDY BEGUN

Justin 12:56: dont hurt her

Sarah 12:58: WALK UP STAIRS BE QUITE

■■

Justin 01:01: forget 2 pay ur lite bill?

Sarah 01:02: GO RITE

Justin 01:02: I dont hear sarah

Sarah 01:03: GO RITE

Justin 01:03: ok

Sarah 01:04: HA HA KEEP FLIPNG SWITCH I CUT LITES OFF

Sarah 01:04: KEEP VOICE DWN OR SHE DIE

Justin 01:05: here i am

Sarah 01:06: GO STRAYT

Justin 01:07: dude buy candles

Sarah 01:07: GET FLASHLITE ON TABLE
Justin 01:07: ok
Justin 01:09: wuts on my hand? blood?
Justin 01:09: whos blood is this
Sarah 01:10: BE QUITE
Sarah 01:10: I SAID QUITE
Justin 01:10: okokokok don't hurt her
Sarah 01:11: YU BE QUITE SHE BE QUITE
Justin 01:11: ok I'm quiet
Sarah 01:13: GO UPSTAIRS
Justin 01:13: again?
Sarah 01:14: YOU WER IN CELLR GO UPSTAIRS
Justin 01:14: it sounded like she was in cellar just now
Sarah 01:15: NO
Justin 01:15: yes
Sarah 01:15: GO UPSTAIRS OR SHE DIE

■■■

Justin 01:16: here
Sarah 01:17: LEFT
Justin 01:18: locked
Sarah 01:19: NO TRY HARDR
Sarah 01:19: LAY ON BED
Justin 01:20: wuts that smell
Sarah 01:20: BED
Sarah 01:20: WEL YU WANTED HER
Sarah 01:21: HAHA
Sarah 01:21: BE QUITE
Sarah 01:21: GET BACK N THERE
Sarah 01:22: DARK HUH
Sarah 01:23: LOOK BEHIND YU
Justin 01:23:

Gloves

By Ellen C. Maze

SHE   CAME IN DRIPPING WET AND WHEN I RUSHED
at her with a towel, she winced as if I'd threatened her with a machete.
Or, perhaps the surgical mask I wear in public surprised her. Either
way...

"Oh!" she exclaimed, arms out, gloved fingers open, ready to
receive the dry cloth. "Thank you. Wow! It's really coming down out
there!"

The woman first dried her face, then patted her graceful neck and
ended by daubing the water that balled up on her clothing. I stood back,
figuring her startled reaction was a sign of a flighty personality.

Just in time, Aunt Edna took over, gingerly retrieving the towel
and leading the woman to the registration desk. I stood by the door to
watch and listen. Easily the most beautiful woman I had ever seen, this
lady was covered neck-to-foot in a stretchy white lace garment lined
with creamy silk. It hugged her perfect upper body, sliding down her
arms and ending at her delicate wrists where it tucked into slim white
leather gloves. At her waist, the lacey clothing became a pantsuit that
reached her ankles and ended in short high-heeled boots. If she'd been
wearing heavy make-up, I would have pegged her for a prostitute or
Vegas showgirl, but she wore almost none at all. Maybe I'd seen a hint
of gloss on her lips or some color on her eyelids, but knowing almost
nothing about cosmetics, I couldn't testify to either. Her soaking wet
hair was twisted tightly up against her head, fixed with decorative pearl
barrettes. I guessed it would reach her waist when down; I'd always
been a sucker for long-haired blondes. She didn't have a purse and she
didn't wear any jewelry. The woman intrigued me beyond words and I
leaned against the stair railing near the entrance and listened as she
checked in.

The woman's name was Roxanne Siren, she was busy telling Edna,
and her brother was outside wrestling in the luggage. I peeked through
the glass inserts in Edna's handsome front door and sure enough, a
shortish, balding gentleman was scooting through the drenching
thunderstorm at a trot, carrying two medium-sized bags. I pulled open
the door, noting through the sheeting rain how sad his Volvo looked
with a may-pop on the front right. I made way for the guy as he jumped
onto the porch and stopped before me.

"Good evening, sir," he said in an unrecognizable European
accent. "May I come in?"

I did a double-take when he didn't automatically cross inside and
instead waited to be invited; it was a Bed and Breakfast after all—

everyone was welcome. But he had an accent, maybe he was a foreigner. I gestured for the foyer. "Yes, sir. Please, come in."

Baldy sent me a pert nod without looking into my face, and slipped in, dripping a trail of water behind him. Overcome with a rare sense of propriety, I pointed him toward reception and he sloshed away. It was odd that he didn't meet my eye, or even glance at my face. Was he afraid he'd later have to identify me in a line-up? That made me smile and I resumed my spying stance by the staircase.

Maybe it was a good thing he hadn't looked up. I'd been horribly disfigured in a car crash at age twelve; my nose had to be reattached and both of my lips had been reconstructed from flesh taken from my caboose. As a result, in combination with my pasty complexion and a struggling mutant five-o'clock shadow that I couldn't keep mowed, I was a fairly ugly specimen. I donned a surgical mask for the comfort of the populace, happy that above the nose, my eyes and forehead were untouched by the accident. I'd lost my old friends and making new ones had so far proven an impossibility. Aunt Edna allowed me to live upstairs in one of her rooms, and I avoided going outside. I would be nineteen in a week and I wished I was dead. That about summed up my existence.

"Billy, please take these bags up to Room 4," Edna called and I smirked. She had a habit of treating me as if I was the most normal kid in the world, as if I wasn't scarier to look at than the Elephant Man. She was deluded.

I did as she asked and walked around the dividing half-wall to make a grab for Baldy's suitcases. I clutched one, but he snatched the other out of reach before I could grasp it.

"I have this one, son, thank you," he said without looking up. The Gloved One turned at his hissing tone and gave me a smile that I felt somewhere south of my belt buckle.

"Jasper, you're so cranky," she said to her brother, playfully slapping the air. She sidled toward me and reached out as if to touch my floppy hair, but Jasper grunted and she lowered her hand. "He's so grumpy," she said to me as Jasper came between us and forced us apart.

I didn't say anything, my mind still playing over the woman's every movement, every word. She mesmerized me, tantalized me, intrigued, and confused me. I wish she had touched my hair.

"I'm afraid you've missed dinner, but breakfast is served from six to eight, and then lunch from eleven to one. Food in the yellow fridge is for the guests, the silver one is off limits, okay dearies?" Edna called everyone "dearie." Isn't that endearing? When no one answered, she put down her pen and managed to catch the Gloved One's eye. "I just wanted you to know because the last guests who came to dinner late missed the chicken. It was awful, only the bare bones remained. They had to subsist on leftover meatloaf. You don't want that to happen to you, eh?"

I grimaced, embarrassed at an old woman's take on mealtimes; not everyone lived and breathed scheduled feed-bagging. Jasper was already to the first stair and he shook his head.

"Thank you, ma'am, but no need for meals; we brought our own food. Come along, Roxanne."

With that, he shuffled up the steps carrying the obviously heavier of the two bags. The woman sent me a flirtatious wink and followed him, and after two strides, I tailed her to the landing. After I'd directed them to the correct room and set down the black suitcase, Jasper stepped between Roxanne and me and held out a fiver. A tip? I didn't have anything to spend it on; Edna gave me a credit card to use online. I shrugged and tucked the bill in my pocket and left the room.

As the door was closing, I glanced back, hoping to get another look at the gloved beauty queen, and saw something odd. Roxanne raised her arms in the surrender position and Jasper moved toward her fast. Then the door slammed in my curious face. I remained where I was in case she called for help, but no noise emitted from the room. After a few more seconds, I took a step away from the door and heard an exhale. It was loud and throaty, more feminine than masculine so I made an about-face and entered Room 3. Somebody had to keep an eye on these two.

♦

It rained through the night and in the morning the front yard was a pond. Guests sloshed through two inches of standing water to get to the sidewalk and there was nothing sweet Edna could do about it. By noon, the water had drained to the tiny and useless backyard, and the Gloved One and her rude brother had not made a peep.

Yes, I was waiting for them to exhale. I had remained in Room 3 until Edna chased me out at midnight and then from my own room, which faced the street, I watched to see who came and went. As indicated, Roxanne and Jasper did not come to breakfast or lunch and now that it was nearing 3 p.m., I was increasingly suspicious that the guy had killed her. Side note: an active imagination and a freakazoid face are always a two-for-one deal.

At 3:30, FM-100 interrupted its Beatles marathon to announce a man-hunt underway for the murderer of three college freshman. They'd been found dead of apparent heart attack in the Mill Town Historical Park. The police didn't think it was possible that all three could die that way at the same time so it had to be murder. Uh, *duh*. Good call.

Mill Town Police, people—can we get a round of applause? The announcer said similar killings had occurred in several states, leaving a trail from California to Kentucky of unusually young myocardial infarction victims. A serial killer? In Mill Town? Why not; it had to happen in someone's town, didn't it?

At 4 p.m., Edna asked me to help her peel potatoes and I reluctantly left my post. Unlike the other two meals, dinner was served once at 6 o'clock sharp. When every potato in Kentucky had been peeled, she released me to return to my spying and I hopped up to still-vacant Room 3 to listen in. This time, our guests were making noise.

"Uhhh, please, please…please," the female voice seeped through the wall and once again, I felt an odd tightness in my gut. It was a sincere, begging plea; what could she possibly need that badly from her brother? *Drugs?* Crap. The beautiful Miss Siren was an addict. No fair.

"Stop!" a male voice hissed. I recognized that tone as Jasper's. "Put your gloves on! Now!" The second hiss was more audible and furniture bumped the floor.

"Jasperrrrrr, pleasssssse…."

Gross; she was purring. Now I was beginning to think something sexual was going on in Room 4. She sounded seductive, not like someone jonesing for a hit.

The door to the hall opened and slammed closed, then footsteps hurried down the stairs. The Gloved One was alone, and possibly horny; did the Masked Mutant have a chance? I left Room 3, and with my knuckles hovering over the brass number on Room 4, I took a deep breath. The door swung open before I knocked.

"Billy, isn't it?" she asked, standing with her hand on her hip. Again, she was wrapped from her flawless neck to her tiny ankles, this time in a soft green jump suit. Also, as before, she wore matching leather gloves and short boots. I'd been quiet too long and she motioned inside. "Please, come in, Billy."

"Okay," I said sounding like a moron. I plodded in, happy she couldn't see my grotesque lips quivering. Thankfully, my mask hid all sorts of unexpected emotional responses.

"Please come and sit with me. Tell me about this town, this Bed and Breakfast. Tell me why you wear that mask." She lighted in the room's only sofa, a decorative, scroll-y job with a rose pattern. That left the pink Queen Anne chair for me. I sat stiffly, wondering which of her topics to tackle first. I was definitely going to tell her anything just to watch her mouth move and have her eyes stare deep into mine—I'd sell my soul for a minute alone with her.

I started with the history of Mill Town, Kentucky's largest small town. The country's oldest Fire Department Dalmatian resided here. The mayor held eleven academic degrees—a world record for mayors. Our public school system stopped using buses in 2009 and now the children walked to school in groups led by the former bus drivers. Crazy stuff like that, I let it all fly.

Then I gave her the run-down on Edna's rocky past. The death of her wealthy husband who inadvertently left his inheritance to his first wife. How when Edna thought she was about to go broke, my mother pitched in and helped her purchase the town's only B&B with cable and Wi-Fi. Aunt Edna had it tough, but she was a sturdy type—I was impressed by her optimism, and I said so.

About the time I got to my own story, Edna's voice trickled up announcing dinner; I was supposed to help serve. I stood and Roxanne followed suit.

"Wait," she said and took a step closer. "Wait…" she whispered the second time and lifted leather-wrapped fingers to my eye-level. Oh, I wished those fingers would touch me. "Wait, just a moment, please…" whispering again, and begging, as I'd heard through the wall earlier. My follicles reacted to the sensation of her touch as she moved the curls aside and then stroked, once, twice, three times, without ever touching my scalp. What and why didn't matter, only that she didn't stop. Then an insane phrase came out of my mouth.

"You can touch me, Roxanne. It's okay." I stood only inches away and when the words left my mouth, a look crossed her face that I'd never before seen. Was it exhilaration? Joy? Perverse fear? I think it was all three.

Roxanne withdrew her fingers and right under my nose, I watched her slowly, no—provocatively—slip the glove from her hand. Oh, yes, she was about to touch me. I made an effort to bend my knees so I wouldn't pass out.

"Billy, where should I touch you?"

Choices? What did it matter *where*? Just do it! My tongue stuck to the roof of my mouth and I wished I had telepathy.

Her manicured pale fingers moved toward my hairline and an electric buzz coursed to my head as if attracted by her touch. She moaned the instant her fingers made contact, and I fell in love with her mouth. Then I lost consciousness.

♦

"So impetuous! You couldn't wait just one more hour? One? Look at this! If you kill your prospects, you'll never be matched up!"

"I have another one lined up, and anyway, he's not dead."

Lying flat on my back, I didn't open my eyes as I came to, but I recognized the voices overhead. *He's not dead...* Did I look dead? I considered my extremities—I felt fine. I decided to listen in while Jasper released his frustrations on my new girlfriend.

"You just had to do it, didn't you?"

"Don't be mad, Jasper. Look at him—he's perfect."

"Perfect? He's deformed."

"No, he's perfect." Based on the direction of her voice, it was Roxanne's toe that touched my hip. "Empathetic, resilient, introverted; what else can a girl ask for?"

"You're not a girl, and this kid is not worthy of you."

Rough hands grabbed me under the armpits and dragged me across the floor.

"Buzz the front desk. We'll say he fainted and we want him out of our room." Jasper placed me on the rosy couch and he was none to gentle about it. Figuring it was time to awaken, I groaned and fluttered my eyelashes.

"See? He's fine..."

"Don't you touch him!" Jasper barked in a creepy hiss, then shouted, "PUT YOUR GLOVES BACK ON!"

I opened my eyes in time to see Roxanne playfully reach for Jasper's arm with her bare fingers. He jerked away, but she'd made the briefest contact. He fell to his knees, facing her, his profile to me.

She looked down on him and shook her pointer near his nose. "What's that Jasper? What do you want me to do? Where are my gloves? I don't remember..."

Jasper remained on his knees, looking into her face, apparently dazed. She tossed me a look and gave me a secret smile before putting her un-gloved hand to Jasper's face. That's when I noticed I wasn't wearing my mask.

"OHMYGOD!" I yelped, covering my scars. I hopped to my feet

and the Gloved One caressed her brother's cheek. He convulsed with what looked like pleasure. Feeling naked and confused, I screamed like a little girl and bolted from the room.

The fact that Roxanne's fingers contained an unexplained power didn't register until I'd made it into my own room, locked the door, and tied on a new surgical mask.

He's deformed. Ugh. Jasper said that about the plastic surgeon's nightmare that I call a face.

No, he's perfect. Wait. Roxanne had said that—whilst looking right into my sleeping monster visage. What else did she call me? I busily worked to remember her every word as my last visual of her came to mind; her touch somehow incapacitated her brother. Is that why I fainted? She was reaching for my hair and the next thing I know, I'm on the floor. Gloves, gloves, gloves...

You're not a girl... Then what was she? *She couldn't wait one more hour?* For what?

In the fog that befuddled my senses, I heard the weighty front door slam. I sprinted to the window in my un-lit room and looked down on the now-dark street. It must have been about 9 p.m. and the widely-spaced streetlights only allowed visual contact every dozen feet. The shadow that left the house at a good clip could have been anyone, but I wanted to think it was Jasper. I wanted him to have left in a huff, to have left the house for good, because that would mean Roxanne was alone, and she had said that I was *perfect*.

I left the room dark so I could continue my surveillance of the front yard. Before long, a soft knock on the door caused me to jump. In the hallway, Aunt Edna asked if I was okay, reminding me that since I missed dinner, she'd saved me a plate in the microwave. She sounded tired, as if running a bustling B&B practically on her own was wearing her out. I couldn't imagine how she'd made it this long. I called out that I was fine and she went away. She was good like that—letting me take care of my own business. I returned my gaze to the night below and scouted for movement. When I put my hands to the sill and leaned close enough for my nose to touch the glass, I sensed someone behind me.

"Billy?"

I yelped like an even younger girl than before and clutched my head. Roxanne stood a few paces behind, illuminated only by the romantic light of the moon, her gloved hands at her sides, the shimmery green bodysuit complimenting her emerald eyes. Who was this woman?

How did she get in? What did she want? It really didn't matter if she was going to remove her gloves.

"Yeah, what? I'm sorry, I'm a dummy," I mumbled, and then said some other stupid things before her smile re-tickled my insides.

"Billy, you said I could touch you. Did you mean it?"

She stood about five feet away. If we both put out our hands, we could touch fingers. I nodded and wondered just what I was agreeing to. Her hand on Jasper's cheek turned him to jelly; her fingers on my hair knocked me out cold.

"Good, because Jasper didn't come through." She took a tiny step forward and stopped. I was curious at her meaning, but my eyes went to her gloves. Was she going to touch me again? Please, please.

"It's his fault, isn't it, Billy? If he'd checked the tires more often, we wouldn't have had a blowout, right?"

She wanted me to agree with her? I tried, but what came out was, "Unless he ran over some debris in the road." Her heart-shaped mouth went to the side.

"If that was the case, he should have been more vigilant when driving a princess across country, right?"

Who knows? Wait, she's a princess? "Maybe," I said hoping she'd come closer. Her touch knocked me out, but the pleasure explosion it caused was worth it.

"If he'd been more diligent, then I'd be with my match right now. I had him picked out, but the window was narrow before he was no longer available." Roxanne moved a few inches closer until her face was washed in heavenly moonlight. Only one of us would have to reach out now in order to touch fingertips.

"Your match?" I asked, hearing her odd musings as if from miles away. I was about twenty percent interested in what she was saying; the rest of me concentrated on her hands dangling at her sides. Any second now, she might lift one and...

"They're so hard to nail down and I located this one a week ago. Jasper promised he'd get me there in time."

Awwww, she looked forlorn. What could I do that would make her smile again? I tried what had worked before. "You can touch me, Roxanne. It's okay."

She beamed me with her famous smile and closed the distance between us. "Okay, I will. But first let me finish with Jasper."

"Whatever," I said aloud, not meaning to do so. I meant, *whatever so long as you touch me soon before I explode.* Roxanne gestured toward the night outside the window.

"You should watch. It will mean more to you if you watch."

I turned and looked out the window, puzzling at her words. She hardly said anything that made sense, but I had a hard time caring. I scanned the dark silhouettes of the trees, the roofs of the neighboring houses, then the sidewalk below and finally detected movement in the street. It was a person, short of stature, with a shine to his bald head.

"I need you, Billy, to either be my Jasper or to be my match."

"I don't follow," I said, watching Jasper intently below. He stood in the middle of the road, facing the house, his details bathed in shadow. Cherry Lane was a back, back, back road; he needn't worry about traffic.

"Watch," she reiterated, close enough behind me that her breath fell on my neck.

Below, Jasper put his hands in his pockets, still staring in our direction. I made as if to lift my hand to wave when an eighteen-wheeler zoomed across my vision, mowing the man down in an instant. I yelped, but then Roxanne's gloved finger touched the top of my hand.

"I need you, Billy." The pressure increased where she touched me and the electricity between us sparked deep within. "Jasper's gone. It's up to you. Choose."

Choose? My brain didn't seem to be working properly; I'd just seen a man run down by a giant truck and all I could do was focus on the heat between her leather-encased finger and the top of my hand. Pinned as I was to the spot, a moan escaped my lips. Roxanne put two fingers atop my hand and pressed down.

"Choose, Billy. Pleasssseeee…"

Oh, she was begging again. Yes, whatever, I'm yours, what do you want? My mind went crazy with answers, but I didn't understand the question.

"I need you, Billy," she cooed, the opposite gloved hand coming to rest on my left shoulder. Instantly, a party raged there and tingles of pure ecstasy traveled down my spine to every extremity. Yes, *every* extremity. What if she removed her gloves? What then?

"Pleasssseeee choooooooose…"

I coughed, facing outside, but seeing nothing. My mouth asked an inane question. "Do you need to touch to live?" Why did I ask that? I'm so stupid.

"Where's the gun?"

Huh? I looked over my shoulder and caught her eye. She fluttered her eyelashes.

"Okay, then, where are the pills?"

Oh, that one hit a mark. In my bathroom drawer I had collected about a hundred prescription pills from dozens of guests over the past few months. Most of them were anti-depressants, and I figured they'd kill you if you took them all at once. I didn't feel like admitting that I had considered suicide on and off since the accident.

"Get them, Billy. Go get those pills. If you take them, you'll be my match." Roxanne's voice was urgent and low. I read the eagerness in her eyes and wondered how my suicide could help either of us.

"What pills? What are you talking about? I don't want to die." I said whatever came to me. Roxanne's face fell and she shrunk away, the tantalizing contact with her gloved fingers disappearing as she did so. "Wait, what's going on? You can touch me, Roxanne." I sounded like a pathetic broken record.

"Suicides match me, Billy. I thought you wanted me to touch you. What's the problem?"

Clearing steadily, my mind raced a mite faster than sludge. "Let me see if I get this: Jasper was taking you to a man who you somehow knew was about to commit suicide and because of the blow out, you missed your window and the man is dead."

Roxanne nodded. "It hurts me not to touch. It hurts them when I do." She gestured out the window. Down below red, white, and blue lights flashed as ambulances, police, and fire medics arrived to peel the dead man off Cherry Lane. "Suicides, seized at the point of death, can be touched and live."

"That doesn't make sense," I sent back. "What kind of person kills people with their touch?"

"No kind of *person* does, Billy."

You're not a girl, and he's not worthy of you... Jasper said that earlier. What did it mean?

"You're not a person?" I asked and tucked my hands under my armpits.

"Not like you are." Roxanne removed her left glove and my stomach roiled, this time in a bad way. In my mind's eye, I saw dead college kids. I thought of the gloved creature's electric touch and was beginning to try out the kind of math where one plus one equaled two. "Did you kill those boys at the park?"

"Billy, pleeeease...." she cooed, her eyes sorrowful, her glistening lips begging me to surrender. "It hurts me *not* to touch. It *hurts* me."

"But why those kids? And why three of them?" Was I the police now? I hated my questions because I didn't want to know the answers.

"Three, three hundred, three thousand, a million—all of them... Billy, I will touch them forever if you don't match me." Roxanne's voice fell to a whisper. "And soon, Billy. I don't usually go this long."

"How often?" I asked barely audible.

"Several times a night, Billy, until I stop hurting."

Roxanne's naked hand traveled to her throat as she spoke and rested there. I was profanely interested in what *she* felt when she touched the college boys to death. Thankfully, that question did not leave my mouth.

"A match can absorb my touch, Billy. A match ends up saving lives."

"So you've had one before," I asked and she nodded. "What happened to the last one?"

"He died of old age. He was with me for forty-five years." Roxanne pulled off her left glove and dropped them both to the floor. "It can be a nice life, Billy. I have land, houses, boats, cars, anything you want. For as long as you live."

"There's gotta be a catch. I mean, I think you just caused Jasper's death." I blinked trying to make sense of it all.

"No, no, Billy. No, Jasper knew my chance with the other man was blown. He also knew that I'd tested you already in my room and that you passed. Jasper is my former match's son. He hoped to take his father's place." Roxanne's countenance darkened with sadness and I took a deep breath.

"Jasper was trying to commit suicide just now? That's why he was standing in the road?"

Roxanne shrugged and then nodded, her eyes never leaving mine.

"You just let him do it?" I was almost speechless.

She shrugged and said nothing.

"Why would he do that? Why?" I asked, shaking my head. Yes, when she touched me, I nearly died with pleasure, but to stand in the road and wait for a car to run you over? Wasn't that insane?

"Because, Billy," Roxanne began as she grasped the hem of her tight top, "the match doesn't die when I touch him."

In a flash, she pulled the stretchy garment over her head and dropped it alongside the gloves. Underneath, she wore a thin scoop-necked tank, her pale skin as blemish-free and perfect as I suspected it would be. Was it just her fingers that caused such excitement in my flesh? What if she touched me with her elbow? Her shoulder? Her knee?

Her lips?

"The match doesn't die," she repeated and pulled the pins from her hair.

As I guessed, her golden blonde tresses fell below her waist as full and as wavy as in my filthiest dream.

"You're not even 20, Billy. You have a long life ahead of you, a loooooooong life, with me." She reached out her naked hand and I protectively clamped down my folded arms.

"What would I have to do?" I asked, trying out the scenario in my head. That was okay, wasn't it? Just a little dry-run to see how the whole thing sat with me?

"Take those pills—all of them, and don't regret it. I will be here to make you my match. In the nick of time, I'll bring you back, and then you'll be able to survive my touch for the remaining years of your life." I must have looked dubious for she stepped forward into the light of the moon over my shoulder.

"Do you, well, would we, you know..." I was babbling and embarrassed to ask—but didn't I have a right to know what I was getting myself into? I sought the right words, but Roxanne filled in the blanks and smiled.

"No, I'm not really a girl, Billy." Then she added, probably because of my expression, "but I'm not a man, either. Remember my touch— that's what you want. Remember?"

"Can I feel it again? Just a tiny bit?" I asked, no better than a druggie trying to choose life over death and death over life. Roxanne didn't delay to put forth her pointer finger and touch my inner elbow. Arrows of delight raced through me with power and I fell to my knees. The contact was severed and I remained where I was, kneeling, staring into her face.

I was going to do it. What did I have in my miserable life that even half measured up to what I could have with this goddess in the form of a delicious woman? Roxanne smiled again, as if she sensed my concession, and she gestured for the bathroom. Drunkenly, I scrabbled to my feet. It would be fine to spend my life with Roxanne. I mean, I'd be helping her so she wouldn't have to suffer. And I'd be helping the world, who'd get to keep their loved ones safe from her wanton touch. It was a win-win all around. I reached the bath and yanked open the drawer. My stash was gone. Unbelieving, I looked in the cupboard below as a crash sounded two rooms down. *Aunt Edna!* The realization almost crippled me. When I spun around to explain to Roxanne, she was gone. I bolted for my aunt's room. I reached it in four big strides.

On the lavender comforter atop her bed, my sweet old aunt lay sprawled out, convulsing and foaming at the mouth. A sheet of paper fluttered to the ground near her head as Roxanne covered Edna's face with her hands.

"LET HER GO!" I shouted, and clawed at Roxanne's white fingers. Immediately, I was disabled and fell backward, rapping my head hard on the end table. Through fuzzy and wavering vision, I watched Edna's body rise to meet Roxanne's hands. Her long fingers traveled down my aunt's chest, her torso, her hips, her thighs, and finally to her toes. Roxanne was reviving her, but this kind of healing was the kind that enslaved the resurrected.

It was useless trying to rise so I yelled for help; nothing came out. All I could do was watch, and by the time the other guests reached the room, drawn by the commotion, Aunt Edna was sitting up in bed, grinning like a Cheshire cat.

Roxanne stood back, her huge smile in place, and waited for Edna to crawl out of bed. The other guests rushed in to inquire about her health and she sent them away, thanking them for their attentions. No one bothered about the masked boy prostrate on the rug beside the bed. Was I invisible? Of course, I was, I'd always been, ever since the car accident that stole my face. I clutched at the errant sheet of stationery that rested near my head. In my aunt's old-lady scrawl, she'd written, "I can't do it anymore. I'm sorry, Billy. The B&B is yours, Edna." I'd been a selfish idiot; I never saw this coming. But Roxanne had. Had she known all along?

If she was drawn to suicides, did she really stop off here by accident and coincidence? Or did she and Jasper come to our specific B&B because there were two potentially suicidal people living here? I glanced at the wall clock. Jasper had chastised Roxanne for not being able to wait an hour. *That* was an hour ago. Could this woman predict suicides that accurately? The questions kept rolling in and there were no answers for any of them.

When only the three of us remained in the room, Edna rolled off the bed and folded herself into Roxanne's open arms, her mouth making sounds a nephew should never hear from his aunt.

"You are my match, Edna," she said in my aunt's ear, just loud enough for me to hear. "Whatever you want, just ask. I'll take care of you. I need you, Edna."

Wait! Stop! That's my aunt! I wanted to shout, but nothing came out—I was still frozen from touching Roxanne uninvited.

Roxanne caressed Edna's back and led her to the door. Once, for a fleeting moment, my aunt looked at me, but her eyes had changed. Her brown eyes were now the palest blue, and she didn't know me at all. I shuddered and tried once more to make a noise; the tiniest whimper issued forth—some victory.

"Come to my room, Edna. Stay with me tonight. Tomorrow, we'll plan a new life together."

"Please, oh, yes, pleeeeeease..." Aunt Edna purred, hanging on to the creature's arms.

"Yes, oh, yes," the Gloveless One answered.

My poor aunt—what did it mean for her? She'd spend the rest of her days absorbing the creature's toxic touch? Carrying her luggage? Tending her daily business as a tactile-addicted slave?

That was supposed to be my job.

What was I saying? I was miserable and incorrigible—a horrible combination.

Roxanne led my aunt to the door and looked back my way. "Go on to my room, Edna. I'll be right behind you." My aunt nodded, still in the happy trance evoked by Roxanne's touch. When Edna was gone, she closed the door with two shapely fingers.

"Don't worry, Billy," she said and approached me on the floor, her eyes shining. "I'll be touching you now."

"What? Don't..." I gasped, finally un-sticking my tongue.

"I don't need you anymore, Billy. I have my new match." She sent me an air kiss as she knelt beside me.

"But—please, Roxanne, I don't want to die!" I yelped, still struggling to form words around my semi-paralyzed palate.

"Don't worry, it'll feel marvelous," the creature named Roxanne said. She rolled her eyes closed and lethargically reached her bare palm toward my chest. I strained to move away, but was securely pinned to the floor by my lack of muscle control. Deftly, she maneuvered her fingers under the fabric where I'd stopped buttoning and lay her fingers directly on my sternum. In that moment, I'd never been happier to die.

I relaxed and lay on the floor and watched the ceiling fan twirl lazily above us. *Let's face it,* I thought, *is it really ever going to get any better than this?* I didn't see how. Soon enough, my body was singing, and everything went black.

Wonder if I get back my face in heaven? It's a legitimate question, after all.

Lab-Rat

By Elizabeth E. Little

Day 1

I have been brought to this place against my will. The others have no recollection of their previous lives, seemingly believing that this whitewashed prison has always been their home. I both pity and envy their ignorance; it seems a great burden to be aware of the world outside, knowing as I do that while I was not born in this place, it is likely I shall die in it.

Our captors have assigned us names for their own amusement. I cannot conceive why they would have named the others Mickey, Minnie, and Bernard otherwise. I, myself, have been given the designation Wormtail. This designation displeases me. Not only is it incredibly erroneous, but it is also insulting.

My tail does not in any fashion resemble a worm. Also, I am not a rat.

I am a mouse.

Day 2

Bernard and I have been deposited in a large prison cell, while Mickey and Minnie reside in a similar location adjacent us. The cell is made entirely of bars, crossing each other in a checkerboard fashion which eliminates the possibility of escape. There is only one exit—a strange hatch-like door situated in the ceiling of the cell which is impossible to access without the use of thumbs. This is unfortunate, but not enough to quench the hope of eventual freedom.

The bars of our cell seem constructed of a strange grey material, and Bernard tests their malleability with his teeth. The bars prove impenetrable, and yet another avenue of escape is closed to us. I commend his dedication to survival, however, as it seems Mickey and Minnie have made no attempt to leave their cell and are content to simply run around like idiots.

Briefly I consider the possibility that the two have recently suffered brain damage of some kind, but dismiss it due to the fact that they had seemed perfectly normal before being placed in the cell.

I take the opportunity before our captors return to examine the cell in which Bernard and I have been placed. The floor is covered in what looks to be wood shavings, and there is a strange contraption attached to the easternmost wall that looks to be a jug of some kind with a metal tube leading from it into the cell. I surmise this must contain water, as Bernard demonstrates his implacable courage by mouthing at the opening until a drop emerges.

I must remember to reward his bravery at some point.

A large metal wheel resides in one corner of the cell, filled with parallel spokes and enough room in the center for one or two mice to comfortably rest. I wonder if this is perhaps meant to be our bed, but as I place a paw upon it I find it moves according to the distribution of my weight, and decide that its nefarious purpose would be better examined at a later date.

The miniature sun that had previously illuminated the space outside of our cell abruptly sets—the speed at which it does so is both awe-inspiring and the single most frightening thing I've witnessed in my entire life—and our enclosure is plunged into darkness. I can hear Mickey squeaking in alarm from his own cell, and resist the urge to do likewise.

It would be terribly undignified, after all.

Day 3

Our captors returned in what I assume must be morning—as the miniature sun rose with the same stuttering swiftness with which it had set the previous night—and study us for an uncomfortable amount of time, taking notes on sheets of paper and on large boards as they stare at us. I am unsure what they are looking for, but attempt to "act natural" in an effort to avoid drawing undue attention to myself.

Bernard apparently decided to follow my lead, for he is currently running a fruitless marathon on The Wheel which draws many approving noises from our jailors. How utterly bizarre these creatures are. Why do they seem so pleased that Bernard is performing such a useless action? He will never get anywhere, and will only accomplish his own inevitable exhaustion. He would be better served saving his strength like I intend to, so as to make the most of the earliest attempt at escape. Attempting to understand how these strange beings think is impossible, and so I cease to do so.

Mickey and Minnie seem to have recovered from their spontaneous insanity the previous night, and scamper away when one

73

of our captors opens their latch and lowers a massive paw—it was bigger than my entire body!—inside, holding a container of brown pellets. I can smell them from here... revolting.

After a similar experience is repeated in Bernard and I's cell, I stare at the pellets with wary fascination. Their purpose is unknown to me, although Bernard seems to have some idea as to their function. He approaches with confidence and, to my utter shock, stuffs one in his mouth. When Bernard does not immediately asphyxiate or begin hemorrhaging from the eyes, I ascertain that our captors have not attempted to poison us—yet—and do likewise.

The pellet tastes of grains and oats, and is not entirely displeasing. Between the two of us the pellets vanish quickly—there is no way to know when our captors would next deem fit to feed us, so it was best to consume as much as possible—and it is not long before I begin to feel a strange lethargy that is entirely foreign.

Immediately, panic strikes. Had they poisoned us after all? Did Bernard know the pellets were drugged? Was Bernard a traitor? Would they kill us while we slept? Would they do unspeakable things to our unconscious bodies? Would they—

—oblivion took me.

Day 4

When I awake again, it is dark. Bernard is draped across The Wheel as if dropped there from above, and the other cell is silent. A glance towards the others confirms the slumbering presence of both Mickey and Minnie, one slumped inside the pellet container and the other unconscious in the center of their cell.

I feel a strange prickling in my left hind leg, as if something had stabbed me there, but when I look the fur is undisturbed and there is no blood and no wound.

My paranoia is not satisfied. If anything, it is heightened. I am utterly certain our captors have done something to us while we were unconscious; it is unlikely I will ever know what was done to me, but I resolve to be more careful with the food pellets in the future. If Bernard is so willing to take all of the risks, I will simply watch him for such reactions in the future. He will be my taste-tester, my shield, and I will not succumb to such trickery again.

Day 5

Bernard was taken from the cell by our captors today, and he has yet to return. I worry for his safety, as they have never removed one of us from the container to my knowledge—again my thoughts flash to that unknown, horrible period of unconsciousness during which any number of things could have happened—and I can only be grateful that it had not happened to me instead.

When he is returned, there is a patch of fur missing from his flank. It is a perfect square, and obviously not an accident. He does not seem to be wounded, but I can tell the missing fur bothers him in some way. Was he aware of what happened? Was he awake? Did they knock him out again? Bernard refuses to speak of what has occurred, and I do not particularly blame him.

I would not like speaking of my perceived failures, either.

The captors do not return again until later, whereupon they remove Minnie from her cell and stab her with a horrible, thin metal weapon with a large canister at its end. I can only watch, frozen, as the liquid in the weapon is forced into Minnie through the sharp metal end. It does not initially seem to cause her undue harm that I can see, but the experience is horrifying nonetheless. Minnie struggles, squeaking— I can hear her voice yelling out for help, begging Mickey to save her, crying that it burned and that she would do anything they wanted if they would just stop*stop*STOP—before she falls limp in the creature's hand. Unconscious, exhausted, or dead, I am not sure. Bernard falls silent even as Mickey goes wild, and I cannot find it within myself to make so much as a sound.

These creatures so overpower us that it is not even vaguely amusing. What had begun as a simple prison has turned into something else entirely. This is no longer a matter of escape.

It is a matter of survival.

Tzadik

By Ellen C. Maze

Hannah

She knew better. A nice Jewish girl would never go to a downtown bar in the middle of the night with a group of women she barely knew, only to be forced to find a ride home because her friends had disappeared in the throng of partiers. Yet here she was, standing center floor in the hottest nightspot Old Prattville had to offer. The place hummed with life; country music alternating with 80's pop boomed from an expensive sound system; men and women, ranging from drinking-age to mid-thirties, swayed as one on the dance floor or snuggled over tall round tables along the perimeter; and Hannah stood alone next to a support beam in the center of the room, wishing she'd, for once, stayed home.

She was *tzadik*—righteous, striving for holiness. Hannah and her friends had taken a six-month pledge to concentrate on ministry and servitude. She even had a ring, a turquoise-and-silver job engraved in Hebrew with her name. It was cool. So, maybe the Big Guy had work for her tonight in the bar. Why not?

An amorous couple, dancing chest-to-chest, one face sucking the other, ambled close. The man smelled of beer and Polo cologne, the woman's hair was kinky and freshly-permed. Hannah looked away, toward the door. She didn't dislike them, she didn't dislike any of them, but she wanted to go home. Every passing second, a sense of impending doom inched closer to her consciousness. She wasn't psychic—not by a long shot—but she communicated closely with God, and it seemed he'd found work for his little crew of *tzadikim* tonight. Hannah wondered if the other girls were up for it.

A loud peal of laughter sounded on her left and Hannah looked over. A gaggle of women guffawed at a joke, slapping each other on the back and sending long gazes toward a similarly-sized herd of stallions a few stools down. One woman laughed again, spilled her glass of beer, and climbed up to the bar for another. Hannah read their intentions: The ladies hoped that with enough beer, wine, and joviality, the men who ogled them would try to pick them up. Hannah sighed and looked back to the exit. Whatever. She just needed a ride home. Where were the girls she came with?

Hannah released the support pole and took a step toward the door. At that moment, a high-pitched scream hit the air and she broke out in goose pimples. Hannah froze where she was and spun toward the sound. Another scream erupted, this one masculine and on the opposite side of the room. Hannah squinted across the dim space, but saw only the rushing movement of bodies. Then, the entire room moved as one creature toward the door as shouts of anger and fright rose to the high ceiling. Hannah allowed the crowd to push and shove her toward the doors. Something untoward was underway and she was as eager as the rest of them to escape now and ask questions later. Maybe, just this once, God would let her off the hook.

Caine

Caine sent the third and final wave into the establishment and stationed men at the front and back doors. The first two groups were instructed to blend in for five minutes and wait for all of the brethren to be in place. Caine checked his watch: sixty seconds until ground zero.

That's what they called this night: *La Zona Cero*, in honor of Jesús, the clan's original leader. Zeus, as he preferred to be called, for obvious reasons, had set up Ground Zero to placate the whiners in the bunch. All year long, the individual members of the brotherhood, forty-five in all, disciplined their hunger and controlled their lust, knowing that one night a year, Zeus would take them on a killing spree bigger and more fantastic than the one before. Until his premature death five years ago, Zeus carefully chose each killing field on every 5th of May, covering all fifty states and southern Canada. As Zeus' duly-appointed successor, it was now up to Caine to direct the boys' long-bottled frustration outward onto the patrons of the Foundry Night Club.

A woman screamed and Caine snapped to attention; the game was afoot. Remaining near the doors, he scanned the crowd, seeking a special prize for himself. His brothers would kill three, four, maybe even five people each, biting, ripping, and tearing flesh until they were exhausted. Caine had no such need; he desired one special girl—one who smelled nice, looked good, and who could withstand his attentions for a few nights to come. Giving his younger brother, Julio, the thumbs-up as he jogged past dragging a woman by her hair, Caine leaned against the door frame and watched. There was always one worthy woman and he was an extremely patient monster.

Hannah

The crowd stopped abruptly all around her and two people slammed into Hannah's back before apologizing and spinning around.

"What the hell is going on?" one asked. The other mumbled the same sentiment with a few added expletives and the duo moved off.

Fresh screams erupted near the doors and Hannah bobbed between the men and women in front of her to see what the trouble was. When she caught sight of the woman who wailed, she wished she hadn't made the effort. A man held her up by the waist and was brutally biting her neck. Hannah's heart leapt and she backed slowly to her original waiting spot. Second-by-second, on all sides, men and women alike were grabbed up and attacked in a similar fashion. As the bodies hit the ground, a way was made for her to see all the way to the exit. Two smiling monsters guarded the door, their faces dripping with blood.

"OhmyGod, ohmyGod, ohmyGod!" Hannah mumbled under her breath as she reached the metal ceiling brace. The violence and frenzy with which the monsters attacked the club patrons stole her words. She couldn't pray, which made the experience unbearable all by itself. Eventually, they'd come for her, wouldn't they? Hannah gulped louder, "OhmyGod."

Shannon Lower, the young woman who'd driven her group to the club, jogged toward her, a mask of terror on her face.

"Hannah!" she shouted and lifted her arms as if to grab her into a hug. Four steps out, she was yanked into an embrace, then right before Hannah's eyes, the monster in the form of a man, sank very long and very sharp teeth into Shannon's throat.

Hannah shouted with surprise and surged forward, grabbing the attacker by his long hair. The moment she made contact with his greasy locks, two steel-like hands took her shoulders from behind and jerked her backward with enough force to cause her neck muscles to throb.

"Caine! A brunette, right?" a voice shouted near her ear as the man who grabbed her maneuvered her around to face him and then lifted her over his shoulder. Hannah pounded his back and screamed for help, but every face she saw that wasn't a vampire was either dead or being attacked. The entire night club was filled to capacity with monsters and the horror of the blood-soaked dance floor caused her to swoon. The last image before everything went black was of a limousine and herself being tossed into it. As she hit the leather interior, Hannah fainted.

Caine

Paulie had chosen well. The slender brunette in the center was odds-on favorite by appearance alone, but the smaller one on the left had the petite build he preferred. Still…the big black one on the right looked hardy enough to last a week under his teeth. Caine remained in the next room and spied on the women through a drilled hole in the wall. Bugsy and Julio were on the job behind him, ready to hop-to when he'd made his final choice.

"The one in the middle—she's gonna be the calmest," Bugsy whispered. Caine sensed Julio's agreement without having to turn. They sometimes placed bets on which woman their leader would choose. Caine liked the women he chose to be frightened, but he didn't like them to make too much noise. Struggling and crying was tolerated; screeching at the top of their lungs, not at all.

Twelve months ago, at the previous La Zona Cero, Caine had chosen a large-framed woman in her forties, whose best feature was her waist-length, dark blonde hair. When she finally expired in his arms, Caine ordered her hair shorn and braided. He draped it across his bedpost and even today, he stroked it often before falling asleep. Sometimes he wished he'd never finished her off; she'd been the best in a long while.

Which one of these women would feed him tonight and how long would she last? Caine ordered his men to hush and focused his attention into the next room. His stomach grumbled, but he could wait. In fact, that was why Zeus handed him the reins before he died—Caine was the only one fully in control of his impulses. The leader of the vampires smiled and peeked through the hole.

Hannah

Snapping awake, Hannah sat up and looked around. She'd been placed on a floral-patterned couch with two other girls. The one on her left was petite, blonde, and unconscious. The woman on her right was thick, African American, and bound at the wrists. Hannah met her eye.

"Where are we?" she asked the woman.

"How am I supposed to know, ya stupid witch?" the woman replied and looked away.

Momentarily speechless, Hannah took a deep breath. The woman was frightened, not particularly rude or unfriendly. Hannah tentatively touched her knee.

"I'm Hannah. What's your name?" she asked, her voice gentle.

"Burnetta, but I don't know why you're introducin' yourself. We're gonna die here. Just a matter of time," the woman said in a rush, facing away. "They killed my girl, Shessy. Just like that." She snapped her fingers and then turned to meet Hannah's eye. "Shessy never even gone out before. She turned 21 on Saturday. I just wanted to help her celebrate a little. Oh, God! We're gonna die!"

"Shhh, shhh," Hannah said, consoling her as best she could. Yes, they were likely all about to die, so what could she say to help the woman? "Burnetta, it's not your fault. Shhh."

"Shessy's momma gonna be so sad. Why? Why?" Burnetta asked the air and then bent forward to cry over her lap. Hannah rubbed her back and turned to the little girl on her left.

"Hey, how about you? Are you okay?" she asked, touching her sleeve. The waif-like woman wore a sheer material top over a white tank and skin-tight white jeans. Tiny, flip-flop-type sandals with rhinestone accents finished her fashionable outfit. The girl stirred slightly and peeked up to meet Hannah's gaze.

"I'm scared, Hannah."

"I know," Hannah said smiling; the girl had been only pretending to be unconscious. "What's your name?" she asked.

"Trisha," the girl replied and sat up. Even sitting beside Hannah, she was small, barely coming up to her shoulder. Hannah touched the crown of her head and spoke to her as if she were much younger than twenty-one.

"It's okay, Trisha. Just be calm, it's okay."

"How's it okay? HOW IS IT OKAY?" Burnetta shouted and got to her feet.

A door opened in front of them and a man with wide shoulders and a hulking stance entered. Hannah assumed he was a vampire by the bloodstains on his shirt.

"You!" he bellowed to Burnetta. "You're out! Bugsy! You take this one!"

Hannah hopped to her feet and grabbed Burnetta by the shackled arm. "Burnetta," she whispered urgently into her ear, "do you know God?"

Burnetta screamed and fell into the couch to avoid being grabbed by the one called Bugsy. Hannah went down with her and asked her question again, right into her ear. Bugsy put a hand to Hannah's shoulder as if to separate them, but Hannah turned and looked him in the eye.

"WAIT ONE SECOND!" she shouted. It worked with the hooligans she came across periodically outside the YMCA where she worked. Evil people were like bad dogs—you stare them down, assert yourself, and hope God will hold them at bay while you make your escape. The vampire looked back the way he'd come as if awaiting instructions, and then fell still.

Hannah squeezed the woman's fleshy bicep. She'd do her best; Burnetta needed to be reminded that her Creator loved her. Hannah took a deep breath and asked God to fill her mouth with words and her heart with wisdom.

Caine

This was a new thing, watching one of his victims console the others with religious mumbo-jumbo. Out of simple curiosity, Caine motioned for his inferiors to hold back and allow the woman to speak.

Decades ago, before Zeus forbade the clan from attending religious services, Caine used to enjoy a Buddhist monastery that he frequented in Washington, D.C. There, he met a delightful mortal Buddhist who taught him how to meditate into a calm state and thus control the bloodlust that accompanied vampirism. It wasn't easy and it wasn't natural, but with Jangi's help, Caine was able to convince his body to rely on animal blood and avoid drawing off humans for the most part. That in of itself was the major challenge for all of the vampires in their clan and Caine had been ecstatic to bring his body into submission.

Zeus outlawed all religious expression fifteen years ago, after three of the brethren were murdered by a Catholic priest they'd trusted with their secret. Father Bob, as they called him, befriended the vampires, brought them close with promises of peace, and then beheaded them in an elaborate exorcism ceremony. Caine abducted the clergyman after the incident and led the interrogation. It was clear after four hours of torture that Father Bob hadn't meant the vampires any real harm, and he truly believed that he was able to save their souls from hell. Still, Caine's brothers were dead just the same; good intentions aside, he ordered the priest's head be removed and buried along with those of his deceased brethren.

Caine listened to the woman named Hannah and sucked his teeth. What religion was she spouting in there? So far, he didn't recognize it. She hadn't mentioned any specific god-names and despite his people's past history with the godly types, he was too curious to make her stop. Plus, wasn't the sound of her voice soothing him, too? Caine swallowed back the last thought and using the meditative skills he'd learned at the temple, he forced himself to ponder the kill instead. Very soon, any minute, he'd see what the girl was made of…literally. Caine smiled.

Hannah

"Burnetta, right now, speak to God," Hannah whispered in the woman's ear. "Ask him to save you. He loves you so much."

Burnetta looked as if she might curse in Hannah's face, but then, her eyes softened and she relaxed a fraction. The one called Bugsy stood with his hands on his hips and looked at the women, a perplexed expression in his red eyes. Hannah ignored him and focused all of her attention on her new friend.

"Sweet," Bugsy growled and reached for Burnetta's arm.

Burnetta was pulled to her feet and she shuffled off her high heels before Bugsy led her out of the room. Hannah watched her go, a sense of peace in her spirit. Burnetta was in God's hands; now to check on Trisha who was bawling into her fingers.

Hannah scooted across the cushions until their legs touched and she gently patted the girl's back. The door opened again and Hannah looked up to see another man, this one narrow, with a long face and flashing blue eyes. He leaned against the doorpost, crossed his arms at his chest, and settled in to see what she would do. Hannah scowled.

"Will you let us go, now?" she asked. The vampire smirked, as she expected, and said nothing. Hannah returned her attention to the tiny Trisha. "How about you, Trisha? Do you pray to God?"

"I used to," she whispered, "but he never answered me."

Hannah smiled and continued to rub her back. "Sure he did. If you ask him to, right now, he'll send you comfort."

"Hey, you," the vampire barked then, gesturing toward Hannah. "Walk yourself through those doors right now." He pointed the way Burnetta had exited and Hannah stayed put.

"Why?" she asked, unafraid. Her earlier fear was due to surprise, but now that she understood the dark nature of her enemy, she was no longer frightened. She hoped she wouldn't be tortured, but beyond that, she trusted God to either save her now or save her spirit upon death.

"Because if you don't walk yourself in there, I'm going to drag you in there and possibly dislocate your shoulder in the process."

Hannah remained where she was, reluctant to leave Trisha alone. The vampire took a step toward her and she inhaled sharply.

"Can I take Trisha with me?" she asked, and the girl looked up from her hands to see what he'd say.

"I'm going to take care of Trisha. You. Go. Now." He pointed to the door and took another step toward them. Hannah pressed her lips together and pulled the girl into a hug.

"Trust God," she whispered into Trisha's ear. The girl nodded and began to cry again. When Hannah stood from the sofa, the girl wailed and curled into a ball against the arm of the couch. Hannah frowned; Trisha was too frightened to pray. Hannah dropped to her knees at the girl's feet and reached for her clutching hands.

"Trisha, I'm praying for you!" Hannah said. The vampire had stepped close and stood over her, his face looking down and in shadow.

"This is adorable. You have until the count of one to get out of here," he said, his voice edgy.

Hannah patted Trisha one last time on the head and stood to her feet. The vampire was so close that before she could back away, she'd been nose-to-chin with him. He did not move against her as she turned for the door he indicated and stepped into the dark hallway. At least Trisha was quiet and perhaps praying now. Were these women about to become vampire food? Was Hannah?

Hannah stepped into the dark and expected the worst.

Caine

"Ah, the verbose one," Caine snickered as the brunette wound her way into the study. Feeling along the wall, she reached the place where he waited. She startled at the sound of his voice, putting a hand to her sternum.

"Oh!" she gasped and blocked the door with her body.

Not in, not out, but hovering half-way, she looked him over as he leaned against the back of the tattered couch he sometimes napped on after a particularly harrowing day of trying to survive in a world not made for vampires. The one called Hannah said nothing more; she didn't scream or beg or cry. More curious than ever, Caine held her gaze and stared her down. She held his eye, and although a few tears slipped down her cheeks, she wasn't afraid.

"Are you crazy or something?" he asked, lowering his chin. "Are you on drugs? It'd be nice to know before we consummate our relationship."

The woman shook her head. Caine sighed, unsure of how to

proceed.

"I'm going to kill you," he said in an undertone, watching her eyes. "Slowly. What do you say about that?"

The woman offered a tiny shrug and didn't look away. Her respirations and heart rate jumped at his words, but Caine saw no outward evidence of distress. Maybe his distance gave her courage. Caine stood off the sofa and the woman stepped backward into the hall.

"Oh, so you do feel *something,* don't you, Joan of Arc?" he asked and followed her into the darkened space between the two rooms.

Somewhere in the house, a woman screamed and Hannah looked to the side, her lips pressed together.

"Sounded like Miss Burnetta, didn't it?" Caine asked. He reached forward and grabbed Hannah's upper arm. She wore a sleeveless pink summer dress that dropped straight down from her bosom and revealed nothing of her figure. Her physical proportions mattered little at this point; it was her blood he wanted, and sooner than later.

Playing with his food, Caine sucked his teeth and waited for her eyes to meet his in the low light. Finally, Burnetta grew silent and Hannah faced him. She first looked at his hand on her arm and then met his gaze.

"Trisha's already dead. She lasted only a minute with my brother, Julio. How does it feel to be such a failure?" he asked in a low voice. This time, the woman's eyes flashed.

"Just do what you're going to do, you devil," she whispered in a wavering voice. "I have places to go, people to see."

Caine smiled. "You going to see God?"

"If you kill me, I am."

"Oh, I'm definitely going to kill you." Caine grinned wider and pulled the woman close, one hand cupping her throat, and the other, her shoulder. She broke out in nervous perspiration and furrowed her brow.

"I forgive you," she whispered as Caine moved in. He backed up a few inches.

"What?" he asked, his voice hard. Hannah said nothing and squeezed closed her eyes. Caine shook her shoulder. "What did you just say?" he shouted into her face.

Caine waited a few seconds, fully expecting a reply. Instead, the woman went boneless and slipped out of his grasp, falling to the floor. Caine bent over and yanked her upward by her long hair. One way or another, he was going to get a reaction out of the woman. One way or another.

Caine viciously jerked her to him and stabbed his fangs into the flesh of her throat. That'll teach her.

Hannah

"Wait!" Hannah yelled as the vampire attacked, miraculously feeling no pain at the wound-site. "Wait!"

Deep in her spirit, a message bubbled to the surface. One that assured her that she would not die this way, and she would not die this day. The vampire didn't let up and the whooshing sound in her ears reminded her of the noise her old truck made in the winter as it warmed up. But she had no time to be distracted. She had to get the guy to stop killing her.

"Mister Vampire, sir, stop!" she yelled again, right into his ear. "You can't kill me! It's not time!"

That worked. The monster's lips left her skin with a smack and he looked into her face, panting.

"I assure you, I am killing you," he hissed. Hannah winced at the sight of her blood staining his teeth.

"No, no, any minute now, something will happen and I'll be released or rescued or…"

"You're crazy," he said and leaned back to her neck.

Hannah screamed as loudly as she could, purposefully pointing her lips to his right ear. The vampire pushed her away and pressed his palms to both sides of his head.

"SHUT UP! SHUT UP!" he shouted, spitting red.

Hannah darted into the study and looked around for an exit. Burnetta had gone through there, right? At the other end, she noticed a closed door. It could be a closet, but what if it was a way out? The vampire reached for her dress, and it ripped as she ran for the door and pulled it open.

"You can't escape me!" he shouted and made another grab for her. Hannah ran down a short hall that opened into a kitchen. Moonlight poured through the windows, and as the monster gained purchase on her loose curls, she spotted the back door.

Two flashlight beams headed up the pathway.

"HELP! HELP! IN HERE!" she shouted, and the vampire released her hair. Hannah dived for the door and yanked it open. Falling into the arms of the first policeman, she gestured behind her. "GET HIM! HE WAS TRYING TO KILL ME!"

The second officer disappeared through the kitchen and back the way she'd come. The one who held her up radioed for help and led her into the cool night air.

"It's okay now, shhhh, you're okay," he soothed, carefully steering her to his patrol car on the side of the house. Hannah clutched what was left of her dress together and fell into the back of the black and white. Moments later, more cars arrived, lights flashing, illuminating the devil's den. Taking a deep breath, Hannah covered her face and thanked God. In the middle of her prayer, the door on the opposite side of the car opened and another person fell in heavily.

"Oh, sweetie! You was right! You was right!" Burnetta cried, pulling Hannah into a half-embrace in the backseat of the cop car. "I prayed for help and I got away! I got away and I got the neighbor to call 911! You was right!"

Hannah laughed and cried with her new friend. Within a few minutes, no vampires or cops departed the big house, but an ambulance rolled up and two attendants ran in with a gurney.

"You think that other girl got out?" Burnetta asked Hannah.

Hannah wiped her cheeks, but didn't respond. The vampire had said she was dead. Was that true? If so, why had she and Burnetta survived? It was a puzzle and both women watched the back door awaiting word.

The police radio cackled to life in the front seat, and hidden within the puzzling police code, Hannah got the idea that the vampires had not been captured. But what of Trisha?

When the gurney came out five minutes later, the sheet was pulled over the head of a very tiny feminine figure. Hannah burst into tears and Burnetta rubbed her back.

"It's okay, hon, she's gone to be with Jesus," Burnetta soothed. "God does things His way. You know better than me. God's got that girl and He's got us, too."

Burnetta was right, but Hannah the Tzadik cried anyway.

Caine

All the boys escaped the house and were scattered across Montgomery. Caine checked the time—ten minutes until sun-up. Some of them would be cooked; it was nearly impossible to find suitable light-tight shelter on such short notice.

Julio was with him and was really sweating it; cursing, crying, and terrified of being melted by the morning sun. Caine soldiered on, older, wiser, and infinitely more intelligent. He'd find them a place to hole up, and at sunset, he'd call the surviving brethren together. For now, he needed a quiet place to meditate; a dark, safe place to calm his frenzied mind. At sundown, he'd move the clan out of state.

Julio overheard his thoughts and grasped his arm. "Where will we go? We just got set up here. It's perfect!"

Caine shrugged out of his grasp. "This place is rotten. Now, shut it or I'll go on without you," he growled and the kid fell silent.

This place is rotten. The phrase danced around in his head. It was truly rotten, and he didn't want to run into the Hannah-woman ever again.

"And no more brunettes," he muttered.

Julio didn't reply. It was just as well, Caine hadn't been speaking to him anyway.

Rotten woman, he sighed inwardly and jogged toward an abandoned warehouse ahead. *Calm, calm, calm...center yourself, Caine...*

Caine cursed and made it to shelter just in time. The Hannah-girl ruined everything and the next La Zona Cero was a year away. *Rotten tzadik.*

Regeneration

By Kevin R. Maze

GIBSON BLALOCK DROVE PAST THE OLD STANLEY
house and this time he had an idea. He pulled into the gravel driveway
in front of the darkened abandoned house and turned off the truck.
The full moon shone through the trees and bathed the "For Sale by
Owner" yard sign in a soft, ambient glow. The driver's door creaked
loudly over the sound of crickets, but with the nearest neighbor a mile
away, it mattered little. Grinning, Gibson walked toward the back of
the house.

The place had been on the market for a year, ever since Willodean
Stanley passed away. Her son Kyle checked the house every Monday
and Friday. Gibson knew this because he repaired windows there that
had cracked before the late Mrs. Stanley departed this world for a world
without broken windows.

Gibson reached the back porch and faced the door, a rectangular
piece of dilapidated wood that revealed its age in the moonlight. A
rotted rocking chair rested next to a weathered stand-alone freezer.
Someone had removed the lid, time and the elements dusting the
interior with a layer of grit, and the decaying plastic emitted a pungent
odor. Gibson peered into the chasm and wrinkled his brow. Why do
people take the tops off freezers, even old ones? He didn't understand
it, but saw lidless freezers often in the south. Was there a run on these
things?

He turned to jiggle the doorknob and leaned in with his shoulder.
With a pop, it was ajar, and he stared into the blackened room. Gibson
stepped slowly into the kitchen and waited for his eyes to adjust. Soon,
his hands scrambled to the left and he carefully inched his way through
the dark until his fingers felt a cold, chiseled doorknob. He recognized
the type, clear glass that every kid made-believe was a giant diamond.
When he turned the loose knob, the latch clicked open and he pushed
the door inward with a screech of metal hinges. Gibson fumbled in his
jacket pocket, produced a flashlight, and pointed the beam into the
basement.

Gibson smiled; it was a clever idea.

Break into the house, find the basement, loosen the water-heater
connections, maybe break a pipe, and release the stored water onto the
floor. When Kyle Stanley checked it tomorrow morning, he would call
on his friend Gibson Blalock, of Blalock's Affordable Home Repair. It
was a great way to generate business. Or, since he repaired the windows
of the house already, he would *re*-generate business.

Gibson smiled; it was too funny.

As he followed the flashlight beam into the cellar, each stair groaned under his weight and threatened to give. A dank, damp odor punched him in the face as he descended. Gibson covered his nose with his free hand and continued on. Suddenly, his left foot slipped out from under him and he fell backwards onto the staircase, crashing with a thud and a yelp. The flashlight disappeared between the steps and Gibson looked up into the darkness.

Mumbling curses, and with his back throbbing with pain, a minute or two passed before Gibson moved. When he did, he turned his head toward the basement floor and saw a dim light emanating from underneath the staircase. Gibson smiled, thankful he had a sturdy flashlight and not one that broke easily like those used in horror movies.

Gibson grabbed the handrail and pulled himself vertical with a grunt. The railing stopped; he had reached the cellar floor. Now to retrieve his torch.

Gibson walked around the staircase to the beam of light shining underneath and dropped onto all fours. The stone floor was cold and pushed through his denim jeans. Immediately, the chill permeated his bones, ran through his joints, and shot up his spine until the tiny hairs on the back of his neck stood at attention. His arms turned to gooseflesh as a shiver danced through his body. Gibson reached through aged cobwebs for the flashlight. His fingers crawled around the black metal cylinder and fumbled for a grip while the sticky mesh wrapped around his hand. When retrieved, he wiped off his hand, turned around, and shined the light in the cellar.

And then he saw it, tucked away in the corner of the cold, dark room. The water heater.

Gibson smiled. Pulling a set of vise grips from his back pocket, he walked toward the appliance. With the flashlight in one hand and the tool in the other, Gibson went to work like a master craftsman. His arms moved quickly, motivated by purpose while the metal grips glinted in the light that flashed across the room. The corner flurried with activity in a room that reeked of bitter stagnation.

Shortly, Gibson stood and smiled at his handiwork; water poured steadily from the broken connections. By the time Kyle Stanley performed his routine check tomorrow there would be enough water across the floor to warrant a phone call. And Gibson would be ready.

Of course he had to make sure Kyle would call him. Why wouldn't he call him? Who else would he call? Gibson Blalock posted signs at both intersections in town and in front of the grocery store. Kyle would *have* to call Gibson; there was no other choice.

Gibson bit his lower lip. Maybe he should call Kyle in the morning for coffee, just to say hi and catch up on old times. They could discuss plans for the day. Gibson would tell him he's going to look at a new truck while Kyle would tell him he was checking on his mother's old house. And then, uh-oh. What do you know? Water damage. Good thing he just saw Gibson Blalock this morning; let's give him a call.

Something scurried in the dark.

Gibson swung his flashlight in the direction of the sound. He didn't see anything, just some boxes covered in dust and a couple of stacks of papers. Then something small scampered across the floor.

Gibson fought the urge to panic and continued to follow the motion with the light. He squinted toward the back of the room and watched the rat dart along the side of the wall. Gibson relaxed his shoulders and let out a breath he didn't realize he'd been holding, and followed the rodent with his eyes. It continued toward the back corner and disappeared.

Gibson cocked his head. How could a rat just disappear?

Curious, he walked to the back of the cellar. Even with the flashlight, the corner remained dark. He waved the light slowly from side-to-side and then he saw the hole. It had been cut into the stone floor, a radius of two-feet, and when he stared down, it seemed to continue endlessly into an abyss. Did something use to be there? Gibson looked up, but the ceiling was undisturbed. He glanced back toward the dark opening and thought about the rat. He fell down there, the poor fella. Gibson shined the light into the hole, but couldn't see anything, not even his long-tailed little friend.

The water trickled steadily from underneath the water heater. Gibson walked toward the steps and paused when the light caught something at the bottom of the staircase. It appeared to be a type of gauzy material riddled with fresh scuff marks. He looked closer; the marks were from his shoes. Now it all made sense; this is what he slipped on coming down the stairs.

Gibson grabbed the sheet-like substance, furrowed his brow, and examined it more thoroughly. It was not soft, but felt more like parchment, and was round, tubular on one side, but expanded into a flat piece at the end. The whole thing resembled a funnel. He examined the flatter piece under the flashlight. The beam diffused the material somewhat, but still provided no answers. The tube, in particular, resembled snakeskin, but was as big as Gibson's arm.

Gibson frowned. It was *exactly* the size of his arm and about as long.

As he measured it up to himself, the flat piece fell parallel to his side and draped against his jacket. The stuff had the shape of an arm and torso, but it was definitely not human.

Something rustled behind him.

Gibson pivoted and aimed the light toward the back of the cellar and caught a glimpse of something rushing from the hole in the corner. Water continued to flow along the floor from the bottom of the water heater and Gibson's heart pounded through his chest.

Time to go.

He turned to walk up the stairs when the rustling sounded again. It was louder than before and although a voice deep within him said to run, he turned the light toward the sound.

The water rippled like a stone thrown into a pond. Then he gasped at the sight of what caused the disturbance.

It was as big as Gibson and fast, scuttling quickly across the floor even though it didn't have legs. The torso moved upright while the tail dragged behind it and sloshed in the water. The creature's head peered down at Gibson, who froze in its gaze. A forked tongue flicked out of a mouth full of sharp teeth. The digits at the end of its arms resembled talons, not fingers, and they flexed and glistened in the halogen light Gibson clenched in his hand.

Gibson glanced at the shed skin by his feet. A fleeting memory appeared from the recesses of his subconscious, a story his grandfather told him long ago. He told of a legend that says whenever a snake sheds its skin, it is a symbol of new life, of regeneration.

The snake-man moved suddenly and Gibson knew it was the last thing he'd ever see. Still, one last thought rushed from some quiet place within his mind just before the darkness enveloped him.

Regeneration.

How ironic…

Shocked

By Pete Turner

HE GRIPPED THE SIDES OF THE CHAIR AND SQUEEZED, hoping to dull the pain even if just a little. He did not even hear the word, "ON!"

As if he were in a cartoon, he gritted his teeth hard enough for them to shatter, but could not shut his eyes any tighter. The initial jolt of electricity connected rapidly to every nerve in his body and exited through every orifice. Even though his eyes remained sealed, he was blinded by the brightest of white light, as if he had been in darkness for a thousand years and had finally opened his lids.

As suddenly as it began, the pain subsided. He relaxed and allowed his hands to loosen their grip. When he tried moving his arms to rub his forehead, he realized that he could; he was no longer bound. His consciousness re-entered his mind and he flicked open his eyes. He was lying down. Abruptly upright, he looked around at his surroundings and gathered his thoughts, taking in clues to register exactly where he was. What happened?

His mind flashed backward, his last thought being strapped into an electric chair. He'd been sentenced to death for torturing and killing nine women in the states of Kentucky, Tennessee, and Florida. He recalled the initial jolt of an electrical current and the smell of burning flesh.

His flesh.

Then he woke up here, on this...

This couch.

He looked around the immense and immaculately-appointed room in which he sat.

This isn't my home? Where am I? And more importantly, how did I get here?

Swinging his feet to the floor, he found he was too woozy to stand. Resigning to remain sitting, he rubbed his hand across his face.

Think... Think... THINK! he screamed inside.

"Hi, babe," a sultry voice said from behind.

He jumped and turned around, staring at the beautiful woman looking back at him. He did not know her. He searched his memories, but could not consign recognition. Yet, a strange and wonderful feeling enveloped him. He was madly in love with this woman. How could that be? He did not even know her, right?

"Hon, are you okay? You act like you don't know me."

He blinked in response.

This must be heaven, he thought, *but how do I deserve heaven?*

His thumb moved across his other fingers and he felt a ring on his third finger.

"Um... yes, love. It's just... You look so beautiful." He wasn't lying; she was stunning. She could have been a supermodel. Still, this was insane. He was married to this gorgeous woman and their home looked like a mansion, but he did not recognize anything? Yet, the feeling was unmistakable—he was in love.

"It's time to come up to bed. You have your investors' meeting tomorrow, darling."

He nodded in agreement, having no clue as to what she was referring. He had to think.

"I'll be up in a moment, dear," he managed. She smiled and he would have sworn that the room they were standing in became brighter.

She said, "Am I still your most valuable investment?"

"Of course. You're the most important thing in this whole world to me." And he meant it. She turned and walked up the winding white marble staircase.

He stepped over to a table displaying several photos. Photos of their wedding day. Photos of them on horseback. Photos of...

"AHHH!" A scream pierced his silent thinking and rang in his ears. He ascended the stairs as quickly as possible, sometimes leaping three at a time. Instinctively knowing where she was, he entered the first bedroom. He tried to pull up as he burst through, but could not as he slid in the blood that pooled on the floor.

She lay on their bed, not only dead, but mutilated and unrecognizable. Running to her lifeless form, he fell on his knees and swaddled her into his arms. Her face, only seconds ago the most beautiful he had ever seen, was now gouged and slashed to bits, marred the way he had marred his last victim. He was reaping the evil of his sown seed.

A jolt of electricity struck his back and he turned quickly enough to see his attacker, covered in her blood, holding a taser. He shut his eyes and the bright flash came again. Rubbing his eyes, he tried opening them. His world was moving back and forth. Not spinning, but moving back and forth. Side-to-side. The unmistakable scent of saltwater filled his nostrils and he forced open his eyes.

He was on a boat. A big boat. A yacht. He sat straight up in the bed. Surely he had simply fallen asleep and dreamed that nightmare.

But he was almost positive that he had been in the electric chair. Was that part of the nocturnal illusion?

In uneasy wonder, he rose from the bed and followed the stairs to the upper deck.

"Did you get enough beauty sleep, my illustrious husband?" a voice asked behind the opposite way he was ascending.

He turned and saw her; it was his wife. The woman from his dreams or his last reality. He still did not *know* her, but the feeling of deep, passionate love squeezed at his heart like before.

"It would pale in comparison to you, my love." He could not extract her face from his memories. It was as if she did not exist anywhere in his recollection. However, this did not quench his love for her.

"It looks like it's going to storm," she said as she pointed over his head. He turned and saw the dark clouds swirling above. When he turned back, her face contorted into a gruesome fixture of utter agony. Within moments, he was baptized in a red liquid that emanated from a gaping wound in her sternum. Unceremoniously, she thudded to the deck.

"NOT AGAIN," he screamed and ran up the remaining steps. He looked all around and saw no one. No perpetrator. No killer. Returning to her side, he scooped her into his arms and wailed. His heart filled with grief; the sensation of having this woman—his wife—torn from him overwhelmed his senses and he cried piteously.

Thunder rumbled overhead and just as he looked up, lightning bolted from the sky, struck his head, and paralyzed him. He slumped beside the body in a pool of her blood, staring at her empty eyes. Still feeling the boat swaying in the water, he blinked back the pain and closed his eyes for a long pause.

Someone called his name, but the sound echoed as if he were in a tunnel. His eyes fluttered open again. His beautiful wife was standing beside him. He looked into her intoxicating eyes and felt the pillow against his ear.

Sitting up quickly, he took note of the majestic bed on which he lay. He scanned the room and looked back at the woman speaking to him in a gentle, sincere voice.

"Welcome back to the world, my sleepy-headed husband," she said softly. He grimaced.

I am not in heaven, he thought, and sent her a weary smile.

Hell: where their worm does not die, and the fire is not quenched.
~ Jesus of Nazareth, the Gospel According to Mark

Thirst

By Stuart Loudon

It's always been about the Blood.

All I have ever wanted. All I have ever craved.

The Blood gave me life. From it I have gained purpose and focus.

It numbed my sense of emptiness. I have been its slave.

I cannot remember when it began. I only recall countless days of craving the Blood. I would spend most if not all of my waking hours seeking it, only to eventually collapse into a version of sleep with fresh blood within me.

This thirst is not quenched.

I have looked around me, barely seeing other people. To me, others were as shadows, without substance or independent existence. I have stood within a crowd and only seen the prospects for fresh blood, my mind empty except for the various games I would have to play to be able to feed.

I have been a deceiver.

A seducer.

A friend, potential lover, and confidant.

I have befriended and betrayed.
I have met so many people. While others appeared to do so with the intention of forming relationships, for me it was only ever about the Blood. I have walked through life alone.

So many years have passed. I have seen fashions change, celebrities and leaders rise and decline. People have lived their lifetimes, blooming and eventually withering before my eyes. I have watched multitudes having an almost limitless range of experiences. In all this time, amidst all this diversity, I merely fed. Above all else, it has always been about the Blood.

And still...I have thirsted...

I forgot everything else as I sought to fill this burning, aching thirst inside me. Every cell of my body cried out in anguish and longing whenever I was unable to feed. A depth of desire, beyond addiction or lust, consumed me from within. The straining and convulsing of my inner being at times almost sounded like a pounding heartbeat. I laughed aloud at the thought that one like me could experience something akin to a heartbeat.

A living, beating heart.

A human heart.

A powerful muscle...pumping blood, infusing a body with life.

A living heart...vital and alive. Unknown to me, as one who was dead inside...except for the Thirst.

Along with the Thirst came the Fear. I could not bear to let the sunlight shine upon me. I lived always in the dark, knowing the light would consume me. I feared it would burn up my dark and cursed flesh, leaving none of me behind. Even in the throes of a maddening unslakened thirst, I would find myself fleeing the Light for the protective blanket of the darkness.

The light of life for some, but for me, a creature of darkness, it was an embodiment of death, a symbol of my destruction. A merciless enemy who would not spare me and from whom I always fled.

On occasion I made half-hearted attempts to learn about the people around me. They looked like me yet were so very different. On occasion I would find myself alone in the dwelling of a person whose blood now pulsed within me. In the solitary emptiness of such moments, I would sometimes speak to a companion who could no longer hear me. I would look over their possessions, exploring, and would sometimes find books of poetry, of philosophy, of religion.

I was surprised to see beings similar to me portrayed in various books and movies. They were caricatures, pathetic imitations, with black capes and affected accents. While I hid my nature from those around me behind a facade, these creatures paraded around in pure melodrama.

I had never known anyone else like me. I was curious about the legends of such creatures, who, like me, could not bear the touch of sunlight on their skin and had no life save that which they took from others.

It made no sense to me that the caricatures could not stand garlic or pieces of wood shaped like the letter "t". Somehow, it seemed, someone had gained a distorted knowledge of beings like me. For reasons of which I was unclear, the "t" symbol (which I eventually discovered some called a "cross") represented the antithesis of my kind, a force alien and in opposition to the essence of the creature I was. A force which could destroy the only nature I had ever known, and which I considered foundational to my being.

One evening I had the rare fortune to discover two people who were frail and unable to defend themselves. I consumed both of them, and slumped into a chair, glutted, the power of their life-force pounding my temples. I was overwhelmed by the sensation. So accustomed to a constant aching thirst, I now found myself filled to an extent I had never known, with several of my waking hours remaining.

This gave me no satisfaction. I still felt the Thirst coiled within me, an insatiable parasite, its demands upon me only temporarily stilled. I knew that before many more hours passed I would again know its torment, again pouring all of myself into finding my next victim.

I had never encountered such a circumstance. My waking hours were never endingly consumed with the hunt, usually without a successful outcome. To find myself filled with two people and with time to spare! I had no other pursuits or interests with which to fill my time. I could not feed again; I had already gorged myself. How could I fill the remaining hours?

The dwelling in which I found myself was fortunately located only a few streets away from a major city centre. I decided to simply wander, to walk the streets in search of some new experience. I turned briefly to look at the two bodies I had left behind, and then shut the front door as I strolled onto the moonlit street.

As I walked I was able to actually notice my surroundings. For the first time, I saw people as people. I beheld families and individuals...the old, the young, each on their own journey and mission. I saw laughter, tears, excitement, disappointment.

Hope.

I caught snatches of conversations in which many spoke without saying anything of depth. Most, like me, seemed to live for themselves. I was surprised to hear others acknowledging their trials, joys, setbacks, and dreams. I heard talk of optimism, of faith, of belief in an intellect, a power, that was more significant and enduring than a mere person.

A deity.

In the hallway of a large stone building, I found a book with the "t" I had wondered about on the cover. I opened it and eventually found the writings of a man named John. I wondered about John, who he was, and how he had come to write the stories in this strange book which some seemed to consider significant.

I read words which spoke of freedom...of deliverance. I read of a woman, who like me was alone, an outcast, who thirsted physically, and who also had a deeper thirst...for significance, for love....for life.

"Anyone who drinks this water will soon become thirsty again."

The hopelessness of the Thirst was one I knew all too well. It constantly promised me fulfillment; told me that all I had to do was take the life of one more person, disregard the evil of such an act, and I would be satisfied. The discomfort of the Thirst would be replaced by the joy and contentment of being filled.

Time and time again I believed this lie, committing evil acts in the hope that in doing so I would be able to satisfy my thirst. When it was over I would look upon the life I had destroyed, upon the evil I had committed, and while my thirst may have been numbed, what was left of my conscience screamed its dismay.

Could I ever be free of this Thirst?

"Those who drink the water I give will never be thirsty again. It becomes a fresh

bubbling spring within them."

Tears fell from my eyes at the thought. Could I be freed of the Thirst? Dare I imagine it? To be free of having to feed on the lifeblood of others and instead have my own lifeblood welling within me? To be able to have experiences of which I was not ashamed, to be able to do more than skulk around, finding ways to take from others the life which I did not have myself? To be able to feel... to exist ... to live....?

I staggered back under the crushing weight of revelation as I thought of the days...nights...CENTURIES that I had wasted in my desperation and aching to satisfy a thirst which never left me... which gave me no fulfillment or satisfaction. Feeding gave me no peace, only a temporary numbing of my longing and thirsting....

I suddenly realised I was a slave. I had no emotions, no life... I felt nothing except the Thirst.

I collapsed, falling over and striking my head against the wall. I felt nothing. Torn in two by the power that controlled me and my desire to break free, I frantically raised my hands, to whom and what I did not yet fully know...

"Free me, please," I screamed. *"Set me free....I want to live...take this thirst away..."*

I railed and cursed against everything that I was, or thought I was, and all that I had become. I longed to be released from this endless cycle of evil and regret. I wanted to die. Were it the morning, I would have willingly run into the waiting destructive arms of the daylight.

Eventually I ceased my ranting and pleading and stood still. I had nothing more to say and there was nothing more I could do. With everything unspoken left within me, I rejected all that I had been, all that I had done, and declared it at an end. All of it, every part of it, died.

I became aware of a growing luminescence. The Light. Far brighter than the daylight I feared.

More confronting.

More piercing.

More pure.

I could not run from it any longer. I could not suffer any more. I raised my face, and surrendered myself to the Light.

I screamed in agony as the Light reached me, then engulfed me. I felt myself being torn apart and laid bare as it pierced me to my very core. It invaded every part of me and flowed through every cell like a wave. The black shell of my emptiness, my darkness, the evil which had cloaked me for so long and which I had come to consider a part of my very self, began to splinter...

I was aflame...yet I was not consumed...

The heat and light intensified as a transition began to occur. I changed, from one form to another...from an imitation of life to a fresh and new expression of life in all its fullness. The dead and atrophied organs within me began to fill out and live for the first time, performing their various functions. My heart, almost hesitantly, but with growing confidence, started to beat.

Blood began coursing throughout my body that was my own, finally my own. A heart, once dead and only temporarily stimulated by the lifeblood of others, now beat strongly with a deep and transcendent life which would not end...

I fell to the ground...

♦

I write these words as I sit comfortably watching the sunrise. Despite my age, I am like an infant. This life is new to me and I am in the humbling position of having to make conscious efforts to learn what is, to many, second nature.

A new day has begun.

For the first time I can anticipate an end to my life. My once lustrous, thick hair has begun to thin. I experience illnesses and diseases, and I have a discomfort in my lower back which will not leave me. I get emotional at times, and am still struggling to make sense of the feelings which sometimes overcome me.

But....at least I can feel. At last, at long last, I can live.

And what's more...

This morning.

This beautiful morning.

I can sit and watch the sunrise, a beautiful cascade of colour across the sky. I feel its warmth on my face, its light dazzling my eyes.

And my once-dead heart...quickens!

Runaway

By Ellen C. Maze

THE 6-YEAR-OLD CHILD IN THE ROAD WASN'T THE

strangest thing that had happened to her that day. From the moment the alarm sounded, Janet fought to keep up with the shenanigans thrown at her by whatever forces controlled such things. Firstly, when her feet hit the carpeted floor of her downtown loft apartment bedroom, she stepped into an inch of freezing cold water. Although a busted pipe turned out to be the culprit, Janet chalked it up to another sign that the universe hated her and had designs on her precarious happiness.

Her coffee pot percolated obediently for the first three minutes, but when she returned from the shower to grab a cup, a leak had developed and dark brown Folgers coated the counter surface and trickled down the groove between the dishwasher and the sink.

The whole day went that way; one disaster after the other, from her flat tire on the way into work at the law office where she was one of a hundred underpaid secretaries, to the fountain pen that exploded in the breast pocket of her favorite suit coat at quitting time. Now, it was 7 p.m., and while rushing home to watch her favorite TV show, *Survive-Alive*, with the very cute and sexy Sterling Hawkins, she'd just come to a screeching halt, nearly flipping her car into the ditch, in an effort to avoid a tiny waif of a boy in the middle of the road.

Janet took several deep breaths and peeled her hands from the steering wheel. The little boy was fine; she could see him plainly awash in her headlights, standing on the dashed yellow line, hands behind his back, swaying slowly back and forth, regarding her with enormous eyes. Janet switched off the car and got out, scanning the road for any sign of a house or apartment from which the kid might have wandered. This stretch of Hwy 231 was plain countryside—pastures, uninhabited barns, a few abandoned diners/gas-stations. Janet looked back the way she'd come; from the interstate to this point, she remembered seeing no houses. Maybe another three miles, you'd get into Houston Estates, but how could this baby have walked that far?

Then an ugly thought hit her: did somebody drop him off here?

Worse: was he *abused* and dropped off here?

Worse still: was he *abused and then escaped* and she was the one the universe chose to rescue him?

Janet sucked in a deep breath and waved at the kid, affecting a wide smile and squinty eyes—the expression she used when talking to puppies or kittens—and approached the boy.

"Well, hi, there, little fella," she cooed, still a good five yards away.

"I'm Miss Janet. What's your name?"

"Lucas," he replied without pause. He wore footie pajamas on which cowboys harassed Indians with violent fervor around a chocolaty-brown stain on the chest. His hair was long, past his ears, and threatening to flop over his eyes. Janet thought he looked thin, but it might have been the low light.

"What're you doing out here all by yourself? Where's your mommy?" Janet asked.

The boy didn't seem frightened or confused. He walked up to her and met her at the front bumper of her Olds.

"Will you take me home?" he asked, looking up at her in such a way that she felt compelled to drop into a squat. "I'm lost."

Janet nodded, her mind racing. Should she take the boy home? Maybe she should call the State Troopers. Pondering her choices a few seconds, finally she made some words come out.

"Where do you live?"

"In the big yellow house," he said, not missing a beat, pointing vaguely to their right. Janet peered into the gloomy darkness and discerned a grown-over road and a keeling rusted mailbox. If anyone lived back there, she'd be surprised. Still, the kid seemed sincere. Janet clucked her tongue, and stood up.

"Sure, Lucas. That's your driveway?"

"Yes ma'am," he replied and moved to the opposite side of the car. Janet watched as he climbed into the passenger side as if he'd done it a million times before and buckled his seatbelt. Janet fell in beside him and cranked the engine.

"How did you get lost? I mean, were you walking alone in the dark?" she asked, allowing the car to heat up a little before pulling out. It was only November, but her Cutlass had its quirks.

"Well," the little boy shrugged and looked away, "I was bad and I ran away." He looked back at her face then, taking on a repentant expression. "But I'm *real* sorry, and I want to tell mommy how sorry I am. I never shoulda run away like that."

"Oh, she'll understand," Janet replied, not knowing if what she said was true. What kind of mother would let her kid walk around in the dark, in the middle of the road, and not be frantically combing the neighborhood for him?

"She got mad when I colored her magazine. I just wanted to see what the president looked like with a mustache."

Janet smiled. Barack Obama would probably look pretty good with a little facial hair.

Lucas continued. "Do you think President Johnson looks better with a mustache? Daddy has a mustache and mommy likes that pretty well. Why'd she get so mad?"

Janet looked at him sideways; did he mean Lyndon B. Johnson? The kid spoke well for a 6-year-old, but had serious trouble with names. Ignoring his obvious mistake, Janet prepared to pull the car into the kid's narrow, weeded driveway. Not a single car had passed and she wondered at the oddity. She came home this way every night, had since January when she moved into her apartment on Harris road. Usually, this particular connector from town to country pretty much roared with traffic at 7 p.m. Weird.

"I told her I was sorry, but…" the little boy trailed off, still talking about why he ran away. Janet thought she'd better listen or risk making him upset.

"I'm sure she forgives you for that. Johnson hasn't been president for a long time," Janet said, tickled by her answer, but Lucas looked out the window.

"That's not all I did," he mumbled and then blew on the window. When it didn't fog up, he tried again, failing both times. He seemed sad about it and looked down at his hands. "I also made a fire in the bathroom. I just wanted to camp out like Captain Challenge…"

"Captain Challenge?" Janet asked, a little surprised. Her father collected toys from the 50s and 60s, and Captain Challenge was one of three soldier toys of Summer 1966 that made up the centerpiece of dad's display. The Captain alone was worth a thousand dollars. If this kid tried to set it on fire, mom certainly had a right to be furious.

"Yeah, daddy got him for me last Christmas. I think I mighta burned up mommy's rug."

"Well, I guarantee that when she sees you tonight, she'll forget all the stuff you did wrong, and give you a big hug," Janet said, smiling, and got the car in gear. She rolled a few yards to the drive and turned down. Branches scraped alongside the car and rocks crunched beneath her wheels as if they hadn't been packed in years. Lucas was still talking to her right and gesticulating with his tiny hands.

"…but Timmy and I didn't know about the bears, so daddy wasn't mad that time. At Valentine's Day, mommy gave me some heart candy and I ate it all at once and got real sick. After that, she wouldn't give me any candy at all. I really miss candy. Do you have any candy?"

Janet considered the Snickers bar in her purse. She'd bought it because on the back it said NOUGATOCITY, the last phrase in the Snicker's Word Campaign collection she'd started last fall. No, she couldn't give the kid her candy. She shook her head. "Sorry, just gum."

"Poop," he mumbled and leaned forward to see the trees lit up in the headlights. "Mommy's gonna be mad, me comin' home so late…"

Janet glanced his way; his voice had fallen a few octaves and she might have heard fear in his words. Was she taking the kid into an abusive situation? Had he escaped from *mom*? That would explain a lot. His odd "grown-up" behavior, his politically incorrect pajamas with the odd rust-colored stain on the front, and his ominous predictions regarding his mother.

Janet slowed the car to a stop. On all sides, the forest pressed in menacingly, the only light came from her halogens, stabbing the night ahead. No structure loomed close enough to see ahead, and the trail had been swallowed up behind her. Janet put the car in park and pulled out her cell phone. She should have called the cops right off the bat. Better late than never.

"What's that?" Lucas asked when she slid her iPhone awake. "Is that a comoonikater?"

"A what?"

"Are you calling Captain Kirk on it?"

Janet looked at Lucas sideways. "You mean a communicator? Like on *Star Trek*?"

"Yeah," Lucas said, and tried on a small smile. "Daddy used to let me watch it, but mommy said it was dumb. I'm goin' to work for Captain Kirk when I grow up. I'm going to the moon!"

Janet touched 9-1-1 as she nodded absently to the boy. He was just about to become someone else's problem. There was little she could do for a 6-year-old boy with an abusive mother.

"I'm gonna go where no man's gone before!" Lucas yelled, zooming his hands through the air like spaceships.

Janet covered her right ear with her palm and waited for the operator to pick up on her left. Lucas grew louder, shouting the Star Trek mantra a few more times, until he fell into singing the theme of the old show in a high falsetto. Janet heard nothing from the phone and she peeked at the bars—no service. She uttered a curse under her breath and Lucas grew quiet.

"Ah-woo," he whispered, looking at her with wide blue eyes, "you said a wordy-derd. Mommy won't let me say that word. Ah-woo…"

Janet held her tongue, the adventure finally souring for real. She started back down the drive, picking up the pace when it seemed level enough. Lucas continued to chatter on lots of subjects, until he mentioned the stain on his chest and Janet's ear perked.

"What? How did you get that chocolate stain?" she asked, stealing peeks at him as she piloted through the blackness.

"That's not chocolate—mommy won't let me eat candy, silly!" Lucas laughed, high and sweet, and then pulled the fabric out. "Mommy got mad and poked me with something shiny. It didn't hurt bad. I wish it was chocolate! Then I'd lick it!" Lucas laughed again.

Blood? Janet glanced at the stain a little longer before returning her eyes ahead. It looked like chocolate, but if it was dried blood, that made sense, too. She decided to attempt another probing question.

"What shiny thing did your mommy poke you with?"

"She uses it in the kitchen, too," Lucas said, more subdued, "and I was bad. I shoulda stayed outta her room. Hey!" he shouted and strained forward. "There it is!"

Janet made out the silhouette of a large two-story house, probably painted a light color, but in the night, it looked gray. The shrubs hadn't been trimmed and the boxwoods that should have been waist high grew wild as trees that reached the gutters. No lights burned, no cars sat out front, there were no signs of life at all. Janet stopped the car and Lucas hopped out as soon as she shifted into Park.

"Lucas! Wait!" she called after him. He should have run around the front of the car, but when he didn't, she called him again. "Lucas? Where are you?" No answer. Janet stood motionless a few moments, considering the dark and spooky house and the clear night sky that the house's lot revealed. When she hadn't heard anything, including a running boy, for three minutes, she headed for the front porch.

The slab of concrete elevated to the front door was brittle and strewn with leaves and litter, as if nature and the local teenagers worked their magic there as often as they could. Janet peeked in the window set in the double doors and then knocked. It was fairly ridiculous; there was simply no way the house was occupied. After another loud knock, she peeked in the window on her left. The clouded glass prevented her from seeing anything past shadows, but before she gave up, the door creaked open, seemingly of its own accord. Janet jumped and pressed her hand to her chest.

"Lucas! That's not funny!" she barked and walked to the door. A small noise tinkled a few feet within, like a glass bottle rolling, and she braved one step across the marked threshold. "Lucas!" she yelled again, examining what she could see of the room's contents. At her feet were a dozen newspapers. Oddly enough, they were distinctly yellowed; so much so, that Janet bent down to read the dates. "1966?" she asked the air and picked up the closest one.

"Local Woman Stabs Son, Kills Self," the headline read. Janet stepped back onto the porch and stumbled toward the car, newspaper clutched in her hand. In the glow of her headlights, she scanned the facts: "Kelly O'Reilly, 28, stabbed her 6-year-old son Lucas last night at 7 pm, dropped his body in the ditch on 231, and then drove her car into Inky Lake…"

Janet looked back at the house. The door stood ajar, but the scene was as lifeless as before.

"LUCAS!" she yelled, loud enough to strain her throat. "LUCASSSSSsssss!" she screamed again.

Only crickets answered, their voices unnaturally loud. Janet whirled around to the driver's side and pulled open the door. Taking an absent glance at the paper before she tossed it to the grass, she caught the date: November 7, 1966.

Yesterday's date, 45 years ago.

Tossing her car into gear, Janet peeled out, sending gravel and dirt onto the porch of the house, and sped off down the driveway. The woods had closed in, making the driveway more a walking trail now, with barely enough room for her car to pass. Scraping branches sounded skeletal and Janet pressed the gas further to increase her speed. At one point, a pot hole she hadn't noticed before swallowed the front end a moment and then vomited it out, creating a violent lurch. Janet gripped the wheel more tightly and zoomed on. When she reached the main road, she barely slowed to yield to traffic. None was coming anyway.

Punching the gas again, she headed toward home. On her right, the night had gulped up a dark ditch. Did she see a small body lying on the edge? A child in footie pajamas?

Janet sped on.

On her left, a quarter mile later, Inky Lake appeared, more sinister and mysterious than ever now that she'd read the newspaper article. A woman in a red nightgown might have waved to her from the miry shore, but Janet sped on.

She'd take the long way home from now on.

It was for the best.

Friends

By Elizabeth E. Little

BEFRIENDING DEATH HADN'T BEEN ON THE DOCKET when Jacob met Zith, a magnanimous Shadow Wraith with amazing dark powers and a secret crush on their Elven friend, Mithrael. Now, Zith was *Aroul*, the Guardian of Darkness, and Jacob did his best to stay on his friend's very unstable "good" side.

It wasn't easy.

Today, they traveled a two day's journey to Aroul's castle on their way to the Elves' territory. Jacob stared up at the huge castle before them, his mouth agape. He barely made out a tattered flag waving in a stale breeze at the top of the tallest spire. If he squinted, he could see a black-winged individual wielding two swords portrayed against a blood-red background.

Aroul stopped at his side and tilting his face, followed his gaze. "I really should replace that old flag."

"Is that you?" Jacob asked without taking his eyes off the impressive and frightening image on the billowing fabric.

Aroul shook his head. "No. Although I can see why you'd think that. That is the likeness of the Guardian before me. It's traditional to put a picture of the Guardian-in-residence up there, but since I tend to change my appearance so often, I just left it as it was."

Absorbed by the sheer immensity of the castle, Jacob looked blankly into space until Aroul shook him by the shoulder and gestured for the entrance. The towering doors creaked open of their own accord, groaning in protest against rusty, unused hinges. As they swung inward, Jacob stared in slack-jawed awe at the impressive interior. Huge arches ribbed the long hallway, bracing the walls and ceiling. Stained glass windows adorned the sides and could be seen between the massive blue marble columns. The light that shone through them illuminated the entire hallway in a rainbow of color, almost negating the dreary atmosphere the gothic architecture emanated.

A white marble statue of an angelic figure stood at the far end, huge feathered wings filling the entire space from floor to ceiling, wall-to-wall. Long, wavy marble hair cascaded from the statue's head and reached past its shoulders to mid-back. The figure stood upright, two-handed sword in her left hand, tip touching the floor because of its length and weight. The hilt spiraled up around her hand, as if it had been made for her and become part of her arm. Crafted with such precision and skill, Jacob could read emotion in the angel's eyes. Her long marble dress brushed the floor and flowed outward, rippling like water. In the statue's free hand she held an open book, bracing its spine with her palm so its pages faced her. Jacob was sure that if the statue hadn't been all one color, he would have seen her move. A huge window behind her was colored just so that it altered the light of the red dawn from outside into pure white beams that shined from behind her like rays of untainted sunlight.

Directly to the right was the statue's exact opposite. Carved from black marble, a tall man with slightly-opened dragon wings and clawed hands that clutched a sword to its chest, menaced the room. A flowing black cape drifted in a long-past breeze, draped forever over black armor. Spiked shoulder pads framed a head of black hair hanging past its shoulders, nearly covering its pointed ears. The statue appeared to glare at the angelic statue to its right, head turned to face her and with intense eyes. Its face was set in a grimace, not of pain, but of playful disgust. Wonderstruck, Jacob's gaze still gathered the details of the space as Aroul closed the door.

"What's wrong with *you*?" he asked, raising his brow with humor.

"This castle is amazing!" Jacob exclaimed, but Aroul dismissed him with a laugh. "I'm serious," Jacob pressed, still studying the statuesque figures.

"You thought it would be like the outside: all death and decaying corpses, right?" Aroul eyed him with amusement. "Well, even *I* grow weary of looking at all that nonsense."

Jacob turned in a slow circle as he observed the castle's magnificence. His eyes found their way back to the two lifelike statues at the head of the room.

"That one looks a lot like you," Jacob said, pointing to the black statue. "Well, the other you…" he finished awkwardly.

Aroul laughed. "It's the Guardian of Darkness that's on the flag, and that other statue is Miloa, the Guardian of Light."

"Why in Sky's name would you have a statue of Miloa here?"

"Because as the Guardians of Light and Darkness, we are as much one individual as the Guardians of Fire and Ice. We are two halves of the same whole. Neither is complete without the other. With no light, there could be no darkness; and with no darkness, there could be no light."

"That doesn't make any sense. If there's no light, then there'll be *only* darkness. And if there's no darkness then there'll be *only* light." Jacob crossed his arms. Aroul smiled.

"If you lived your entire life in fear, would you know what fear was? If you were always hungry, would you know what hunger is? If you were always happy, would you know what happiness really is?" Aroul asked him. Jacob hesitated. "No, you wouldn't. If you lived your life without the light, then you would not know what darkness is so it cannot exist."

"That still doesn't make any sense."

Aroul chuckled. "Wisdom comes with age. Believe me; I'm old enough to rival the intellect of a dragon."

Jacob pondered his words and followed behind as Aroul led their way into the bowels of the castle. Aroul fulfilled his job as Death-Giver with a calm Jacob couldn't comprehend—what must it be like? Granting death to whoever asked? Jacob had seen him deal death more than once, and it was a chilling experience to say the least. As he rounded a corner, he lost sight of Aroul. He looked around in despair; getting lost in this particular castle would not be a wise thing to do. He spotted his host a few paces ahead and jogged up behind him.

As they resumed their side-by-side tempo down the marble hallway, Aroul glanced over at Jacob. "You are troubled."

"I don't want to die," Jacob said suddenly, "ever."

"Of course you don't, Jacob." Aroul looked at him incredulously. "But, you, above all, should know that death is a mercy, not a punishment."

"You once said you'd welcome death, if given the chance. Did you mean that?"

A smile tugged at Aroul's lips. "Death is a mercy, Jacob. With all my heart. I have awaited death since the day I took this form. I'm actually envious of those who receive death from my hand. It's hard for me to give freely that which I cannot have."

"I'm still trying to get used to this." Jacob shook his head in wonder. Here was a man, or creature, that could actually help people die. Jacob had difficulty grasping the concept. "Do you know your future?"

Aroul crossed his arms. "No one knows for sure, Jacob. Judging by my life thus far, I can imagine my afterlife won't be a nice one." Aroul chuckled. "Being the Guardian of Darkness and seeing so much death… it'd be nice to finally be able to know what it's really like. Pain I know. Suffering I know. But death? I'm a stranger to death while it is no stranger to me."

Jacob took in for a moment the wisdom in this last statement. "I still don't want to die."

"Then that's where we're different." Aroul smiled. "You're still young; you haven't even *tasted* the true bounty of life yet. I'm far past my due date and my life has all but spoiled."

"I don't think your life is rotten," Jacob said defensively. Aroul chuckled and shook his head. "I'm serious."

"That's why *I'm* the Guardian, and you're not."

The simple poke at Jacob's pride made his face flush with color. Aroul turned and started walking again, so Jacob was forced into step behind him.

"Enough talk of death. Death, itself, grows tired of the praise." Aroul waved the topic away with his hand.

Jacob nodded in silent agreement. So many more questions were burning on the tip of his tongue, but he refrained from asking them. He knew from experience that Aroul/Zith had a hot temper that was easily aroused. Jacob followed him wordlessly down the endless corridor, realizing that he could walk down these halls forever and never find their end. Aroul caught his glance and grinned.

"Goes on forever, eh?" he asked casually and Jacob shook his head in awe.

"It sure looks like it."

"It's a trick of the mind," Aroul said, tapping his head for emphasis, "but if you go long enough, you *will* find the end."

"What's at the end?" Jacob asked him. He half expected there to be a secret entrance to a treasure room or something, like at the end of a rainbow.

"My room," Aroul said with a wry smile, then added when Jacob looked curious, "it's nowhere you want to be, Jacob."

Jacob accepted this silently, already forming images of the horrors Aroul might have in there. After a while, Aroul stopped by a door and fiddled with the knob for a moment before it opened. Inside was a simple bed with a table and lantern.

"This will be your room during your stay," Aroul announced and gestured inside. "Mind your wandering. This is *not* somewhere you want to get lost."

"I don't doubt it," Jacob agreed as he headed in, grateful for a place indoors to lay his head for a change. "I think it's lovely," Jacob exaggerated. His friend wasn't fooled, but smiled anyway.

"Just don't go exploring." Aroul turned to leave, then remembering something, turned back. "Oh, and Jacob, these halls tend to appear different every time you leave a room, to discourage people from escaping. Just remember that you came from the left and you should be fine."

"Got it."

Aroul nodded at him and headed out, politely closing the door behind him.

Jacob sat on the bed and pondered their adventure so far. Traveling with a friend he only recently discovered was the Guardian of Darkness was proving to be extremely interesting as well as exhausting. When he lay back on the rather stiff blanket, he fell into a deep sleep.

Before midnight, he awoke and looked about the dark room, remembering his situation. Eyebrows raised with resolve, he opened his door and nodded approvingly at the torch-lit hallway. At least if he wanted to stroll about, he'd be able to see where he put his foot. Keeping in mind Aroul's advice to remember he came from the left, he headed down the long hallway.

An hour passed and Jacob's frustration had reached a breaking point. The same hallway he'd entered at midnight continued on without apparent end, and his legs were tired of walking. He spotted a turn up ahead and eagerly hurried forward. As he rounded the corner, he was met with a huge door locked from the outside.

"Great," Jacob mumbled, staring up at the tall door before him. The intricate black iron door was barred four times, locked five, and had a large wooden plank slung across it. A stench from inside the room reeked of death. It occurred to Jacob then that he might have stumbled across Aroul's "room" and he shuddered.

A gentle tap on his shoulder caused him to start and whirl around. He reached for his sword, but frowned when he realized he'd left it back in his borrowed room. Jacob puffed out his chest and stared into the eyes of the beast before him.

"Who are you?" he asked and a blank stare was its reply.

The tall creature's face hung below its shoulders due to a brutally broken neck and it stared at Jacob sideways. It was humanoid with ears longer than an elf's and a tattered suit covering its ruined body. Both of the thing's eyes worked, but they were emotionless and it had a severe burn on one side of its face and the corresponding arm.

"Neth'rakl balish?" the creature asked him. Jacob maintained his gaze and the creature tried another language. *"Velnelsha kai? Ba'al'am melthir? Kerreesh cleippss?"*

"What are you trying to say?" Jacob asked shakily. The last one had sounded like insect chirps. The creature sighed in exasperation.

"So it's the human tongue you speak, is it?"

Jacob nodded slowly.

"Finally. *Who are you?*" the creature repeated slowly, as if Jacob wouldn't understand if it were said any other way.

"I'm Jacob," Jacob said defiantly. "Who are you?"

"I am called Melthim." It straightened its back and winced as its neck was moved. "If you want to visit Death you'll have to wait your turn. I'm overdue."

Jacob took a moment before answering. "Overdue?"

Melthim looked him over. "You don't look like you should be here."

"I shouldn't. I went the wrong way."

Melthim's sideways mouth smiled weakly. "Then you should flee before Death mistakes you for a visitor. This door," Melthim gestured to the locked door, "is what will take away my pain. I've heard that Death himself lives beyond it and offers his gift to those who ask of it. I broke my neck…" Melthim felt the twisted neck with a burned hand. "I broke it trying to escape from a fire. Fell into a hole and hit my head on the ledge. I awoke to find myself outside in that horrid place." Melthim shuddered at the thought. "I'm not sure why I'm not dead yet, but I'm hoping whoever's behind this door can finish me off."

"Well, I'm not going to stop you." Jacob stood aside. Melthim eyed him curiously before he pushed against the door, testing its solidity. "How in the world am I supposed to get *in?*"

"Beats me," Jacob admitted, backing up. "Maybe there's a password."

Melthim looked back at him incredulously. Jacob couldn't take the look seriously since Melthim's head was parallel to the ground.

"A password? Are you serious?"

Jacob shrugged, maintaining his safe distance. Aroul warned him to stay away from his room, and that advice seemed sound. Melthim turned back to the door and counted the locks silently.

"It'd take a giant to unlock these."

With a sudden thought, Jacob crossed to stand beside him and felt of the cold steel. If it hadn't burned his skin, his hand would have frozen there. He rubbed his burned hand and eyed the door.

"That's weird. It didn't burn *me*." Melthim put his hands back on the door and strained against it, but it would not budge. "Maybe if we pushed together."

"It'll burn me again!" Jacob protested. The look on Melthim's face clearly stated that he didn't care, and if Jacob didn't help him that he would follow him around the rest of the night bugging him. "All right, all right."

Jacob braced himself and shoved against the heavy door, while Melthim did the same. The door creaked and groaned as they heaved against it and burned like fire on Jacob's hands.

Finally, when he could take no more, Jacob shouted without thinking, "For Sky's sake, Aroul! Open the door!"

There was an audible screech of metal on stone as the door flexed outward, knocking them back. As they watched, the locks snapped open and the bars fell to the ground with a loud clattering. The large wooden plank caught fire and burned away to ash before their eyes. After a silent moment, the air stilled and the doors creaked inwards of their own accord. Jacob squinted into the darkness and helped Melthim to his feet. The sad creature looked at Jacob, and then at the door.

"Guess you were right. Sounds like 'open the door' was the password," Melthim said smiling.

Before Jacob could turn to leave, a gust of wind from behind forced them both into the darkness of the room. Jacob struggled against the pressure, but was soon knocked from his feet and slid through the doors on his backside. Once they were both through, the heavy doors swung closed behind them.

Uh oh… Jacob thought miserably, straining to see in the darkness. Melthim's hand landed on his shoulder, he was as blind as he was.

"Jacob, please tell me this is you."

"Yeah, it's me."

Melthim sighed of relief. "You know, I was so eager to get in here, but…" Melthim whispered, "…I'm pretty nervous."

"*You're* nervous?" Jacob demanded in a hiss. "I'm not even supposed to be in here! He's so going to kill—" Jacob stopped himself short at the irony. Melthim removed his hand and from the heavy footfalls, Jacob guessed he was working his way forward through the darkness.

"Augh!" Melthim shouted, leaping back.

It took only a second for Jacob to figure out what happened; for at that moment, two flaming blue eyes leapt out from the darkness. Following the deafening roar of a dragon, the rest of the beast came into view. Blue fire leapt from its jaws, licking its face with the flames. The entire dragon was made of bone, and blue fire burned in its ribcage, from its feet, in its jaws, nostrils, and eyes. Skeletal wings with fire for membrane flared in the air at the intruders.

Jacob began to scramble away when Melthim grabbed his arm. "Be still, Jacob! It has eyes only for the dead."

The unfortunate being's words were true. The huge dragon had its gaze locked on Melthim and Melthim alone. It tracked his movements as a predator stalks its prey. The massive skull lowered and sniffed Melthim's face and shoulders, lingering longest at his twisted neck.

While the dragon continued to sniff Melthim, Jacob took a moment to look around. Using the faint light from the dragon's fire, Jacob could make out decomposing corpses piled as high as the ceiling. He recognized the shapes of elves, humans, ogres, some that looked like Melthim's kin, and many other races Jacob had never encountered. As his gaze drifted across the melee, Jacob locked onto Melthim once more and tracked his movement. The one with the broken neck moved as if in a trance as the dragon maneuvered him onto a platform and snarled to make him stay there.

Unable to look away, Jacob spotted Aroul on the opposite edge of the platform. He wanted to call out to his friend, but stopped himself as Aroul doubled over in pain, falling to his knees and holding his chest. Jacob's eyes widened as Aroul howled in agony and visibly gnashed his teeth. His hands caught fire and burned with blue flame, and his black tunic ripped open as boned dragon wings flared from his back, matching those of the dragon that threatened Melthim.

His eyes now burning with blue fire, Aroul clambered to his feet. In one clawed hand, he held a shining sword, and in the other, an ancient book unharmed by the flames. Jacob held his breath; this was *not* Aroul.

This was the Guardian of Darkness. *This* was Death.

"Melthim Shadowblade," Aroul began, reading from the book in his hand as he advanced one slow step at a time towards Melthim. His voice echoed with power and, although it made little difference, Jacob covered his ears. "You have come before me this night seeking counsel."

Clearly frightened, Melthim stuttered a reply. "I-I've heard rumors…" Melthim hesitated as Aroul came to a rest a few feet from him, still reading from his book. "…rumors that you could end my suffering."

"Your suffering means nothing to me." Aroul regarded the crooked visitor, but Melthim held his tongue. Aroul shook his head and consulted his book again. "Is death truly the answer you seek from me?"

"Yes," Melthim answered, carefully choosing his words.

"Is that so?" Aroul held the book pages out so Melthim could see what it said. Jacob could barely make out a name being burned into the page. "Your name has now been written into the Book of Death," he said, his tone final.

Jacob shuddered, sorry he was privy to the entire discourse.

"Now is the time to decide how you would like to die."

"I don't know," Melthim blurted. "Just cut my head off or something. I really don't care!"

Aroul studied him carefully, flaming wings burning silently behind him. "Death is not your desire, is it Melthim?"

Melthim hesitated.

"No. Your soul still burns with life and will not accept any death I can offer you." Aroul looked back into the Book of Death and erased Melthim's name.

"What are you doing?" Melthim asked in a soft tone.

"No death I can give you will quench the fire in your soul. You have left me with no choice but to remove your name from the Book." Aroul looked up at him with a wolfish grin. "And if Death will not have you, then may Life take you back."

The bone dragon pushed Melthim to his knees with a clawed foot and he cried out in alarm. Breathing blue fire over the man, it snarled and rumbled deep within its belly, filling the cavernous room with sound. Melthim shouted out for help and Jacob wanted to rescue him, but interfering could kill them both. When Aroul held up his hand moments later, the dragon fell silent and stepped off Melthim's chest.

Melthim gagged, coughed, and then inhaled deeply several times. Jumping to his feet, he retreated several steps, his hands inspecting his neck. He'd been restored—his broken neck corrected and his burned flesh a memory.

"You…you revived me! But, you're Death!"

Aroul smiled and closed the Book with authority, the ominous sound shaking the room and causing dust to rain down upon them.

"Death would not claim you this day, Melthim. One day again you will stand before me, and then your soul will be ready. Now leave my sight, lest my mind be changed."

Jacob heard the heavy steel doors sliding open again, and he bolted for them. Aroul noticed him for the first time and pointed at him with a long, claw-like finger. Jacob froze, every muscle in his body refusing to move. Melthim walked dreamily toward the exit and out the doors, which swung shut behind him. Jacob fell to the cold ground and groaned. The bone dragon advanced towards him and bared its broken fangs. Faint-hearted, Jacob watched as Aroul strolled calmly his way, the closed Book of Death in his hand.

The bone dragon stepped aside as he approached and Aroul casually opened the Book again, scrolling through the names listed within. He shook his head and frowned playfully. He did not close it.

"Ah, Jacob, you come seeking Death?" Aroul asked, his voice no longer booming, his flaming bone wings at half-mast, like the statue outside.

Jacob shook his head, assuming his friend knew he'd not enter of his own accord. Aroul laughed.

"You are in *my* realm, human. What shall I do with you?" Aroul studied Jacob as if he recognized him for a moment before consulting his Book again. He flipped forward a few pages and turned the book for Jacob to see. Jacob almost didn't look. He glanced up and saw a list of black names that were not burning with blue fire.

"These," Aroul explained, "are those whose times have not come."

Jacob spotted his name on the list alongside his Elven friends who he'd left behind to travel with Aroul.

"As you can see, everyone is in my Book of Death. There is simply no way to avoid it." Aroul flipped forward a few more pages and turned the book back around so Jacob could see. Two names in particular caught Jacob's attention. *Matthew the Butcher* and *Jarsha Shadowsong* were written side by side. Jarsha's name glowed with green fire. The being he knew as Aroul had been the Shadow Wraith, "Zith," when they first met, and over time, he learned that Matthew and Jarsha were his identities during his arduous transformation from human to Wraith to Guardian, as fate directed.

Jacob gulped. "You wrote yourself in the book?"

Aroul chuckled, his fire eyes flickering bright. "*Everyone* is in my Book."

"Why is it in green?"

"Because I am immortal," Aroul said, a chill to his tone. "Death will never grace me. My name already burns because my time has come, and it burns with green fire because that time has passed and I missed my appointment. Zith stopped me from meeting my appointed time, Jacob. Being a Shadow Wraith has erased my chance for a mortal death."

"Then shouldn't your name be erased from the Book, too?"

Aroul sighed with careful impatience. "I am both in the Book of Life and the Book of Death, for I walk the line between them." At Jacob's glance he continued. "Miloa, however, is not in my Book. As a full-fledged Guardian she will never face a mortal death. I was drafted into the position, as are all Guardians of Darkness, and so my name is written in them both."

Jacob tested his muscles and was able to sit upright on the platform, but not stand. Aroul eyed his attempt and shook his head.

"Your being here has posed a problem for me, Jacob."

"Problem?"

"Yes. You see, only those who desire Death come to me, here. I warned you that this was not a place you wanted to be."

"I got lost! My room changed sides of the hall overnight so I went the wrong way!"

"It matters little now, Jacob. No living man has left this room, well, *alive*." Aroul cringed at the awkward wording. "And so therein lies my dilemma."

"What dilemma? Just let me go," Jacob pleaded.

"If I let you go, then I wouldn't really be called Death then, would I?"

"There's got to be something you can do."

Aroul grinned. "What's this now? Pleading with Death? How very original."

"I'm serious." Jacob mustered up all the courage he could. "We're friends, right? Am I to be held accountable for what could not possibly be construed as *my* error?"

Aroul froze as if struck through the heart by a lance. Whatever bitter world the creature walked in, a vestige of camaraderie remained as well. At that moment, the invisible bonds that held Jacob down were loosed and he stood to his feet and respectfully faced Aroul.

"Jacob," Aroul said coldly, "as much as I would love to let you walk out of here and pretend nothing happened, it is impossible."

"What are you going to do?"

Aroul thought a moment. "The usual punishment is the removal of the mortal soul, but seeing as how we're friends, maybe there's a way to lessen the punishment." Aroul grew silent before he drew his sword from its sheath and slowly ran his fingers down the flat of the blade. Jacob watched him uneasily.

"Wh-what are you going to do with that?" Jacob stammered,

watching the bony fingers trace the blade's length.

Aroul's shining gaze locked with his. "I'm going to make you bleed."

Jacob squeezed closed his eyes and prepared for the worst, deep down wondering about his choice of friends. As the blade neared him, and the charred air filled with a disturbing buzzing noise, Jacob wished he'd never met Zith at all. Before another moment passed, Jacob lurched forward following a sharp explosion of stinging pain.

"Death is a mercy," Zith/Aroul was fond of saying.

And so is fainting, Jacob thought, and was gone.

Quack

By Pete Turner

"THIS IS THE FIFTH PERSON GONE MISSING IN TOWN," the sheriff said.

"Yeah, and what are you doing about it, sheriff?" someone yelled.

"Do you think that someone is killing them?" another asked.

This was followed by another ten indecipherable questions hurled at once to the haggard and worn lawman. He looked down from the podium, tugged at his hat, and shifted the cigar in his mouth from left to right.

Raising his hands, he said, "Please, please. We're doing all we can. There're no bodies, therefore we believe there're no murders. We've five missin' persons and we're working every lead."

"That means you don't know any more than we do!" a woman protested.

The sheriff inhaled enough cigar smoke to fill both lungs, completely exhaling it in large smoke rings. Ripping off his black sunglasses, the sheriff narrowed his eyes and pointed toward the throng, growling, "No, it doesn't. I swear to you, citizens of Redwood Lake, there will be no more disappearances in our town! Even if I have to personally work twenty-four seven!" Removing his oversized hat, he wiped the sweat from his brow. He then returned the glasses and replaced his hat.

"Thank you all for coming out today," he said, pulling the cigar from his lips, "but I ain't answerin' no more questions. This press conference is over." The sheriff tipped his hat to the crowd. Again the onslaught of questions barraged him. Ignoring them, he put the cigar between his teeth, stepped away from the podium, and walked toward his police-issue SUV parked behind the stage.

Dr. Isaiah Sixx saw him approach and straightened from leaning against the police truck. He shuffled his feet toward the man and said, "Good afternoon, Sheriff Rogers," and thrust out his hand.

The sheriff dipped his head. "Afternoon, Doc," he replied, shook his hand, and continued, "Sumpin' I can do fer the town shrink?"

"Nah, I'm alright sheriff, but I did want to talk to you about the disappearances."

"Now, who'da guessed that?" the sheriff snapped.

"Sorry about all the dead-end leads, Sheriff, but I do have a theory about it."

"A therrry?" he cracked.

"You know, what scientists say for an educated guess."

"I know what a theory is boy, I ain't stupid, but we townsfolk like to shoot straight 'round here, so I don't talk in theory and psycho babble." His last few words he quipped in a forced Northern accent.

Sixx smiled nervously and continued, "Sorry for the implication, but I just meant that I think I know what's happening to the missing people."

"Sure ya know, cuz yer the feller who's killin' 'em," the sheriff snarled, tapping his right hand on his gun. "And so now, you's ready to confess?"

Sixx saw his reflection in the sheriff's black glazed sunglasses, stepped backward, and replied, "What? No…! What…? Why would you think that?"

"Cuz yer a weird one, boy! And usually the bad guy is the weird one! Besides I ain't the only un that thanks that!" he said as he unsnapped his gun holster.

"Whoa!" Sixx quickly raised his hands in defense. He looked around behind him and then back to the sheriff. He continued, pointing to himself. "I'm a suspect now, Sheriff?"

"Right now, Doc, everybody's a suspect." He closed one eye and blew smoke in Sixx's face.

"So does that include you, too? Are you a suspect in your own town?" Sixx backed up more.

Sheriff Rogers swore loudly and stepped close enough to the doctor so that Sixx could smell the vanilla flavor of the man's cigar. The sheriff pushed his index finger into Sixx's chest and the force caused him to momentarily lose his balance. He stumbled against the sheriff's SUV with a thud.

"You ain't as funny as you thank youself to be, Doctor Quack," Sheriff Rogers said, spitting every other word.

"Um, no. No sir… I mean, I know sir. I respect you immensely, Sheriff Rogers. This is your town, I get it. I just had an idea that might help."

"Good. Glad that's cleared up." His tone softened and he stepped back. "Sorry, Doc, this thing is stressing the devil outta me and I guess I'm coming off a li'l gruff and short with everyone."

"Oh, I understand. Business has been booming for me, too. I guess paranoia makes for good therapy cases," Sixx chuckled dusting off his backside as he stood.

"Okay, so what's yer theory, Doc?"

"Well, I might sound a little crazy—a little *counseling humor*—but I swear, strange things are happening at that church down by the lake."

"The power of God ain't strange, boy!" he snapped again and continued. "That Conners kid is a good preacher."

"I agree, he's quite charismatic, but I'm just saying that his message doesn't seem all that godly to me. I mean, Conners has everyone believing that any day now, Jesus is coming to take them up to the clouds."

"And He is! Doctor Sixx, you just went an' got yer fancy degree and became one of those atheist folks."

"I'm not an atheist, I'm agnostic. There's a difference," Sixx protested.

"Don't matter. Conners is a prophet of God, and yer fool therry needs work!"

Sixx nodded and held his tongue.

The sheriff shook his head, swore again, and pushed Sixx to the side. He opened the truck door and pulled himself inside before looking down at Sixx, finger pointed.

"Boy, I'm watchin you."

Sixx nodded again and watched the sheriff peel off and speed away.

♦

"The God I serve has power!" Conners said and sliced his hand through the air emphasizing his point like an old-time Pentecostal preacher. "This is tangible power! You gotta *feeeeel* it deep down in ya bones! I don't serve a little God!" Conners shook his head, and continued. "My God is big enough to meet your every need! But He does require something! Something from…. You!"

He pointed to the enraptured crowd for a dramatic pause.

"He wants your soul! So, friends, let me ask you… Just… ONE… QUESTION!" Conners paused between each word, taking deep, long breaths. His face was blood red and sweat dripped from his chin. He pulled a handkerchief from his back pocket and wiped his brow. "Are you ready to move up to this next level? The next step in our transformation into God's people?" He waited for the applause, dropped his head, and smiled, finishing with, "Who is ready to feel this tangible power of my God tonight?"

The congregation erupted as one; show over.

The Reverend Ben Conners did not look like your typical pastor. He was tall, 6' 6" at least, 250 pounds of chiseled muscle, his hair long and raven black. Some described his pale blue eyes as mesmerizing, some said he looked like an angel. Yet there was much more to Ben Conners than his rugged good looks. He was comfortable in the pulpit, as if it was his calling, his purpose. He had a deep R&B singer's voice and an enigmatic, super-powered persona. His words flowed easily, hypnotizing everyone in his wake. The audience sat captivated, hanging on his every word.

The "show," as Sixx labeled it, did not affect him. He was too smart to drink the kool-aid this conman was serving. God wasn't real, especially the God Conners preached. *I'd never fall under the spell of this charlatan,* Sixx scoffed to himself. He saw through Conners' façade and was not at all caught in the deceptive web of his golden tongue. The churchy phrases "a wolf in sheep's clothing" and "false prophet" applied to Conners more than anyone he knew. However, Sixx remained in the pew. While he was not impressed with the preacher, he was amazed at the influence he wielded over the crowd.

Like lambs to the slaughter, Sixx thought, trying to psychoanalyze Conners from his seat. Something was wrong; he could not yet label it, but the feeling gnawed at his reasoning, his intellect. He would discover the truth. Frustrated, Sixx looked away and forcibly suppressed his suspicions for the time being.

The preacher approached the doctor and placed his hand on Sixx's shoulder. "Isaiah, aren't you ready to come back to God? Before His return?"

He sounds genuine, Sixx thought. But the realization sank in; this was the hand of the killer on his shoulder. He couldn't prove it, but in his heart, the sick uneasiness was all the proof he needed. Anyway, knowing people, reading people, was Sixx's strength, his specialty.

Sixx thought about the preacher's words; they penetrated his heart unlike anything had in years. How did Conners know he'd once been a believer? Did he know that Sixx was a teenage convert, despite a staunch atheistic father? Or that he abandoned his beliefs while attending college? Sixx managed an answer.

"No, thanks, I'm just here as an observer."

"A seeker, perhaps?" Conners pushed.

"No, I'm not seeking anything except the truth." Sixx immediately regretted his choice of words.

"Well, you've come to the right place to find the truth," Conners replied and extended his hand.

Yeah, the truth that you're behind the disappearances, freak! Sixx thought, but could not say.

He pushed Conners hand away and brushed past him. The uneasy feeling had not let up, and he watched with disgust as the townsfolk made their way down the aisle to the altar. How did they not see the deception in this false prophet? Paying homage to a deity that doesn't even exist? Disgusted, Sixx stood to leave.

Conners bellowed again loudly, as if he wanted Sixx to hear. "He's calling us home soon; don't wait til it's too late!"

Sixx walked jerkily toward the door, inconspicuously looking over his shoulder. Had he forgotten something back in the church? He couldn't put his finger on it; maybe it was leaving those people with the killer. Hopefully, his proof would soon appear and everyone would see Conners for who he really was.

♦

Sixx woke early the next morning, even before the clock radio roared alive. He rubbed his face, breathing a long sigh. Something about last night still lingered in his head and he looked at the red numbers that shined brightly in the darkness. He still had ten minutes. Sixx sat up and decided to get out of bed anyway. His morning routine was typical of many young professionals who worked stressful jobs: find something productive to participate in to relieve stress. He turned off the alarm and was out the door five minutes later for his morning jog.

Sixx's shoes pounded out a regular rhythm as he followed the long stretch of blacktop that would take him well over two miles from his house. When he'd been house-hunting in Redwood Lake, this potential jogging route was the main selling point. The curve ahead rounded the lake and he anticipated the view of the sun on the water. Once there, though, on the other side of the lake, something was happening. The someone involved was Reverend Conners.

Sixx slowed, but did not stop the momentum he had achieved after his first mile and half. Once he concluded that Conners was behaving strangely, he slowed even more, finally jogging in place. Conners was carrying something long and seemingly solid, although the preacher exerted no effort handling it. He switched the long item from one shoulder to the other and Sixx stopped moving altogether. Narrowing his eyes to see, he gasped; it looked like the preacher was carrying a body bag.

Conners dropped the sack on the ground. Squinting further, Sixx saw what looked like a hand trickle out of the end. The preacher stooped and stuffed it back in, and then looked around as if paranoid that he was being watched.

Just then, someone crested the horizon of the hill above where Conners stood. It looked like a lawman, but the uniform indicated he was not county or state. Sixx thought he might be an FBI agent. Hunkering down to watch, he hoped the guy was about to arrest the conman, Ben Conners.

The two men argued, but since Sixx needed to remain hidden, the words were lost in the distance. It was a strange event, considering the pseudo-religious persona Conners wanted the town to trust. But Sixx knew all along: Conners was a phony and the good people of Redwood Lake were all under his spell. If Conners was arrested by this lawman, then they would see the truth as he did.

Sixx cleared his mind and tried to read the two combatants' lips. When that failed, he analyzed their kinetic-body language, although he was no expert in that field, either. Wishing he had more training, he cursed silently and watched.

At that moment, an odd weapon materialized in Conners' hands. He gripped it tightly behind his back, and Sixx gasped as it took the form of a sword. Afraid he'd been heard, he ducked behind the tree and held his breath through clenched teeth. After a long minute, he peeked out in time to see a burst of light illuminate Conners as he plunged the sword into the stranger's chest. Sixx froze; shocked, sick, but strangely vindicated. Wasn't it only fitting that he be the one to witness an actual murder? And how would he describe the weapon without sounding like a nut? Was it one of ours? Some top-secret military jewel that Conners stole or otherwise procured illegally?

Sixx shrugged; the important thing was that he saw Conners kill someone. As he fixed his eyes on the shining sword, it disappeared and shrunk back into a book-like square. The mystery was solved; Sixx was now convinced.

Reverend Benjamin Conners was an alien.

Sixx jumped up. He had to contact the sheriff, but... What if the sheriff was in with Conners? The other day, he was the man's biggest defender. Should he call the FBI, or would they just think the shrink had become the crazy one? Sixx headed home.

After debating nearly an hour, he finally contacted the sheriff and demanded that he search the grounds of the church and the person of Conners. When the sheriff agreed to do so, he headed back to the scene of the crime.

Shortly thereafter, the police SUV rounded the corner slowly and without its sirens blazing. Pretending as if he'd just jogged by, Sixx bounded back up onto the road toward the church and met the sheriff in the drive. When their eyes met, the sheriff shook his head.

"Doc, you have no business here," he bellowed and pulled the cigar from his mouth.

"I thought you may want to interview me face-to-face before confronting him."

The sheriff cursed loudly and walked into Sixx's space. "Boy, you need to keep yer nose out of police business." He punched his finger in his chest.

"Sorry, Sheriff. I was just out jogging, I meant no harm."

"Hey, brothers, what's up?" a voice behind them spoke.

"Sorry to bother you, Rev, but I was just dropping by to see ya. And the witch doctor here was just leaving."

Sixx's countenance enflamed as he sputtered, "Now wait…"

"Gentlemen," Conners interrupted, his voice soothing and sincere, "let's be kind one to another."

Sixx couldn't deny the effect the man's voice had on him. His face softened and he looked at the rugged preacher without speaking. The Sheriff complied as well.

"You both are welcome to come in," Conners invited.

"Well, I'm here on police business, Reverend Conners," the sheriff insisted.

Sixx continued to stare at Conners' face. He knew he had just witnessed him murder that lawman, but his face, his eyes were intoxicating. Sixx blinked and looked away.

"I would like the good doctor to come in as well. I've done no wrong and whatever is done in the dark will be brought into the light."

Was he planning to kill us both? Sixx wondered. Conners answered as if Sixx had spoken his fear aloud.

"I mean you no harm."

Sixx looked at the sheriff, who shrugged.

"Whatever," Sheriff Rogers said and then narrowed his gaze at Sixx. "You better not git in my way."

Sixx brushed by him and followed the preacher inside.

♦

After explaining what he'd seen in the sanest possible way, all three men stood from the dinette and followed Conners outside to the scene of the crime. They found no blood, no corpse, and no evidence of anything out of the ordinary.

"But I definitely saw you arguing with a man right here," Sixx said.

"You must be mistaken," Conners said with a sad smile. "There was no man here earlier."

"I'm not a fool, Conners. I saw that lawman come over that hill and argue with you. I saw you pull out a weird sword and murder him."

"Doctor, the only sword I own is my Bible, the sword of the Spirit," he replied, smiling.

The sheriff stared at Sixx. "There ain't no evidence to support the contrary here, Doc."

"Okay," Sixx snapped. "Then what about the body bag you were carrying? I saw the *hand*, Conners."

"Oh!" Conners laughed. "You must have seen the mannequin pieces I've been working on as part of Sunday's dramatized sermon. I have them right up here next to the barn."

"No! It can't be!" Sixx screamed. He cursed loudly and pointed his finger at the preacher. "You-you're not what you seem! I know who you are!"

"Get behind me Satan," Conners replied.

"All right, that's enough, Mr. Sixx," the sheriff drawled, choosing to drop Sixx's title. He stepped between the two other men. "Reverend, I'm sorry to've troubled you…"

"You're a murderer! I saw you kill that man and I saw the other body too. You have been killing the people of this town! It's you! You may fool everybody else with your hooey voodoo crap, but I am not a fool!"

"For which good deed do you try to strike me?" Conners said.

Sixx's face reddened more and he lunged. The sheriff grabbed his collar before he reached the preacher.

"I said *enough*, Sixx. Yer harassing this man!"

"At least ask him to show you these so-called mannequins," Sixx barked, dangling from the sheriff's meaty paw.

"I have nothing to hide, Sheriff, Doctor. I'll show you."

The sheriff dropped contact with the doctor and held him back with a hand to his chest. He turned to the preacher.

"No. Reverend, that won't be necessary. We don' wanna ruin the surprise. I think it's time the doctor and I took our leave."

Conners smiled and shrugged his shoulders. "Ruining the surprise is no fun now, is it?"

The sheriff gave the preacher a nod, pulled Sixx's arm, and walked toward the SUV.

◆

Sixx paced the floor of his home. Conners was definitely a fraud. How could the sheriff be so blind? Quoting all those scriptures? Being too cocky for words?

BEING TOO GOOD!

"Yeah, that's it," he thought aloud. "TOO GOOD TO BE TRUE!"

Sixx needed proof; he needed pictures. What was *really* in that barn? Sixx squared his shoulders; he'd go down there and find out for himself. Grabbing his cell phone, he headed out the door.

◆

Sixx parked his Jeep far enough from the church so he wouldn't be overheard. Slinking around the side of the church building, he looked for any sign of the preacher. The coast was clear. Sixx popped over the hill, but Conners wasn't there either.

Maybe he's in the church preparing for tomorrow's sermon, he thought.

Sixx tip-toed to the back door, and finding it unlocked, he opened it a few inches and slipped inside. Standing in a back office, he readied the camera on his cell. What if he came upon Conners performing some kind of human sacrifice? Isn't that what he was always preaching? That the people of Redwood Lake should come on down and give their souls to a conman in the guise of the clergy?

On the other side of the door, in what was most likely the sanctuary from this location, Sixx heard voices overlapping. Was it praying? Whichever it was, Sixx did not understand the language. He listened closer and heard Conners say, "We are ready to join you! Please bring us home!"

The praying increased and Sixx cracked the door open to peek inside. As the altar at the front of the church became visible, Sixx froze, unable to fathom what he was seeing. His knees buckled and he snapped as many pictures as he could. He was getting his proof; no doubt about it.

◆

"Sheriff, I know this sounds crazy! I finally have proof," Sixx shouted shrilly into the phone, "Conners was glowing! Blazing white! His clothes and his hair were as white as snow! And there were two other creatures with him dressed the same way! They have got to be aliens or something!"

He waited.

"No, I don't want to be arrested for trespassing! It's a public church!"

He waited as the sheriff spat a string of expletives from his end of the line.

"I printed them out. I'm going to bring them to your office."

More cursing.

"No sir, you'll believe when you see these pictures."

♦

The sheriff shuffled the photos in his hand. He went from one to the other, chewing his cigar, and grunting now and then. He pulled the cigar out of his mouth, dragged off it, and then shuffled through the pictures once more.

"I know they're blurry," Sixx admitted. The sheriff looked up at him. Sixx frowned. "I was nervous when I took them."

The sheriff shook his head and puffed on his cigar. Sixx snatched the pictures from his grasp and pointed at the white blob on the paper.

"See! Right there! He's glowing!"

"Listen up, boy," Sheriff Rogers grumbled. "If you go near that man again…"

"It's plain to see," Sixx interrupted. "He was glowing too brightly for a clear picture."

The sheriff cursed, grabbed the pictures, tore them in two, and jammed them into his shredder. "I'm telling you, you crazy quack, if you wanna keep yer doctoring license and stay outta jail, then you better not get within a hundred feet of the Reverend Conners!"

Sixx blinked at him. "You're forbidding me from going to church?"

The Sheriff stood and grabbed Sixx's shirt collar. "ONE HUNDRED FEET!" he yelled followed by more expletives.

♦

Sixx could not sleep. Finally giving up, he got out of bed and sat on the couch. He clicked the remote control repeatedly, not interested in what was on. He just wanted to stay occupied. Keep his mind off the alien killer loose in his town. After a few useless minutes, he rose off the sofa and looked out his big bay window. Peaceful as ever, the lake shimmered like a blanket of diamonds. Sixx walked onto the balcony. From there, he could see most of the lake and its surrounding homes. Just over the crest of the far hill, he could make out Conners' barn, but the monster's church sat just out of sight.

It had been three days since he saw Conners' glowing alien skin and he could not get the image out of his head. Even his own treatment methods and a few extra shots of whiskey failed to blot out the memory.

Suddenly, in the direction of Conners' barn, a light exploded across the sky. He strained his eyes and gawked; Conner's barn glowed like a nuclear explosion. Why wasn't everyone running from their houses in terror? Was he the only one witnessing this? Sixx threw on his robe and headed for the Jeep.

♦

Parked outside of the large, wooden edifice, Sixx wondered at the light still burning brightly, as if stadium lights were installed inside of the barn. When he pulled at the door it swung open as if pushed from the other side. Sixx shielded his eyes, focused on the event taking place inside the barn, and gasped. A gigantic spaceship filled the barn, its hull nearly too bright to observe head-on. Sixx fell to the ground, his heart pounding.

A million thoughts flooded his senses.

And then he did the only thing that felt right. Jumping to his feet, he dashed up the small metal steps attached to the side of the vessel and pounded on the door. His blows thudded as if hammering cement and dread spilled into his thoughts. What if Conners was right? The preacher's disturbing and mesmerizing sermons came back to Sixx in a deluge. Was he being left behind to something worse awaiting their planet?

Terrified, Sixx increased his efforts and added his screams to the cacophony. Yet nothing caused the door to open. Instead the steps began to retract and disappear within the structure.

Sixx leapt to safety and slumped against the barn wall in time to watch impossibly cool fire explode beneath the spacecraft. As he watched, it rose up past the trees, the mountains and into the clouds out of sight.

Wiping tears from his cheeks, Sixx continued to cry in the corner of the now-empty barn, until a small sound caught his attention.

"Tsk, tsk," a voice clucked near the door. Sixx stood off the wall and looked into Reverend Conners' face.

"But? What?"

The preacher shook his head.

"Here, Isaiah," Conners said, ambling close. "You're the sheriff now," he said and dropped a six-pointed police star into Sixx's palm.

"Wha—" Sixx had no words.

"We'll head to the next town. I hear they're looking for a new sheriff, and the truth. Together, we'll gather another bunch for home."

Sixx just stared at him.

"You're either with me or against me, Isaiah," Conners said, his voice as sweet and soothing as ever.

Sixx looked up to the night sky through the missing barn roof.

"Why stand ye gazing at the clouds? Together, we will go and tell those who do not believe what you have heard and seen. What do you say?"

Sixx had discovered the Truth he was seeking. And he realized he was both right and wrong about Reverend Conners. He *was* preaching the truth, and while he was not an alien- he was definitely not of this world!

Sixx felt something change inside of him and closed his hand over the star. He nodded his head and pinned the star on the lapel of his robe.

Sheriff Sixx had a nice sound to it anyway.

He was in the world, and the world was made by him,
and the world knew him not.
John 1:10

Canaan

By Ellen C. Maze

CANAAN PARKED THE CADDY IN THE UNDERGROUND garage and made his way to street level. His pace was forward and his step light; an evening with Westley always put a smile on his face.

The Shell Zone was a quiet bar for men situated on the lazy end of a popular Nashville by-way. In a world without Cows, Canaan had found a young man there six weeks ago who let his blood eagerly, as if those days hadn't—like his whole way of life—gone the way of the Dodo. His people, once a proud and strong race that ruled the night, were now scattered to the wind, separated, and in hiding. Most of his brethren avoided the human blood donors they used to depend upon, for fear of the police. But Canaan had Westley, and it was Tuesday, midnight; they had a standing date.

The most delightful thing about Westley was his hardiness. He could be visited every two weeks without suffering any of the weaknesses of most Cows. In the old days, they rotated Cows on strict schedules, sometimes going up to eight weeks without seeing the same donor again. To Canaan's delight, Westley was one of those rare youngsters who's constitution loaned itself readily to Canaan's visits and responded well to his healing and rejuvenation efforts. He could draw an entire pint off the kid, sew up the wound with his touch, and then give him a restorative jolt, all in the space of five minutes and every fourteen days.

Then again, Canaan didn't like to hurry. Tonight, if everything went according to plan, he'd take it easy. A live buzz went down best when drawn off slowly and Westley was extremely patient.

Canaan left the shelter of the U-Park and turned up his collar to the wind that whipped between the buildings. The traffic on Church Street was intermittent at that hour and he crossed the wide road at a leisurely jog.

The club was too small for an official bouncer, but one of the original patrons, a towering black individual named Orion, manned the door most nights of his own accord. He was fond of Canaan and waved as he approached.

"K-man! What's up?" Orion wiped his palm on the black Tee that stretched across his over-pumped pecs and shook hands.

"Same old, same old, Orion," Canaan replied, amused that the identical script replayed every visit without fail.

"I hear ya. Westley ain't here yet. You goin' in anyway?" Orion hooked a thumb to the entry behind him and Canaan nodded. "You one brave soul, Kay. One brave soul."

"What makes you say that?" Canaan asked with a laugh. Orion chuckled and shook his regal head.

"Just get in there if you're goin'." Orion stepped to the side and pushed open the chipped wooden door. "Jill'll protect you. Don't be afraid."

Canaan grinned and headed in, making a beeline for the bar. He met a few glances from the dark recesses of the room, but acknowledged none of them. He'd wait for Westley, and all of the regulars knew better than to distract him from his mission. The only customer who had the stones to approach him was a jellied tub named Cawley, and although Canaan could smell him on the premises, he was nowhere in sight.

Jill the bartender was one of the few females in the establishment and she didn't care for Canaan one bit. But that didn't faze him; her personal feelings were of no interest whatsoever. He checked his watch, clucking. It was 12:03 and not like Westley to be late. Canaan slipped onto a cushioned stool and tapped the bar.

"What'll ya have, Canaan." Jill drawled like a member of the Johnny Cash clan and offered no smile, her terse tone clueing Canaan in that she was beyond perturbed.

"Budweiser. Why are you hatin'? If looks could kill..." Canaan whistled jovially, but the woman didn't lighten up. She turned without a word and drew his beer. When she dropped it to the counter, a small amount sloshed out, which Jill wiped up with a towel and turned away. Canaan thought about her behavior a millisecond more and put it out of his mind, not interested in the least.

"Hey, Canaan, how's it hanging?" A coarse baritone sounded behind him and Canaan didn't turn.

Christian Cawley had entered the main salon to once more try his luck. Canaan never minced words with the guy, but was still forced to physically deflect his advances every time. Last week, Orion dragged a dazed Cawley outside after Canaan slugged him. With a low-burning rage building in his middle, Canaan made plans to finally kill the man. How to do it? Getting away with murder wasn't easy since his people disbanded. He was on his own and he didn't want to get pinched.

"Heard your little twerp girlfriend can't make it tonight. That's a shame." Cawley lifted his triple digit mass into the next stool and slapped his empty shot glass down on the bar top. "Jilly! Whiskey! One for me *and* for Canaan, my illustrious wall-flower friend."

Canaan swigged his beer a long five seconds and then set down the empty glass. "Cawley, what happened the last time you sat next to me at this bar? Have you such a short memory?" Canaan didn't meet the man's eye, but looked at him in the mirror that covered the bar wall.

"Oh, I forgive you," Cawley smiled and straightened the knot on his too-wide tie. "You were drunk. So, how 'bout it? Goring's not coming. I overheard Jilly telling Sol about it before you came in. Car trouble or something."

Canaan looked Jill's way, but she'd already set down two shots and crossed clear to the other side of her station. The thought of not seeing Westley turned Canaan's already precipitous mood decidedly sour. He pushed Cawley's peace-offering away and started to slide off the stool. Cawley put a meaty paw on his shoulder and squeezed it playfully.

"I just don't get what you see in that waste of space. He's not here. I'll happily pay you some attention tonight. Hell, I'd *pay* you period." Cawley downed his shot and reached for the one Canaan disregarded. He never made it.

Grasping the fat man's hand with his left, Canaan lifted it up while simultaneously stepping behind him. The judo move left the gelatinous fool pressed hard against the bar with his arm pinned painfully in the small of his fleshy back. Cawley yelped and Jill called for Orion.

"I want you to listen to me real close, Cawley," Canaan whispered into the man's ear from behind. "I don't like you and I've warned you before. Do you remember what I told you would happen if you ever touched me again?"

Cawley grunted, his chest pressed into the sharp bar edge by Canaan's weight pushed against him. Canaan didn't care to hear a response. He was angry now and it had more to do with Westley not showing up than the miserable insect he was about to crush under his boot. Orion lumbered in and Canaan gave Cawley's arm one more good upward shove and backed away.

"Come on, Christian, get." Orion stood four inches taller and his bulk was muscle unlike the blubbery Cawley's. Canaan straightened his clothes and met the man's reddened gaze as he acknowledged Orion's command and shuffled off the stool.

"Ya'll pamper that jerk," Cawley hissed under his breath as he passed Canaan's position and headed for the door. "I guess a pretty face will buy you a free ride every time. This place sucks."

Canaan's rage still simmered deep down and Westley came to mind as he caught Jill's eye.

"Why didn't you tell me Westley was held up?" He made an effort to control his tone, but as he spoke to the woman, she shuddered nonetheless. "Jill? Answer me." Canaan picked up the odor of nervous perspiration and she backed away, even though the bar itself kept them apart.

"Leave him alone, Canaan. Please, just leave him alone." Jill's voice wavered, captured as she was by Canaan's icy blue stare.

"So, you sabotaged him?" Canaan didn't read humans, but her intentions were obvious. She was, after all, the kid's big sister.

"Can't you choose someone else? I mean, he's just a dumb kid. He doesn't know what he wants. You think you picked him up here? He was visiting me, did you know that? Bringing me a package from home. He's not a customer here—he's pretending for your sake."

"I know all that, Jill," Canaan said, already bored by her histrionic display. It didn't matter what Westley did with his free time, so long as he didn't miss their date.

"He can't even choose his own clothes, Canaan." Jill crossed her shaking arms and ignored a patron who called for her down the way. "I just about had him in college before you showed up. He picked out his classes, paid his tuition, and then bam! He meets you here one night and is like a man possessed!"

"He's 25 years old, Jill," Canaan bantered back. "Isn't it about time you pushed him off the teat?"

In the back of his mind, Canaan pondered the other patrons he'd noticed when he came in, calculating the likelihood that any of them would measure up to Westley. With the snap of a finger, any of the lonelies that lined the far wall would follow him to the over-sized washroom and beg to make his night. But how many of them would voluntarily give up their blood and keep it to themselves? It was tough to say. Plus, Westley worshipped the ground he walked on. That was a hard act to follow.

"He thinks you're some kind of superman," Jill whispered, and even leaned in a few inches, probably in an effort to protect her brother's reputation. "He's got you way up on a pedestal, Canaan. If you cared about him at all, you'd walk out of here and never come back."

Canaan chuckled.

"Well, Jill, I am quite a catch," he replied and gave her a wink. Certain that none of the goons behind him were going to do the trick, Canaan was finally fed up. Hardening his gaze, he put both hands on the bar, palms down.

"Give me your address."

"Canaan!"

Sounding like a meek Elvis Presley and looking like a young George Hamilton, Westley Goring burst into the room. "Oh, my god, I'm sorry! My car wouldn't start and I had to take a cab. Have you been waiting long?"

Canaan turned and the kid turned to jelly when their eyes met.

"Please, don't be mad. It won't happen again. Dang, I don't know what's going on today. It's been just one thing after another!" Westley reached the bar and paused before sitting down. Canaan stood up and he had his answer—no time for chit-chat.

"Well, it was touch-and-go for a few minutes there, Wes." Canaan ruffled the kid's hair and put an arm around his shoulders. "Almost got picked up by Christian Cawley. It was a close call," Canaan joked and Westley paled noticeably.

"Oh, you'd never go with him, would you, Canaan? Please don't hold this against me. I couldn't stand it if you were mad at me."

"Grow a pair, Westley!" Jill said a little too loudly and then lowered her voice. "You sound like a little girl. God! When will you grow up?"

Westley looked at his sister, dumbfounded, and Canaan tugged him away from the bar.

"Come on, buddy," Canaan spoke in the kid's ear, leading him to the semi-privacy of the bathrooms. "It's wayyyy past my dinner time, and I'm almost mad with you for keeping me waiting like this."

Jill continued to berate the both of them as they left the room, but the boy wasn't listening. All he could hear was the sound of his master's voice. If he was a Cow, he'd call Canaan master, but those days were long gone.

Canaan listened to the boy's apologies all the way to the stall where he would draw his blood. The other occupants paid them no mind as they passed through their midst and retreated into the tiny space. Westley begged to be forgiven until his tongue grew numb from blood loss, and he fell silent.

When Canaan had drawn off all the boy could afford to lose at one time, he healed his wound with his touch, and held him up under his arms. The boy was a looker and with his head lolling back and his eyes at half-mast he could have been a teenager.

The minutes wore on and Canaan supported him and watched the pulse through the skin at his throat. Finally, his respirations evened out, he regained his own feet and looked up languidly to meet Canaan's eye.

"Cawley tried to get you, huh?" His Southern accent was even more pronounced when running low on fuel.

"I'm going to kill Cawley, Wes." Canaan spoke low so only Westley heard. "He's crossed me for the last time."

A plan formed, he now knew when, where, and how he'd dispose of the obese ox, and he looked forward to the adventure of it. Since his people parted ways and scattered, it was no longer easy to manipulate the mortal authority. He'd have to commit the perfect murder and throw in enough supernatural clues to thoroughly baffle the Nashville cops. His plan was good, but there would be drawbacks.

"That means I won't come around the bar for a few months."

Westley's eyes widened and Canaan continued before the boy could become hysterical.

"I can meet you at your house until then. Just give me the address."

"Oh, thank you, Canaan. Of course, at my house." Westley spoke in little gasps, but his gratitude shined through. "Thank you for sticking with me."

Canaan smiled down on him and allowed him to stand on his own. His knees knocked a little, but he wavered only twice and stood tall. Placing his palms on either side of his face, Canaan waited for the boy to acknowledge he was ready. As soon as Westley nodded, Canaan willed a portion of his energy into the boy. It didn't take much and momentarily he stood straight up and exhaled as the contact was severed.

"Okay, so next time, your place, same time," Canaan whispered and Westley nodded with enthusiasm. "If your sister is home that night, we'll make other plans, but she usually works Tuesdays, right."

"Yes, sir, yes."

"Okay, see you then, Westley." Canaan unlocked the door and stepped into the room. Many of the other patrons glanced at him approvingly and then at the young man who followed behind, but Canaan didn't notice, his mind now on murder.

A full gut did that to him every time.

"Canaan" is a character from Ellen C. Maze's The *Rabbit Saga*.
www.ellencmaze.com

88

By Ellen C. Maze

MICKEY'S TINGLING GOITER WOKE HIM AT PRECISELY 4 a.m., signaling the waking moments of his 88th year. Without hesitation, he reached for his bifocals in the dim lighting of pre-dawn and once located, placed them atop his nose. Now, to get out of bed. More than usual, his blood felt thick as molasses and his head swam woozy. Back when he was 78, rising from bed was still a simple process. These days, he was forced to psych himself up. Not mentally, no, he was excited to prepare for his big day; rather, he worked for several minutes convincing his muscles that they were still pals. *Back muscles, contract and help me sit up. Hip and leg muscles, help me swing my feet to the carpet. Arms and hands, reach for and grab my cane. There ya go; we're pals, you know. Best pals.*

Their symbiotic relationship apparently intact, Mickey came erect and surveyed the distance to the bedroom door. It took only seconds for his slippered feet to obey the command, and he smiled as he reached the hallway. A noise from behind caused him to turn and glance at his rumpled bed. The comforter was lumped high, propped up by extra-feathered pillows and a thick electric blanket. Mickey grinned—it looked like he was still in bed. Giggling now at the image, he turned to leave the room, feeling in his spirit much younger than his flesh would allow him to demonstrate.

Oh, the day would be grand, the party a sensation. It wasn't every day that a man reached such a pinnacle of life with all of his faculties, most of his marbles, and four fabulous children who loved him and would gather in his honor to exhort the day.

Mickey reached the kitchen and flipped the light switch, filling the brightly-painted room with a yellow glow. First things first. Reaching into the refrigerator, he pulled out a tray of tiny tuna-salad sandwiches he'd prepared the day before and set it on the counter. Next came out the nacho cheese dip of salsa and Velveeta, mixed and ready for the microwave when the first guest arrived. Mickey smiled as he placed paper plates, cups, and napkins on the conservative dinette his youngest son, Bill, had given him the Christmas before last. Or was it Evan who gave it to him? On Father's Day? Maybe it was Mona? Or the baby, Frank? It didn't matter—one of his young'uns gave it to him so he'd stop eating off TV trays in the den.

The paper goods matched—cheery yellow balloons on a dreamy sky-blue background, with the words "Happy Birthday" floating in and around the balloons. Mickey had found them in a drawer a week ago, which was the catalyst to plan the party. The table set for eight (in case the kids brought their spouses), Mickey grinned at his handiwork, his single remaining upper tooth pressed against his bottom lip. It was going to be such a glorious party.

Mickey checked his watch: 4:45 a.m. Good, plenty of time left.

Before heading over to the phonograph to select music for his party, Mickey shoveled two of the sandwiches down and took a swig of tap water. He couldn't taste them, but shrugged—he'd murdered his taste buds years ago with tobasco sauce and jalapeño peppers. Carbs and proteins inside, he headed for the record player.

Bill, his oldest, was a proper musician—had even cut an album before he washed up musically and opted for law school instead. Mickey determined to choose at least one jazz album in the attorney's honor.

Mickey's son, Evan, dropped out of high school at 17, went to work for McDonalds, and today owns eleven franchises. For him, Mickey lined up an Eric Clapton album, as Evan matched the guitar great's motto: If you're going to be something, be the best.

Mona, his only daughter, turned 60 a month ago and she trained horses for a living. For her, he pulled his only Willie Nelson album from the cabinet, accepting that like Mr. Nelson, Mona was as comfortable in the city as she was on the farm. That made Mickey smile since he never much got used to the big city himself.

Lastly, the youngest, Francis, had followed in his old man's shoes and became a preacher. For him, Mickey selected an album of gospel tunes the boy had given him as a gift a dozen years back. Satisfied that the 33s stacked atop the player covered all bases, Mickey nodded and turned for the sofa.

The time was 5:15 a.m. The kids could arrive any minute.

Mickey lowered himself into the couch, facing the closed front door, and sighed. The remote control to the television fit his hand like a glove, but the darned thing wouldn't come on. Mickey shook the remote, opened the back, and rolled the batteries around, but no-go. The TV was out.

Mickey smiled and shook his head. Nothing was going to dampen his spirits. No, he'd take a nap. It was going to be a glorious party.

The sharp poke of the osteoarthritis in his hip nudged Mickey from a light doze. The clock on the near wall could be read if he raised his head slightly and activated the bottom of his bifocals: 7:30 a.m. Did he oversleep? Mickey peered at the table, visible at the kitchen-end of his three-room apartment. No kids, not yet.

No worries, Mickey settled back into the cushion, shifted his sore hip to redistribute the weight, and closed his eyes. Just a little snooze. They'd be there any moment and he wanted to be fully rested.

The phone on the end table to Mickey's right rang and he snapped to attention. It didn't ring twice and when he lifted the receiver to his ear, a dial tone answered back. Mickey checked his watch: 11:15 a.m. The quiet house affirmed his assumption that his kids hadn't arrived. It didn't worry him. They probably stopped for lunch and were heading over afterwards. It made perfect sense when all Mickey kept in the fridge was frozen dinners and chocolate Ensure.

Mickey spoke to his body and convinced it to lift him to his feet. Once up and feeling confident, he crossed to the front door, his cane quiet on the thick carpet his daughter insisted he install when he moved in. He was thankful for her advice; the cold floors in his previous home irritated his bunions something fierce.

Mickey left the house and settled onto the eight-by-six front porch. The retirement complex was quiet today as he settled into the lone wicker chair beside the door. There was not a soul in sight, but the oddness of that fact did not dampen his spirits. He was 88 today and all four children would arrive momentarily for the best party ever.

Mickey's stomach grumbled and he wished he'd brought a can of Ensure outside. After grumbling back once or twice, it hushed and he fixed his gaze on the road.

Bill would probably arrive first. His wife, a basketball coach at the high school, ran the household military-style. His eldest would never be late if she were in tow.

Evan was divorced, but his current girlfriend had three teenagers and he'd likely bring the entire clan. This was, after all, a grand occasion and not a simple visit to daddy's.

Mona would bring her lesbian lover, a gangly chain-smoking fifty-something Mickey had met only once. Mona had been married three times before she gave up on men altogether. Mickey smirked and shook his head; his daughter's choices had always confounded him, since her youth. She picked jerks to marry and then a lazy lesbian to shack up with. *Whatever.* Mickey loved her and would learn to love her friend as well.

That left the baby. Frank would arrive last, his meek and gentle bride of fifty years at his side. Their five kids were grown and spread across the country so Mickey didn't expect to see them. Of all the children, Frank wrote to his father most often, but visited the least. Mickey understood—of all the kids, Frank stayed the busiest, traveling to desperate countries, and ministering to the lost and destitute. Still, despite all that, he'd be here today. Mickey had no doubt of that.

A buzzing in his ear woke him from a dream about ice cream and Mickey checked his watch. 3:45 p.m. By the lack of cars in his short drive, he knew they hadn't arrived. No worries; they'd arrive by dinner.

Mickey rose and entered the house. After visiting the toilet only to watch nothing happen, he affixed a new Depends anyway and settled at the square, laminated dinette table. The crust of the sandwiches had stiffened from sitting out and the cheese dip had congealed into a solid. Nonetheless, Mickey poked in a pretzel and nibbled it like an ear of corn. After four of those, he decided to count out one pretzel for each year of his life. Carefully grasping the salty sticks from the bowl, one-by-one, he placed them in rows on the balloony plate before him. When he reached eighty-eight, he sighed and leaned back into the wooden chair. His watch read 6 p.m. at his next glance and he looked at the closed front door.

They'd come after dinner. Mickey chuckled and slapped his head. Of course! It was a work day, after all, and nobody would be able to come until closing time. Only Bill was retired and he still worked full time at the pro-bono clinic downtown. Yeah, Mickey shook his head and sipped the stale water from his morning cup. He'd see them about 7:30. That was when he was born, anyway.

In 1923, at 4:30 in the morning, his mother went into labor in their tiny cabin home. That same day, at precisely 7:30 in the evening, she gave birth to him, surrounded by chirping relatives and the town's only doctor. He'd been a strong, healthy baby, never balking at the instruction of his parents. At sixteen, he apprenticed with a local carpenter. At eighteen, he left that job to work for the church. At first, he played the ever-ready handyman, but eventually, by the time he was twenty-five, he was preaching full-time. At thirty, he met Sally Mae Garby, and asked her to be his bride. When she agreed to marry him, Mickey knew more than ever that the God he preached was real and wonderful. Mickey smiled. It had been a happy, laugh-filled life.

Knock, knock.

Mickey started and glanced at his watch: 7:30. His heart seemed too big for his chest as he carefully rose to get the door. To see Bill and Evan, Mona and Frank in the flesh again, tears came to his eyes at the thought. Mickey pulled open the door and gasped.

"Sally Mae!" he whispered not believing his eyes.

"Hi, Mickey," she said, her blue eyes twinkling just as he remembered they did when she smiled. She was young, maybe twenty, the age she was when they met in that tiny Tennessee town.

"Sally Mae?" he asked this time, blinking in rapid succession in case he was dreaming.

"You're not dreaming, hon, it's me."

"What are you doing here?" he asked, still not inviting the apparition inside.

"You're late for the party. We waited all day and you never showed." Sally Mae peeked over his shoulder and seemed to consider his decorated table. "We set you a much bigger table back home."

"Home? What are you doing here? How are you here? I buried you eleven years ago," Mickey explained, keeping his cool, but just barely.

His wife's likeness smiled again and touched his arm. She was real, three-dimensional.

"What in the Sam-hill is going on here?" he insisted.

"Hon, you need to come with me," she said. "Your guests are waiting."

"Oh? Bill and the other kids are there?" Mickey asked, confused. His deceased wife was speaking of his current birthday party. Which way was up?

"No, hon, they'll come to another party. But everyone else is there. Everyone who left before. Even some you don't know will be there. They are such a beautiful crowd, and they're all waiting for you."

"Wah," Mickey stuttered, "you're talking crazy."

Sally Mae sighed. "Mickey, hon, go look in the mirror."

Mickey started to argue, but backed out of the doorway and stepped a few feet to his right. The wall mirror reflected a familiar man, maybe his son, Bill, as a young man with a few pounds shaved off. Who did it resemble? The guy was thirty, lanky, with soft brown eyes and a respectable brown crew cut.

"It's you, Mickey," Sally Mae offered from the threshold.

Mickey shook his head and mumbled, "I must be dreaming." But Sally Mae shook her head, too.

"Go look at your bed, hon," she said softly. Mickey leaned on his cane to turn and she laughed. "And you can drop the old-man act, dear. You don't need that walking stick any longer."

Mickey looked at the ebony handle of his hand-carved cane. Was she out of her mind? His knee replacement. His rickety hip.

Sally Mae giggled into her hand. "Just go hobble to the bedroom and you'll see what I mean."

Dumbfounded and more than a little confused, Mickey carefully wove his way to the bedroom and flipped on the light. Doing a double-take, he gasped at the figure lying on the bed. The lumped-up covers disguised a corpse. It was Mickey, all right, very obviously dead. What was going on?

"You see, hon," Sally Mae's voice filtered to him from the front of the house, "you are young. Now let's go to the party. It's for you, and we're all so excited!"

She was excited? Mickey considered his cane. His hands and arms were those of a young man, strong and lined with hard muscle. Without knowing precisely what it all meant, Mickey dropped the cane and turned away from his remains on the bed. The ease with which he maneuvered his body amazed him and he reached the door in a fraction of the time it normally took.

"What's going on, Sally Mae? I'm dead? Are you a ghost, then?"

Sally Mae shook her head. "No, silly nilly, I'm not a ghost. I just came to get you for the party. They knew you'd be scared if anyone else came, so I volunteered. Let's go home. You're going to love it."

"Home? Heaven?" Mickey asked, ashamed at the trepidation in his voice. He believed in heaven, right?

"That's right. You were supposed to meet us last night. We were all set for you. But, you had it stuck in your head that you were having your 88th here on earth and you refused to come." Sally Mae blew her bangs up and smiled. "So, how about now? You ready to come Home?"

"But Bill, and Evan—" Mickey began.

"The kids aren't coming, Mickey, but don't worry. You'll see them again, at their own parties in their own times." Sally Mae reached for his arm and he allowed her to pull him from the house. "So, how about it? You ready?"

"I was born on this day eighty-eight years ago, Sally Mae. If I died last night, does that make this my Death-day, too?"

Sally Mae laughed like the sound of church bells and squeezed Mickey's hand.

"No, silly. Today is your *Re*birth-day. Now let's go celebrate."

Mickey pulled closed the door behind him and followed his wife off the porch and into the yard, strong, young, happy, and smiling. Rebirth-day Party in heaven? Nice.

Valéry

By Krisi Keley

I DON'T KNOW WHAT I WAS EXPECTING, AND I WAS
even less sure of what I wanted, as I watched Angelina pause at her
front steps. The one and only phrase I had read from her mind, "Be
warned, Valéry, there are some mistakes you might regret," repeated
itself over and over again inside my mind, as did the images from her
doctor's records of her dreams. Which of these was affecting me most,
I did not know, but the tempest in me had reached an unbearable point.

Angelina turned around then, as if it was the most natural thing in
the world for her to do, and she waited for me to show myself to her.
And so, fighting an excruciating combination of excited anticipation
and deep reservation, I stepped out of the shadows which so easily
cloaked me, and I let myself be seen.

She seemed not at all surprised to find that all along her inability
to see me had simply been a matter of my will. No, the expression on
her face was not one of surprise, nor was it one of fear. Though God
knows, she should have been afraid. Not only because seeing the
murderous creature of her dreams and the monster of a thousand myths
should be frightening, but also because I had no insight at all into what
I might do now. Of course, I supposed she could have had no way of
knowing how volatile my emotions were right then. But then again, she
should have had no way of recognizing the being who stood before her
either. And yet, she did.

I made no move toward her and I did not speak. I only stared at
her face, studying the most minute of its details. I wanted these details
to explain why she felt as her expression seemed to indicate that she
did. Why I saw no fear as she looked at me, only pleasure, and affection,
it incredibly seemed. It wasn't that I'd never been gazed at in awe and
fascination by a mortal before, but this girl *knew* the creature her eyes
were seeing. Physical beauty could mean so very little to one who had
seen what she had seen of me in her dreams.

I thought I could explain some of what I saw in her face. Explain
it away as her frightened doctor had explained away her dreams. And
the irony of the comparison was not lost on me, I assure you. But I felt
certain that, in part at least, Angelina's feelings contained some element
of relief. Over the years of her life, however short that life had so far
been, she must have had grave doubts about her sanity. She'd had
dreams, ever since she was a small child, of things that could not be. Or
could not be in the mind of rational mortals, anyway. What must it have
been like for her then, when she'd opened her first book about the
mythical creature known as the vampire? When, despite all the

inaccuracies such literature contains, she'd recognized and had been able to put a name to the creature she'd already known through her dreams? Had she been frightened to find that the man of her dreams, this god-like thing, was, in fact, a cursed creature? Something of evil, a murdering monster to be feared and reviled? Or had she only been relieved to find that she was not insane, that what seemed so real in her mind was, though fiction to mortal man, a well-documented creature that possibly could exist? But, did the expression she wore on her face as she gazed at me indicate that all the gruesome tales changed nothing of how she felt for the man in her dreams? Even now that she knew he was no man? Or had she grown to despise the god she'd so loved in the years that had passed since she'd spoken of him with such joy and pleasure? Had all the lore on the evil vampire turned me into a monster in her eyes? But why then this lack of fear and revulsion, if she truly saw me as a monster? Why did she study me as I studied her – with fascinated interest and awed wonder?

I did not know what I would do or how this night might end. Could I let her live until every mystery was solved and all of my burning questions were answered? Or must I satisfy the hunger that was a lust for life and even more? I needed to hold her very essence in my hands, and to make her a part of me in a way I'd done with no other. It was a longing so deep and all-consuming, it was difficult to believe I could make the choice. It almost seemed then, that it would be a choice between her life and mine.

"*Tu viens, Valéry?*"[1] she asked softly, and I could hear the pleasure she took in calling me by my name. That she could finally speak to the one she felt she'd known all her life, I suppose. In any case, my pleasure was as great as hers. A rush of heat passed through my veins and possessed my body as I imagined what it would be like to hear that voice say my name as my mouth closed on her throat and I was locked to her life, my teeth sinking into her warm, tender flesh. But, this image seemed to be overlaid with another, and my mind reeled with this strange double exposure of her in my arms, not as the type of lover I would make of a victim, but in my arms and safe. And I could put my mouth to hers without the demon inside's demand for life. This other image terrified me, not just because it was a foolish delusion, but because I knew that I had not only discovered how to live with what I was, in many ways, I actually reveled in it. Not in the death, but in the

---

[1] "Are you coming, Valéry?"

life… I would no longer change it if I could, not even for this Angelina, I was certain of that. If there were a price to pay for immortality, then I would pay it, for I couldn't pretend that I could give it up.

Angelina looked into my eyes as no mortal should have been able to do without losing him or herself there, and another thrill passed through me as I thought, she knows what I'm thinking, or at least what I'm feeling, and still she does not turn from me.

She watched me closely for a moment longer and then she did turn, but only to continue up the steps to her front door. Without allowing myself to think of any possible ramification – in essence, denying there could be any ramification – I followed closely behind.

As I crossed the threshold into her short and narrow front hall, it occurred to me how like any gentleman caller I appeared, escorting home the lady after an evening out. I laughed aloud at the supreme idiocy of the thought that tonight could possibly be akin to a twentieth century "date."

Angelina glanced back over her shoulder at me, and a tiny smile played on her lips. I decided then, with that quirky smile, that she could not read my mind; she could only guess a very close approximation of what I was thinking, a gift very much like that supplied by immortality. I supposed that this heightened awareness was also what made her able to sense my presence, though I was not confident it was sufficient explanation.

She led me into her bookshelf-lined living room and laid her purse down on one of the end tables. She removed the lightweight jacket she wore and draped it over the back of a chair close to the front windows. My eyes followed her every graceful move as she went to the sofa and sat down, pulling one leg up under her. Every action so relaxed and so unafraid!

She bowed her head, tilting it slightly to the side, her expression thoughtful. As she moved, her long curls fell back against one shoulder, exposing just the barest glimpse of the inside curve of her neck. I stared at the way the room's dim lighting cast a shadow on the hollow of her throat, accentuating the vein which pulsed there. My dark desire rose in me again, in slow and painful waves.

She raised her head and met my eyes with her own. They were bright with emotion, but with what emotion, I couldn't be certain.

"Valéry," she said, her voice light and musical to my ears, "it seems etiquette should force me to offer you something to drink… But, other than to make you laugh, I can't see how that would actually make you more comfortable."

I had remained standing thus far, and as she spoke, I moved soundlessly to the back of the sofa, behind her. Though I did laugh softly at her words. The double meaning in them – she would offer me a drink as would any good hostess, or would she offer me a drink, knowing full well the only kind that could quench a vampire's thirst? Despite my precarious emotional state of the past several weeks, and especially this night, that she found humor in this did not offend or anger me. Strangely enough, it seemed only to attract me to her more. Possibly because the only other creature I knew who would find amusement in something so profoundly unfunny was me.

I stood behind her, my thoughts now non-existent, only emotion in control. I let the back of my hand very lightly stroke her long, thick, spiral-waved hair. The light, however dim, turned it into smoldering embers and each silky strand that passed through my fingers became a small spark of fire.

Every instinct in my vampire's body commanded me to begin the seduction I'd perfected on countless mortal victims, making each my lover in a way that, though it may be less *sexual*, was nonetheless far more intimate than they could have otherwise experienced or dreamed. But for the first time, I was stunned to discover, I harbored doubts in my consummate ability. *She* had already seduced *me*! How then could a seduction performed on just any mortal ever be enough? For her and, even more so, for me.

I wound my left hand tightly in her hair and pulled her head back and to the side, with a concentrated gentleness. I leaned forward, bowing my head low, and I put my lips to her throat. They brushed the warm, soft skin just above her collarbone and I could detect the faintest trace of that light perfume, mingling with her own much stronger and more maddening scent. I closed my eyes and opened my mouth against her, but did not bare my teeth, only kept my parted lips to her skin until I could feel her pulse quicken there. Then I ran my tongue over the vein, tracing it from the hollow of her throat up to the curve beneath her jaw, with an excruciatingly sensual slowness. Tasting her, without *really* tasting her. My heart thumped painfully in my chest and there was an ache inside of me that seemed to have no origin and no release.

"Will you kill me now?" Angelina asked softly, in a tone that sounded nothing more than conversational. Her total lack of fear in the murdering creature who touched her and, even more, her lack of fear in facing the very real possibility of her death, made me feel disconnected from myself and extremely unreal. As if I was not the being I thought myself to be. I clamped my free hand down on her shoulder, my fingers biting deeply into the soft, tender flesh.

She did not cry out however, though I know I must have caused her terrible pain. My grip would be like steel to her, and suddenly I was furious, absolutely furious, that she refused to see me. Really see me, for what I was. She had seen me in all her dreams, I was certain. Every evil I'd ever committed and yet, she chose to remain blind to it. For one brief moment, the deepest confusion and self-loathing I've ever experienced turned to rage inside of me, and that rage turned all I saw to darkness. Too dark to see my foolish self-contradiction, to be sure. A mortal who would see past the monster indeed.

Angelina turned around abruptly and, completely stunned and unaware of what compelled me to do so, I automatically let go of her, lest I break her shoulder bone. She then knelt facing the back of the sofa, her stomach pressed against the cushions. Seemingly without reservation, she caught both of my hands in her own and held them. I was surprised beyond all reaction and I could only stare, somewhat dazed, into her eyes. So liking the feel of her small, soft, and warm hands holding my large, strong, and cool ones, I did not try to pull away.

"Why are you not afraid of me?" I asked her wonderingly. It was the only question that found its way to my mind, and I couldn't tear my eyes from her face. So beautiful, so delicate, so fragile. I was hypnotized by the shimmer of her skin, so smooth, only the light's reflection, as if on dewdrops, made the pores in that skin perceptible.

She lowered her eyes at my question and I was newly fascinated by the inky contrast her lashes made against her porcelain skin. A few light freckles over the bridge of her nose and the slight blush on her cheekbones were the only interruption in the creamy whiteness.

She raised her eyes to mine again and I think I just plainly refused to believe what I saw there. Instead, I lost myself in those eyes, bluer than any I'd seen. Bluer, certainly, than my own blue, despite the unnatural brilliance mine owned.

Bluer than any I'd seen, it would seem, but was that really so? Something tickled at the back of my mind, but not pleasantly, and this was because it was an itch I refused to scratch.

She shook her head slightly as if she recognized my self-imposed blindness and was saying that my refusal to believe did not matter. At least for the moment.

"I could never be afraid of you," she told me and her voice was so gentle and soothing. I wanted to let it hold me, stroke me.

I closed my eyes briefly and opened my hands in hers, turning them over, so that I was holding her hands instead of her holding mine. I was trying, much too hard with the gesture, to act as if I were the one in control. I opened my eyes again rapidly to observe Angelina's reaction, but she was only watching me closely as before.

How could she know what I was, what I'd done and would do again and still not be afraid? Perhaps I was already starting to form a rational answer to the question, but my intuition was rebelling against it. She seemed much too intelligent for what I was beginning to suspect.

"Why?" I asked her, my voice no more than a whisper. "Why can't you be afraid?"

"Valery, would you be afraid of someone you knew could never truly harm you?" she questioned, her eyes still studying me with deep intensity.

"I came here to kill you!" I roared at her suddenly, and the black rage was back and painted every word I yelled. But I knew the rage was not truly directed at Angelina. The anger in me not really anger. And the words were, in fact, a lie.

She flinched at the volume of my voice, which, if I wasn't more careful, might injure her eardrums. I could speak with unnatural power as easily as I could produce a tone as calming as a lullaby. Other than her unconscious pain-response, however, Angelina made no indication she was either disturbed or surprised by the force of my voice. Instead, she slid her hands free of mine and locked them together behind her back. She waited, intentionally vulnerable, to allow me to do what I would. Once again, her actions shocked me into near immobility.

I forced my eyes from her face and let them drift down once more to her throat. I placed the fingers of my left hand on the side of her neck, exerting a gentle pressure on the vital artery there. The blood coursed under my fingers, and I could feel her heartbeat strong in its pulse. Her skin glowed pale pink in the light of her small lamp and my hand grew warm where it rested on her flesh. There could be no other proof, as much as I wished it. Despite the dreams, despite her blindness to what those dreams had shown her, Angelina was still just a young, mortal female, at that age when a woman still looked alluringly too much like a child.

I grabbed her with a sudden, blinding speed, clutching her under her left elbow, and I pulled her up firmly so that she was standing on the sofa, her barely more than five foot stature making her height now just slightly more than my own. I tilted my head just a fraction, so that it was under her chin, and with my left hand I stroked her nearly waist-length hair, until my fingers were hopelessly tangled in the silken tresses. I let go of her elbow and reached to cradle her face, tilting her head as I did so. Once again I pressed my lips to her throat and when I did, I could feel how her heartbeat quickened its pace, because the blood now raced through the vein pulsing against my mouth. I wondered, with a ridiculously triumphant sense of satisfaction, if I had finally evoked some fear in her.

I pulled my lips back and let, not the sharp points, but only the outer curved smoothness of my fanged teeth touch her skin. Angelina's flesh quivered at this contact and her small body trembled against me. But not, I realized, in fear. The lust for her life was a small spark next to the raging fire of my desire for her. For taking her as I have never wanted to take another. It seemed my growing sense that she could not be quite so intelligent as I'd imagined, had little effect on the desire.

"Valéry," Angelina whispered, her breath warm and soft in my ear, "anyone can supply this, the desired life. But if you try to fulfill that desire with me, there will be no one ever to give you what I would give."

I shoved her away from me then, abruptly and very roughly. But it was not because her words had angered me. They had not come even remotely close to doing so, despite that it seemed this further confirmation of my suspicion ought to be terribly disappointing indeed. Rather, it was because as I had held her, stroked her, even felt her blood coursing hotly through her veins, I realized I couldn't do it. I couldn't do it! I could not take a life I wanted more than any other. Something inside me that I did not recognize and could not begin to comprehend was overpowering the incontrovertible command to taste the blood and know the life which would give me more pleasure than I'd ever known.

I paced like a caged animal behind the sofa, but there was no room for it, and I finally stalked around to the front where Angelina was straightening up, after somehow managing not to have fallen from my push. I could feel the menacing glare on my face and my teeth were bared, but she seemed unaffected by what I knew must be a terrifying expression. I glowered with frustrated rage and Angelina just gazed back at me calmly.

The enraged confusion again slowly began to melt away, though against my will, but I could not hold it up to what I saw in her eyes. I couldn't deny the patient understanding I saw there. It appeared so much in contrast to the foolish adolescent blindness I'd been more and more suspecting. She *did* understand me somehow. I cannot describe the feeling in knowing this. This mortal child who seemed unable to be touched by any evil. It wasn't possible that she understood me; it wasn't even *right* that she did, it seemed to me. But she did. Somehow she did.

"Angelina," I said, keeping my voice as even as I could manage, "I would take anything you have to give, if that would bring you pleasure, but there is only one thing any mortal can give *me* to do the same. That is the essence of what I am."

Angelina rose from the sofa and started to walk toward me, but something stopped her. Maybe the expression on my face, or maybe that she wasn't as entirely unafraid as she would have me believe. Or so I persisted in my inane delusion.

"Valéry," she began and then paused. I couldn't tell if she was looking for the right words, or if she was worried about how I might react to what she wanted to say. But as she studied me carefully for a long moment, I again relished the simple pleasure in hearing her speak my name.

Finally, she continued.

"Valéry, the essence of what you are is only one who does not have what he needs."

She watched me very closely as she spoke these words, and God knows what response she'd been anticipating. I could feel frustration and unfulfilled desire turn passion back to fury, and I wondered how long any being could support such rapid and intense fluctuations in emotion. I stared at her incredulously.

"There is nothing else I need but the heated rush of mortal blood preparing a life for my taking," I hissed at her savagely. "What you've chosen to believe of what you've read, it's misled you, and colored your dreams as fantastic illusion," I continued, my voice low and threatening, but I saw no surprise register on her face to learn that I knew of her dreams. I bared my teeth again, ferociously, to prove just how wrong her image of me. I never stopped to consider that I was doing with Angelina the same thing I'd done with Jules, the same thing I'd done with many. That is, trying to force her to see an evil she obviously didn't believe was there. More, I didn't really believe my own words true. That there was nothing else I needed, that is to say.

"It takes a man to be the martyr you would have in me," I told her coldly anyway, thinking of not just some newer romantic fiction, but of her dreams and how, as a child, she'd seemed to consider me something akin to a saint or a god, suffering but still somehow glorious. A saint I definitely was not, and a god? *Ah oui*, I may be very good at playing one, but then it seemed to me, those who refused belief in one always were.

"But I am not a man, Angelina," I continued, even more bitterly, "I haven't been for more than seven centuries."

Her expression still did not change and I had the sudden urge to shake some sense into her. What was wrong with me that I professed a wish to meet just one mortal whose vision of me was not sullied by the frightful myth and lore and yet, now that I apparently had, I wanted her to see that I was indeed the monster the larger percentage of writers had described?

"Your dreams are illusion," I repeated, but I was feeling more and more unsure of myself.

Angelina lowered her head and studied her hands, but not before I saw the glaze of tears in her eyes.

"I have no illusions about you, Valéry," she whispered and lifted her eyes to meet mine. "And I would never have you *be anything*, but what you are. I only wish... I only wish to ease your pain," she finished almost helplessly.

I moved towards her again, so fast it was difficult for her human eyes to track me, and I heard her startled intake of air when I grabbed her upper arm. Despite the dreams, despite all she had read on the vampire, truly there was no real adequate preparation for coming face to face with an immortal being. I found that I was not as pleased as I'd expected, now that the unnaturalness of what I was had impacted her, however slightly.

"You play a dangerous game, gamine," I growled in a low warning voice, my face bare millimeters from hers. "You would attempt to seduce me as you would any mortal man? All you can incite in me, chérie, is a lust for your life."

A single tear fell from Angelina's eye and slid slowly down her cheek, causing the throbbing ache inside me to intensify even more. She tried to shake her head and deny my words, but I wouldn't allow her the chance to speak or to explain herself. I leaned closer still and with a sadistic lasciviousness that appalled even me, I licked her face. I ran my tongue up her cheek, tasting the salty tear, and then with a low, growling moan, I forced my mouth down on hers. I pried her lips apart, rudely and violently, with my tongue, even as each of my own actions drove a knife deeper into my heart. But I ignored the voice inside that screamed for me to stop. With every fiber of my being telling me 'no,' I bit down, sinking my fangs deep into Angelina's tongue, and tearing some of the tender flesh on the inside of her mouth as well. A rush of blood, hot and salty, and oh so sweet too, filled her mouth and mine, as I held her locked in this venomous kiss. I moaned aloud with a want so overwhelming, it was more agony than ecstasy.

I pulled back suddenly and violently, however, when the end result of this impulsively passionate act became a too vivid image behind my closed eyelids. I gasped with the pained shock of my withdrawal and turned my face away from her. But not before I saw her put her hand to her mouth and tentatively touch the blood that had spilled over her lips and run down her chin. The sight of it actually sickened me, and I couldn't force myself to look at her as I whispered, hoarsely, "Is that what you want, then? To taste *that* on your lips for all eternity?"

Angelina let out a stifled sob which drew my eyes back to her with a concern I did not wish to feel. Tears flowed freely from her eyes now as she stared, raptly, at the blood on her fingers, as if she couldn't believe it was truly hers. Or couldn't believe that it had been I who had made it flow.

"You'll convince yourself then that this is all you want of me?" she asked, her voice filled with sad wonder. "This *blood* which would bring you to your pleasure?"

I put my hands to my ears, trying to shut out that sound, the wish to understand I could hear in her voice. *Ah oui*, it would be so easy to pretend, at least for a while, that I was what she wanted me to be. This ravishing creature of mystery her dreams and, more, too much recent fiction, had deluded her into believing me to be. I had played that role before, and many others. That was the essence of seduction, after all – without a single touch, it was simply the art of making oneself another's fantasy. Eight hundred years and thousands upon thousands of lives and there were few of *those* I hadn't seen. If only mortal man would realize how little of his sexual desire was actually physical, perhaps then the vampire would not have such a frightfully simple time of it, taking any life he chose. And what pleasure might it give, if only for a brief time, to fulfill *her* every fantasy? For hers were pure, sweet sensuality, were they not? What man didn't want to lose himself in the lie of that role – the hero, the saint, the fairy tale lover? But I was none of those and she could not make me be, no matter how I might try to let the pleasure of playing that part blind me to the truth. Oh, and if I'd only been able then, as I convinced myself that I heard all of this self-deception in her soft, compassionate voice, to turn that sharply perceptive eye on myself. But I was just a man really, as much as I always swore otherwise.

"There is nothing else you can give me," I answered her tiredly, though, strictly speaking, I did not know this to be true. "There is no other pleasure. Seven centuries ago I died a mortal man and all mortal desire died with me. The desire I possess now? Nothing natural can fulfill it. What I am…"

I shook my head, feeling utterly drained and wondering what had possessed me to come here this night. I had learned nothing. Nothing but that, despite past claims to the contrary, there were still some things I envied mortal man. One of these things stood before me now and scarred me with every word and every look she gave me.

"You knew your death," Angelina responded, pleading with me. "But you are not dead. *Valéry* is not dead. No matter what is done to the body, who you are remains the same. Valéry is not only flesh and blood. He is essence and that can never change. A man is always a man. What one is created to be is what one always is, despite anything and everything that happens to the body. And life, life is not simply what the flesh experiences and knows through the senses. It is all the person wants and needs and hopes."

I sank heavily onto the chair across from her and shook my head again wearily. Why was I listening to this mad child? I'd heard it all before in one form or another, hadn't I? How many would I know in my existence who would try to convince me of a similar ridiculous delusion, and how many times would I let myself fall for it? To want a thing a man wanted did not make a man of one, and I'd learned to my great pain more than once that any human desires left to me were not yearnings that could be fulfilled. What I wanted and hoped… that mattered not at all.

"Essence?" I whispered in fatigued disbelief, locking on the one word of her many that would most inspire my bitterness. "Soul, you mean. Well then, Angelina, has the devil a soul? If he does, then I suppose so must I. But if that is what you seek to know as human still, I can assure you, you search in vain. My spirit may still live, but that makes me nothing which even closely resembles a mortal man."

Angelina looked to the ceiling as if she were asking God's help to talk to me – to explain the answers she had, in words I could understand. I felt a shiver of something that wasn't quite fear go through me, despite how ridiculous I thought the impression to be. Or perhaps how ridiculous I wanted to consider such an action.

"Valéry, I know that it hurts you," she began softly, and I tried again to pretend I didn't hear the compassion in her voice. To pretend it was not that, but only curiosity in the mortal viewpoint which kept me listening so closely. But Michel's words came back to haunt me. 'You can call it curiosity if that will make it easier for you,' he'd said. And he'd been right, of course. I already cared too much.

"You think because you cannot fulfill desire as mortal man does, you are human no more," Angelina continued, voicing an opinion I'd never even allowed myself to consider. Was that the *real* reason I saw myself as something inhuman? For I had to admit it, murder was not a sin committed by the monster alone. Therefore, was it not really that a human must die to feed me that made me certain I was one? Was it instead that the taking of a life fulfilled another human hunger, one which had nothing to do with an anatomical need for nourishment? Could it truly be that – something so moralistic, so... so... Catholic?

She brushed her hand back over her forehead almost violently, pushing her hair away from her face. She shook her head several times before she spoke again. "But, it's only that you've forgotten that what you always truly wanted was not that at all. The reason that physical desire is such an incredible thing for mortal man... it is only because he is not ready for what is beyond that desire..." She paused again and clenched her fists, pressing them against her thighs. Her expression was one of frustration and deep concentration as she searched for the right words.

"You don't feel anymore the human desire you think you should because of the very corporeality of the thing, not because of any unnaturalness of your body. Only a mortal finds one of his greatest pleasures in that which is a bodily experience because that is the extent of what he knows. That is the forgetting. This pleasure has not been taken from you. It is simply that... that now you come closer to the fulfillment man seeks in the flesh in a more elemental part of yourself. This is not unnatural because it is evil – not in itself, in any case – but only because it is more than any living being was meant to know..."

I shook my head again, not because I didn't understand what she was saying, but because I was afraid that I might.

"Valéry, what you want does not require a mortal man's body. It never has. What *mortal* human beings truly want requires nothing physical. What they try to achieve again and again? It cannot be found. Not in its fullness, at least. But it is all they know. And that you've brought the memory of another kind of desire into this existence of yours... That is only pain. It is not a punishment. The cause of so much of your suffering, it's that you find inhumanity in no longer needing what is necessary only in mortality. There is no demon in you, Valéry. You are not a monster – only a man who has been made to know what no living being was meant to know." She paused yet again and then said with extreme caution, although it seemed awfully late for such caution to me, "You wanted more than what your body could give you when you *were* a mortal man, so why look to it to give you anything now?"

I stared hard at Angelina, thinking I could end this confusion and pain and longing. I could stop her words forever, and though I would have no more answers than when I'd come, the ecstasy of taking her would be worth the loss. But it was a thought of pathetic desperation, wasn't it? I wouldn't do it, couldn't do it. And to my even greater anger and frustration, I knew it.

"You think I hold humanity still? Despite knowing what I am, knowing what I've done and will do again?" I asked her, with more weariness than incredulity and, in essence, ignoring the very apparent implication in all that she'd just said. And be assured, I did understand what she was implying. All the theology the Church had not supplied her uneducated flock in my mortal lifetime, I'd spent a great deal of time reading and contemplating over the centuries that followed my denial of her and her God. Ironic, perhaps, but I find it no more so than that the Church had declared matrimony a sacrament seemingly long before she had any true theological understanding of why she believed it was one. And that was what Angelina was making reference to, was it not, however obscurely? I had always understood, unlike Michel, unlike almost every story written on the creature, that neither the feeding nor the fulfillment of a vampire was in the drinking of blood. That was just a means to an end and the end sought was to hold life. The union of us and them, of killer and victim. To drink blood was to deliver slow death, intimate death, nothing more and nothing less. The real satiation was in the life. I had never seen it exactly as Angelina now portrayed it, but the idea had been there, surely, behind what I did know. Mortal man experienced his greatest pleasure in the union of the flesh. The vampire, for him fulfillment was in the union of something more fundamental.

But then, what would she have you believe? I asked myself irritably. That a vampire knows the truer union, the truer marriage, if you will, in the taking of a life?

I have come here for this? I thought disgustedly, although perhaps only to mask my real sentiments from myself. I sought answers in her and what I find now is some corrupted form of the very faith I spat upon seven centuries ago? I thought she had only fallen for the fairy tale version of the legend. Wasn't this fantasy more depraved still?

"*Viens,*"[2] I commanded her softly and watched with curious dismay as she first tilted her head to consider my request. There seemed little victory when she did at last obey it, completely of her own free will. Completely unaffected by the lulling, hypnotic tone to my voice, that is to say.

I leaned forward in the chair as she neared it and took her by the wrist, pulling her before me. She simply stood there, unmoving in front of me, to see what I would do next. Infuriating.

"Is that what you long to know, *ma mignonne?*" I asked her with seductive sweetness. "Oneness with your dream?" I stroked the inside of her wrist with my thumb, knowing the feeling it would incite in her. She was a human female, after all.

"But why say you can give me more then, *m'amie?* If you know you cannot consummate this union in the flesh, but would instead give me my true fulfillment… when you know that is in your life? Or shall I say, in the very passing of it you claim will not satisfy me?"

She smiled ever so slightly. "Valéry, why do you still attempt the demon seduction when you already know it will not work on me?"

I tightened my grip on her wrist angrily, but not too much, not enough to hurt her really, I was miserably aware.

Fool, espèce d'idiot, andouille[3], I berated myself.

"To give me this pleasure greater than the flesh, you must die," I told her tightly. "You yourself have said so in your own twisted theology, *ma chère.* So come, I will give you your ecstasy and you can give me mine."

"It's not my theology, Valéry," she responded softly, still not angry, still not frightened, and I relaxed my grip unintentionally, defeated. At least for the moment.

"Then what do you want?" I asked her wearily, conveniently forgetting that it was I who had come to her.

"To give you what you need," she answered simply, not pulling her arm from my grasp, though she certainly could have at that point.

"And what do I need, my love, since you know me so well?"

---

[2] "Come (here)."

[3] espèce d'idiot=stupid idiot, ass; andouille=dummy, dope, literally, a type of sausage

"To believe," she whispered.

I shook my head impatiently. "To believe what?" I almost snapped.

Angelina looked at me for a long moment, like one who debated with oneself whether or not to lie. Or one who tried to decide how much of the truth might be too much, in any case. That was the impression her look left on me, anyway, and the feeling of foreboding rose in me again.

"You're not a monster, Valéry," she told me softly.

I stood up abruptly, almost knocking her backward in doing so. I caught her around the waist before she could fall and pretended I had intended to do it as part of my threat, for my own benefit as well as for hers.

"You think not?" I growled menacingly. "I believe I can disabuse you of that folly rather easily," I threatened.

She shook her head. "No, you can't."

I glared at her, but at that moment I was actually more alarmed than angry, hoping she meant solely that I could not change her mind in this and not that her response indicated she knew I felt powerless to make her my victim.

"You are insane," I told her flatly to hide my fear. "You know what I've done, what I do, what I will always do. You haven't just read some romanticized version of it. You've *seen* it! And still you refuse to see what is plain before you. I am a killer."

"Yes," she said and the pain to my heart to hear her confirm what I'd always believed was unbearably intense. And I'd called her insane.

"Yes," she repeated. "As are all men in some manner or another."

I stared down at her, pretending not to notice that I well noticed I was still holding her. "Oh, what madness do you speak now?"

"You think you are so very different from other men? Which of them does not put an end to some life so that he may guarantee his own?"

"You compare the taking of a human life to the slaughter of cattle or to the threshing of wheat?" I asked incredulously.

"But why don't you?" she asked in return. "If there is no God, what more worth the life of man? Is he not just one more animal fighting for survival, the most highly adapted predator? And so, if a more evolved species were to exist, well…" She trailed off.

"I did not come for theological debate, *chérie,*" I warned in controlled rage. But not too controlled.

"No? You did not come here to find answers?"

"Answers, not some perversion of Catholic drivel!" I shouted. "I have known more philosophies in eight centuries than you could possibly ever imagine." But then, that wasn't true, now was it? She could well imagine it, apparently. She had dreamed it, after all.

I shook my head violently, silenced for a moment. Defeated again.

"So if one were to suppose, even without the admission of God, that man is, for some reason, more... what of the soldier who fights for his country, the country which fights for its freedom or against tyranny over the people of another? What of the victim who turns on his attacker...?"

"But that is not the same," I cried out in frustration. "A vampire kills the innocent!" Of course that wasn't true, strictly speaking. My victims were not sinless by any stretch, but who was I to decide their punishment ought to be the loss of their life?

"And in all the so many wars you've seen, no innocent has ever died? What right has anyone to decide one life is more valuable than another, one cause so just it is worth the sacrifice of a fellow man?"

What right indeed? I thought wearily, but though her reasoning was hard to argue, there was something... something. I might want to believe and be freed of centuries of ever-growing guilt, but I did not believe it, any more than I ever had, and I felt certain that she did not truly believe it either. So why was she saying such words?

"Why are you so sure you recognize evil, Valéry, when all your existence you've felt that an understanding of goodness has always remained just out of your reach?"

I tightened her to me and grabbed her hand, holding it to my heart. Could she feel how she was breaking it? No, I could not easily be killed, but I could be made dead, couldn't I?

I closed my eyes for a long moment, cursing myself for once again being so blind and foolish. Why had I thought this girl could never hurt me? I had just not had the imagination to realize how she could.

This fantastically feckless novel excerpt is chapter five of
On the Soul of a Vampire, by Krisi Keley.

Bully

By Ellen C. Maze

FRANKIE VARNY, JR. INCREASED HIS PACE; OF ALL

days to be running late for band practice. The worst part of it, Frankie was being watched. From his smoking perch across the street, Leroy Tanner's narrow eyes followed him as he jogged down the sidewalk. Frankie knew as well as anyone that nothing good could come from that.

Frankie played bass in a small easy-pop retro band that met above the coffee shop, Tuesdays after dinner. Tonight, directly after dessert, his dad handed him the phone and told him to call his grandmother. A twenty-minute captive conversation later and Frankie would have to really hustle to make it to practice before eight. Now that he'd cut through the alley between Mack's hardware and Janet's Flowers, and the footfalls of the town's meanest bully sounded louder and louder behind him, Frankie regretted leaving the house at all.

"Hey, Nancy, what's the hurry?" a voice barked too close to his ear as a rough hand spun Frankie around. Leroy was not huge, maybe 5'9", but he was wide and mean. He'd flunked out of high school. Even though Frankie was a freshman in college now, his childhood enemy continued to haunt him.

Feigning a semblance of courage, Frankie tried a new tact that he'd been practicing.

"Oh, hey, Leroy. How are ya?"

Leroy didn't seem to have heard him. He shoved him violently with both hands and Frankie stumbled back into the dark shadow of the alley.

"You think you're better than me? Huh? Huh?" The thug didn't want an answer, for as soon as the question left his mouth, he struck Frankie across the jaw with a left hook. Frankie's head snapped back and slammed into the brick wall and his vision blurred.

"Hey, man! No, I don't think—"

Slap! Leroy hit him open-handed with his right palm and then jabbed a body blow into his gut. "Smug bastard! I'll show you who's better and who's a worthless turd!"

Frankie shielded his face with both forearms and withstood multiple blows to his abdomen and a kick to his groin that dropped him to his knees. Through a moving red haze, the shape of his enemy filled his vision. A fist in his hair forced his face into the ground and he soon felt Leroy shuffling through his back pocket for the wallet mom gave him for his 19th birthday two nights ago. Let him have it; Frankie could get another one.

Frankie breathed through his mouth as Leroy shouted curses down on him. When the bully's camouflage work boot came down on his head, Frankie whimpered and the lights went out.

♦

Leroy left the alley, fanning out the ten dollar bills. Seventy bucks meant a fairly comfortable beer binge with Jake and Gary. Leroy walked faster, shoved the money into his front jeans pocket, and wiped the nerd's blood from his knuckles to his shirt. Like a war wound, the blood would show the stupid cows passing him tonight on the street that he was dangerous. Leroy growled and faked a lunge at a man and his wife who stared at him too long as he passed. *Jerks, all of 'em,* he thought as he fell into a trot.

Gary's garage was only a block away and the boys could hit the town as soon as he arrived. Only Jake had a running vehicle, and Leroy vowed under his breath that if he got to Gary's before their driver he'd mess him up plenty. Nobody was going to screw up the evening Leroy had planned for them. After a few rounds of beer and pool at Kippy's Bar & Billiards, they'd walk the bartender, Polly, to her car. The woman got off at eleven and she had it coming. Last week, when Leroy and the boys followed her into the parking lot after work, they'd scared her pretty good before Kippy came out and ruined the party. Tonight, Leroy and Gary would grab her, throw her into Jake's car and take her back to the garage. Private parties were best, after all.

Leroy slowed to a fast walk as he reached 5th Avenue. He wasn't even breathing hard; it paid to hit the gym in the mornings. His sad-ass mother paid for the membership in an effort to connect with him, but she could go to hell. He'd take her money, but he'd never return her affection. She just didn't deserve it; ran off his father when he was only five and never stopped trying to make it up to him.

Leroy cursed his mother aloud and then stopped dead. A shadow had passed his position and disappeared again to his right. It was large, upright, and moved like a man. Who in their right mind would stalk Leroy Tanner? He was the king of the night here in Jackson Heights. Leroy looked both ways and then up to the fire escapes of the flanking buildings. If anyone was there, he was mighty stealthy. Just to cover his bases, Leroy called out a taunt followed by a stream of expletives and threats. When no one answered and the alley remained still, Leroy sighed angrily and resumed his pace toward the light at the end of the dim alley. Sounds of laughter wafted toward him from Gary's straight ahead and he grinned until the shadow crossed his path and disappeared once more. Leroy whirled around, brandishing his hastily-opened switch blade at the same time.

"I'm sick a playin' with you, jerkwad!" he hissed, his eyes darting back and forth. Twenty feet behind him, his pals whistled at something and laughed. Leroy thought about calling for them. He considered turning and running out of the alley as fast as he could. But he did neither. He repeated his previous statement and spat into the darkness.

Ooph!

Without warning, a fist knocked out his breath and Leroy stared into the hard gaze of his attacker. Hooded, Caucasian, and very angry, the killer removed his fist and thrust it again, deeper this time, his opposite arm holding Leroy in place. Leroy spat blood onto his enemy's face and noticed, for the first time, a searing pain in his gut. He'd been stabbed, and by a much bigger knife than his own.

♦

Almond tightened his grip on the hunting knife and rotated his wrist forcefully both ways until his surprised victim mumbled twice and gave up the ghost. It was a good kill, a clean kill. Wiping the eight-inch serrated blade on his pants, Almond let the dude drop to the littered cement and backed into the shadows. The grunt might not be discovered until morning, but there was no way of knowing for sure. Almond hugged the brick wall with his back and made his way back to the main road in shadows. When he reached the end of the building, he shrugged off his hood with a swift movement of his shoulders, and fell into the flow of jolly pedestrians.

The night was a comfortable 68 degrees and a dozen locals walked arm-in-arm or side-by-side all around him. Theaters, clubs, bars, and restaurants lined the street, and Almond walked nonchalantly to avoid drawing attention. He blended in, a rugged build—not fat, not skinny, a common face—not handsome, not ugly, and tired clothing—faded navy-blue hoodie over shredded black jeans and dusty black boots. He never turned heads, which worked out fine since his dream was to be invisible. He had a mission and drawing attention to himself only interfered, never helped.

The thick thug in the alley was part of his mission. The beady eyes, swaggering manner, and buzzed-off dirty blond hair made the moron in the alley the perfect target. Every time Almond ended one of those types, his soul was soothed a little bit more than before. Each time he watched the life drain from those soulless eyes, Oppy was once again laid to rest.

His mother's father, Oppy took seven-year-old Almond in when his parents were killed in a plane crash. Almond's childhood ended the first weekend after a jaunt to Oppy's secluded lake cabin. When Almond was old enough, he fought back. When he was strong enough, he stabbed his grandfather in the gut with the guy's own hunting knife. Now, twenty years later, killing Oppys was the only thing that gave Almond pleasure.

Almond reached his Geo Metro and fell into the cracked vinyl seat-cover. It wasn't long before he passed the "Come back soon!" sign as you head out of town. After two miles of open farmland, the dark sky blanketed thick forests that bled into the Tuskegee National Forest. Almond considered his condition, but all he felt was bliss. Utter joy at ridding his universe of another disgusting Oppy clone. A smile touched the edges of his mouth and he relaxed into the stiff chair just as flashing blue lights up ahead snagged his attention. *The police!*

Thinking fast, Almond sat erect, fastened his belt, and slowed the vehicle. It would be virtually impossible for the cops to know he'd just dispatched the jerk back in town. A bit closer and he noted the shield on the closest patrol car: sheriff's department. This was some local crap, not a concern of his. Almond came to a stop at the makeshift road block and rolled down his window. A snappily-uniformed deputy met his car and leaned casually in to speak.

"Sir, we're stopping everyone heading into the Forest," the deputy said, one hand now pointing into the dark trees. "A farmer was mauled to death tonight and we don't know yet what kind of animal we're dealing with. Could be a bear or a rabid wolf. You headin' home?"

Almond nodded and purposefully loosened his grip on the steering wheel to appear calm. "Yessir. I live on Birdie Lane, just before you enter the Forest."

"Uh-huh, okay. Go straight home, get inside, and lock your door, okay? In the morning, we'll come by and check on you and your neighbors."

"Yessir," Almond said as the cop stood off his car and took a step back. "Thanks. I'll be careful."

The cop waved him through and Almond minded the rules the rest of the way home. When he reached his cabin, he left the car and stretched toward the full moon. He loved to look for Oppys on a full moon—he always seemed to have the best luck then.

A howl split the silence and for an instant, Almond's breath hitched. He recovered almost immediately and completed his stretch. Taking a step toward his unlit porch, the howl sounded again, much closer. Almond pulled his knife from the sheath in his lower back and faced the woods. He feared neither man nor beast, and tonight, he felt strong enough to overcome anyone who dared oppose him. A rustle to his right egged him on and he stepped toward the tree-line. Before he took three steps, a large black shape leapt from the bushes and slammed into him full force. Almond fell hard onto his rear, flipped himself over in an instant, and prepared to stand. Before he could bring his knees under him, a weight, heavy and moving, landed on his middle, forcing him to abandon the thought of rising, and instead, pushed his lower half into the moist leaves.

"Get off me!" Almond shouted, but the thing continued its attack unimpeded.

Fire erupted across his shoulders as knife-like claws scraped repeatedly across his spine and a wicked growl filled the clearing. Almond's hoodie and T-shirt were shredded within seconds and his bare back couldn't withstand the attack. With deep lacerations profusely leaking blood, Almond collapsed to the wet earth, his mouth filling with mud. Roaring now more like a lion, his attacker increased its efforts to skin him alive and Almond lost consciousness.

◆

An explosion from the not-too-distant north distracted Kuma from his fugue. The crimson-haze that filled his mind as well as his soul filtered slowly away as he became aware of the possible danger approaching from behind. Leaping off the dead human, Kuma took cover in the tall, unkempt bushes that lined the cabin's clearing. He couldn't recall how he knew to avoid the ones with the loud stick, but he knew with every fiber of his being that he should run. The ones that carried the stick carried lights in their hands and wore a curious star on their chests. Kuma hunkered down as low as possible and watched the stick-men arrive.

The first to pass his position seemed familiar. His scent, his shape, even the sound of his voice triggered memories from deep within, but Kuma could form no coherent thought regarding the sensation. It was almost as if he *should* know him and know how to react, but Kuma saw only red and desired only to open the human up with sharp claws.

"Over here!" the stick-man said, and Kuma marveled at the words. He understood them, and morbid fear possessed him at the same time. More rustling brought more stick-men to his proximity and Kuma considered bursting out. Before he could make up his mind, the one he recognized pushed into his cover and called out loudly for his fellows.

"I see him!" he yelled, his loud stick coming up to Kuma's eye level. Kuma roared at the top of his voice and leapt straight for the human blocking his escape. With a deafening sound, the stick erupted fire.

◆

"I got him! By God, I got him!" Frankie Sr. shouted as his fellow deputies reached his twenty. For a week, local farmers had been reporting missing sheep, and most recently, mauled livestock. Tonight, Farmer Mason was found mutilated outside his barn two miles away. Frankie Sr. cocked his rifle and fired one more round into the animal's chest. It was down, and as he half-expected, it didn't look quite animal enough for his taste.

Without sharing his theories with his fellow officers, Frankie Sr. had been suspecting a supernatural perp from the start. As soon as he noted the strange man-wolf footprints left at all of the mauling scenes, Frankie Sr. figured whatever was doing the killing was neither man nor beast, but something in between. Tonight, just in case he was right, he'd loaded his Remington with silver bullets. They seemed to have done the trick. Before his eyes, the wolf-shaped man began to shrink, shrivel, and mutate back into the man he'd been before his transformation. By the time his pals shined their beams on the bloody mess, they recognized the Mason kid. He'd been a sweet guy, a little slow in the head, but friendly and generally helpful around the farm.

"Joshua Mason?" the deputy on his right asked the air. "That kid's been doin' all this killin'? That don't make sense."

"That weren't no Joshua Mason made them slashes in Farmer Mason's back, I tell ya." The other deputy offered and spat a wad of tobacco.

Frankie Sr. didn't add his two cents. He was city enough to know when to keep his mouth shut and country enough to believe in monsters. Joshua Mason had somehow gotten himself mixed up with a werewolf. Now…how to find the one that made him…

177

Buzzzz!

Frankie Sr. whipped his walkie from its holder and pressed the button. "You got Varny, go ahead."

"Varny, Doc Miller called. Your son was beaten unconscious tonight. Some kids found him in an alley. He's okay, but you might want to go by the hospital and see him."

Frankie Sr. calmed the nervous knot in his belly and told the dispatcher he would. Leaving the body of Joshua Mason to his coworkers, he headed for his patrol car.

"Damn bullies," he mumbled, "the world would be such a nice place if everyone would just be NICE."

In his car, he phoned ahead to alert his wife of their son's condition. Wouldn't do to have her find out from a neighbor. Small towns, small minds, and all that. Frankie Sr. zoomed back into town and ran his lights for good measure. Tomorrow morning, he'd arrest that no good Tanner, who'd been picking on his boy for the better part of ten years. Tomorrow night—he'd hunt down the other werewolf.

It was going to be a busy day.

Excursion

By Kevin R. Maze

"WAKE UP, SLEEPY HEAD," SHE SAID.

Slowly, I opened my eyes, batted my eyelids to chase away the morning fog and stared into the blue eyes of the smiling face above me. Her golden tresses dangled toward me as she brushed my hair off my forehead. I smiled and for a moment I did not know where I was. My head swung a little to the side and I saw I was lying on a green sofa. Her green sofa. I was at her apartment. "What time is it?" I asked.

"Seven thirty. Time to get up and at 'em. I just made coffee."

She walked into the kitchen and I sat up and stretched. "I take it I slept over last night."

"You don't remember?"

"I just woke up. Give me a minute."

She smiled as she poured a cup of coffee. I rubbed my eyes, ran my fingers through my hair and looked at the pillow I had slept on. "I take it I was a perfect gentleman?"

"Perfect," she said as she poured sugar into her coffee.

"Was I drunk?"

"Let's just say you were in no condition to drive."

"I'm sorry. Are you ashamed of me?"

"I wouldn't be here if I was. Or rather, you wouldn't be here." She winked.

I smiled and lifted myself from the sofa, stumbled into the kitchen and poured myself a cup. I took a drink of the hot, bitter liquid and grimaced.

"It's kind of strong. You might want to put some sugar in it."

"I usually do, but after last night… Yeah, sugar." I added a couple of teaspoons until the coffee was palatable.

"So what do you want to do today?" she asked.

"I guess we've got the whole day, huh?"

"The whole day. Anything you want."

I took a drink and tried to sift through the cobwebs in my head. "Well, what do you want to do?"

"Okay, I was thinking about the botanical gardens. It's so pretty this time of year."

"The gardens?"

"I know. It sounds a little silly, but it's so beautiful and it looks like it's going to be a perfect day for it. What do you say?"

"Sounds good. I can't remember the last time we've been there."

"Perfect! I'll get dressed and you can freshen up in the bathroom." She kissed my cheek, went to her bedroom and closed the door.

The garden was alive with plants and flowers, a blanket of green dotted with sprinkles of colors, a kaleidoscope of red, yellow, pink, orange, and blue hues. Sunbeams trickled through the canopy of treetops and danced on the stone path before us. A soft hum of insects drifted through the air as I inhaled the fragrance of the flora around us. We walked hand in hand, stopping at every other flower. She bent over a bouquet of colored flowers, closed her eyes and inhaled. She smiled and slowly exhaled. She opened her eyes and looked at me. "This one smells beautiful."

"Does beauty have a smell?"

"This one does."

I leaned over and smelled. It was sweet and… well, beautiful.

She said, "You gotta stop and smell the flowers."

"I guess so."

A lone bee worked busily on the petal. I stared a moment and watched its tiny legs walk softly along the inside center. I reached out for it, and then stopped, but the bee quickly retaliated. It stung my finger and flew away. I recoiled my hand and exclaimed.

"Are you okay? What happened?"

I looked at my finger, red and beginning to swell. "Bee stung me. I don't know what I was thinking."

"Let me see." She took my hand and examined it. "Does it hurt?"

"Not really. I'll be okay. I'm not allergic or anything."

"We'd better keep an eye on it."

"Julie!"

We turned to see a man walking toward us quickly.

"Wait here," she said to me and met him down the path.

"I just got served."

"What are you doing, Tom? You can't be here. You'll mess everything up."

"When were you going to tell me?"

"I think I just did."

"Ha ha. If you want a divorce, at least have the guts to tell me to my face."

"Seriously, Tom. We'll talk about this later."

"We'll talk about it now."

"Look, if you're mad at me that's one thing. But you can't come here now. The corporation is not going to accept you interrupting the experiment. There's too much at stake here for you to follow me at work and discuss our personal lives. I'm sorry, Tom, but it is going to wait. Get out of here now or I'll call the police, and then you'll have some real legal problems."

He clenched his fists then stormed off.

She stared at the ground a moment, took a breath and then walked back to me.

"How's your hand?"

"Who was that?"

"Nobody. Just a guy from work."

"Work? He said something about a divorce."

"You heard us?"

"Yes."

"It must've only sounded like 'divorce.' He said... 'divert.' We had some sort of diversion at work."

"I know what I heard. He said something about a divorce. And you said something about an experiment and the corporation."

"Experiment? No, I said... excursion. I told him you and I were on an excursion. That place just cannot manage without me for one day, but they're going to have to try until tomorrow. That's all. Don't worry about it."

I furrowed my brow and looked at a yellow flower. Something wasn't right.

"Why are you lying to me?"

"I'm... I'm not lying. We work together at the same corporation. Understand? We work together. He followed me here on our excursion because something at work had to be diverted. But we are here, together, on this excursion. I'll see him tomorrow. Everything is okay. Now let me see your hand."

"Oh, it's fi..." I showed her my hand and noticed it had swollen more in the past few minutes and was a dark pink color. "What the heck?"

"Come on," she said. "We'll go to the lobby. They may have something we can put on it. I'm sure they're prepared for bee sting allergies. Follow me."

We walked briskly back to the front of the gardens. I kept looking at my hand. "I don't understand it. I've never been allergic before."

"Not that you remember anyway." She paused. "I mean not that you know of."

"What are you talking about? I've been stung before. When I was... I was only... I..."

"Try not to think about it. Stay calm. We'll be there in a minute."

Moments later we sat in a back office. The garden attendant examined my hand, mumbled something about medicine and left with a promise to return in a minute with something to help the swelling on my hand.

"Are you okay?" she asked.

"Yeah. I'm fine."

"Look, she'll be back in a minute with some stuff for your hand. Now I have to go to the bathroom, but I'll be back in a jiffy. Keep an eye on my purse for me?"

"Sure."

"Will you be all right?"

"Sitting in a chair? I'll be fine."

"Back in a jiff," she said and left.

I looked out the office window and saw the beauty of the garden outside. Whatever this person's job included, the scenic view must've made working here better. Then again, perhaps the picturesque scene served as a reminder of what waited several feet away, but seemed unattainable.

A ringtone interrupted my thought. I looked around and noticed the sound was coming from her purse. I hesitated and then opened the clasp, looked inside and took the phone from one of the pockets. The display on the screen read "Work." I answered the call.

"Hello?"

"Who's this?"

"It's… Tom."

"Tom? You sound different."

"I'm a little hoarse today."

"You're… you're not interrupting the experiment, are you?"

"No."

"If he sees you it could raise too many questions. It could jeopardize the whole project."

"No, I just told them… I'm from the corporation."

"Good thinking. Where's Julie?"

"She's in the bathroom."

"Have her call me when she gets out, okay?"

"I sure will. Hey!"

"Yeah?"

"He doesn't know about the… experiment, does he?"

"Of course not. He is the experiment."

We hung up and I placed the phone back into the purse and

clasped it. The man on the phone was right: There were too many questions. What did the man on the phone mean "He is the experiment?" Who was Tom? For that matter, who was Julie?

Who was I? Why couldn't I remember how I got to Julie's house? Why did I not know I was allergic to bees? What was going on here?

Too many questions.

Julie walked into the office and sat on the chair next to me. "She hasn't come back yet?"

"Who am I?"

Julie looked at me, startled. "What? What do you mean...?"

"Don't lie to me. Your work just called. What is the experiment?"

"They called?"

"Just now when you were in the bathroom. The man said 'He is the experiment,' and I know he was referring to me. What is the experiment?"

"They talked to you?"

"I told them I was Tom."

"You told them...? You shouldn't have done that." Julie paused. "I mean, it's not funny. At least you still have your sense of humor."

"Stop it! Tell me what's going on. Who is Tom, the guy wanting the divorce? Who am I that I can't remember where I was last night, how I got to your apartment or that I should avoid bees? Tell me what you're not telling me."

Julie looked at the floor and cursed. For a moment she didn't say anything. She just stared at her feet, her mind clearly racing. When she finally spoke she said something that did not make any sense.

"What the hell. We'll just start over."

"Start over? What do you mean 'start over'?"

Julie shook her head. "That Tom has really screwed up now. If he thought the divorce was something, he ain't seen nothing yet. You don't mess with OmniCorp."

"What are you talking about?"

"First of all, Tom is my husband. I'm divorcing him."

"What the...? I didn't know you were married."

"Of course, you didn't. But don't worry. It has nothing to do with you. He's a controlling, heartless... never mind. He knows better than to visit me when I'm working."

"But you're not working today. That's why we're here, remember?"

"No, this is part of the experiment. Memory recall."

"What?"

Julie took a deep breath. "You are the fifth generation of a physiological cellular reproduction designed to retain higher brain functions, namely the development and preservation of memories."

"Wha…?"

"You are an experiment designed to produce a new artificially structured human that will eventually serve as labor forces, military personnel, or even as a vessel to continue memories and self-awareness of terminally ill patients with failing physical bodies such as the elderly, the cancer-ridden, those with blood diseases and so forth. You are the latest in scientific advancement and achievement. Or you were. We're going to have to start over now. "

"Wait a minute, Julie. You are insane. Do you expect me to believe that I'm… I'm some sort of guinea pig?"

"You're the fifth, actually."

"The fifth? Really? And I guess you've been doing this since I was a boy? Is that what you've been doing? That would make you really old, though, wouldn't it?"

"The cells generate quickly, but deteriorate just as quickly, too. The clones live for only about eight days for some reason. There's another lab working on that. I only do brains."

"Eight days?"

"Today was Day One for you. It usually takes a few hours for the memories to generate completely. We've been to the gardens before, but the earlier tests were never stung before. I don't know why you're allergic. I'll have to bring that up to Physiology."

"This doesn't make any sense."

"Do you remember more now than you did this morning?"

"We met in college. You wore that green shirt. You like Italian food, but you don't like onions. The day I helped you move into your apartment, the electric company wrote down the wrong date to turn on the lights. You didn't have power until the next day. Your furniture was still in the moving truck. We ate take-out rotisserie chicken on a blanket while the room was lit with candles."

Julie smiled. "That was interesting."

"Did that really happen?"

"Yes. With the first generation. Everything you remember from before this morning happened to previous generations. You've retained the memories. You're a success. And in case you're interested, the apartment is a test facility."

"You don't really live there?"

185

"No. But your memory is improving. And now we're going to have to scrap the whole thing and start over because of my frustrating soon-to-be ex-husband. Oh, he is seriously going down for this."

"I don't believe this. It's not true. This can't be happening."

"I'm so sorry."

"Wait a sec. How long did you say I had?"

"The subject has to be euthanized on the seventh day so nothing gets lost in the transference. Once the body begins to fail we have to act quickly before all is lost. But we're confident all this will be rectified in time." She paused a moment. "Again, I'm sorry."

I looked at my hand. The swelling was worse now. Slowly I made a fist and felt the tightened skin stretch as it pulled the spot where the bee stung me. Pain shot through my hand, followed by heat and an unbearable itch. The soreness made me feel alive. I was alive. Memories flashed before my mind. I turned toward the window and gazed at the vivid colors of life outside, like a palette waiting for an unseen artist, so bright, so vibrant, so brilliant. I stood up and looked out the window at the explosion of life in every direction. "You said I have seven days?"

"Yes."

I turned to Julie and smiled. "I'll see you in a week," I said and ran out the door.

Magier

By Ellen C. Maze

"LASSEN SIE UNS ZUM KARNEVAL GEHEN! COME! *Es ist Spaß!* Fun, Britt, fun!"* Anna exclaimed even though Britta didn't understand half of it. She was visiting the tiny village with her riding buddy, hoping she didn't anger Zander by skipping the week-long Show-jumping Clinic he'd purchased for her.

"Anna," Britta said, "are you saying 'carnival'? Like a circus?" Britta imitated the sound of an elephant, using her arm as a trunk. Anna smiled and nodded, repeating her earlier exclamation.

"Fun," Britta echoed and kept pace with her friend.

"Magier," Anna whispered with a mysterious inflection and Britta smiled, not understanding. Anna tried again, more spookily, and wavering her voice. *"Magie,* Britt, *hokus-pokus."* She waved her hands before her eyes. Britta finally understood.

"Oh…*magic,"* she said, relieved. "We're going to see a magic show. Okay, great." She smiled, but remained unimpressed. Not a big fan.

"Ja…magic-k," Anna repeated, over-enunciating the end of the word. Britta nodded again and craned her head around a couple in front of them to view the overpass of a huge tattered banner. Announcing the entrance to the impromptu fairgrounds, the sign read *Die größte Schau in Europa.*

"Die Greatest Show in *Europa!"* Anna semi-translated with hands held wide apart, as if she agreed with the sentiment wholeheartedly. Britta sent her a tight grin and snugged up right behind her as they navigated the entrance with a hundred other eager souls.

Townsfolk and city slickers mixed like oil and water, and Britta was aware of how much she stood out in the throng. Painfully Caucasian, her white-blonde hair and pink-hued skin made her very visible among the dark-haired, dark-eyed people on her every side.

Anna led her past tents with garishly-painted marquees printed in a language even more bizarre than German. Making a bee-line to the largest tent of all, Anna led Britta to the end of the narrow dirt road.

"Magier. Hokus-pokus, Britt." Anna pointed to the hand-painted sign hanging on the tent flap. The badly-done sign revealed a rendering of a magician waving his hands over a crystal ball. Anna pulled her by the wrist to a swarthy man collecting the small entrance fee. A few of the local coins later, they were inside.

The area inside was the size of a tennis court and every seat was occupied. With her eyes glued to the stage, Anna pulled Britta to an open chair and they sat down. On Britta's immediate right, a matron cradling a fat baby in her arms smiled at her with brown teeth. The woman roughly nudged Britta's shoulder.

"*Dieses wird groß sein,*" she barked loudly to be heard over the boisterous crowd.

"I'm sorry, I don't speak German," Britta replied touching her right ear and hoped that was the end of the conversation. But it wasn't. The woman laughed and nudged her again.

"*Ja! Englisch!* Have you seen this *magier* before? This is going to be good!"

Spoken around a thick German tongue, the woman's English was pretty good and Britta was happy to finally understand someone clearly.

"What's the big deal with this magician?" she asked, "The *Magier?* Is he that good?"

"*Ja!* Shhh…here he comes! Shhh."

Britta rolled her eyes absently and turned to face the stage. The slightly-elevated platform sat at the head of the multicolored tent, so that the performers entered through the flap in the far end. Beth watched as a stocky and stern-looking man stepped past the flap and tromped up onto the stage. He had no microphone, but he didn't need one. Taking a deep breath, he began his announcement. Not a word of it was in English, but Britta heard the word "magier" at least once. When the man stopped speaking and motioned for the flap, the crowd went wild. Britta smiled at their enthusiasm and watched the opening.

Within moments, the magier came onto the stage and the room fell silent as a tomb. Then he spoke in the local tongue with a softer, more rounded accent than she had heard since she'd been in country. Britta found herself mesmerized by his voice, lilting and floating to her ears from a dozen feet away.

His dark complexion was clear and smooth, his clean-shaven cheeks daubed with a hint of stage rouge. His hair touched his shoulders and was brown with red highlights that flickered in the weak spotlight. Britta found herself seeking out his eyes, to catch his attention as she sat entranced by his undulating narrative and the fluid movement of his hands as he performed his magic tricks. But his eyes flitted all over the room, never seeming to land in one place more than a second. Britta was forced to abandon her ploy and watch the show when she realized her feminine skills pulled no sway with the handsome performer.

His magic started off simply enough; a few sight gags using floating silk scarves and then an oversized deck of cards. After that, he moved to coin tricks, proving the dexterity of his long fingers, more than anything else. Absently, she glanced briefly to the crowd on all sides and found them as spell-bound as she was. Maybe more. They loved him. Maybe they were all under his spell.

Maybe he was a *real* magician…

Britta's mind was just beginning to wander and allow her to fantasize further about the mysterious man on the stage when he began to speak in English. She snapped to attention and realized that he was looking dead at her.

"And you, *fraulein*…what do you think of my performance thus far?"

Britta's throat momentarily closed as her mind raced for an intelligent reply. The magician's English, like his German, was lovely, and it flowed up out of him like smooth water.

"Or does the cat have your tongue?" the magician asked coyly and hopped off the stage. He walked toward the third row and stopped only a few feet away. "*Lassen Sie diese Frau durch Sie gehen,*" he said to the crowd, and then fixed his eye to hers for the translation. "Let her join me on the stage. *Frau?* Will you help me perform my next trick?"

Britta's eyes grew wide and she shook her head. The audience urged her along and Anna pushed her to her feet, barking foreign words that she figured she did not want translated.

"Sir, *Herr Magier*…I don't speak German," she stammered, having risen reluctantly and was moving past the woman with the brown teeth. The *Magier* held out his hand for her without releasing her from his gaze. An odd tingle vibrated through her body when she took his hand. When their eyes locked, she suddenly thought of Zander.

"A German tongue is not necessary to do magic. *Magie,* Fraulein, is in the eyes."

Britta thought about that as he led her back up to the stage. In her experience, the eye *was* pretty powerful. Even before she became aware of the wonderful world of the supernatural, she had power over men with her eyes. But as with Zander, she did not seem to have the same power with this magier.

As she hopped up onto the stage and allowed the man to spin her dramatically to face the audience, she realized that she was still wearing her riding attire. The very same dusty and stained outfit she had ridden four hours in already. Her breeches were form fitting, as if sprayed on, and her snug Polo shirt was stained with sweat and horse slobber. Britta took a deep breath and cleared her mind. She was part of the show and she'd give it her best shot.

◆

"Ah, my new American fan. Come in. Come in."

Britta blushed and took a look around before stepping into the man's caravan. She'd attended his show four nights in a row so it was no surprise he invited her backstage. Inside, sat a kitchen on one end and a bed on the other—this was his *house*. How would Zander react if he knew she was standing in a strange man's bedroom? A Gypsy magician, at that? Britta pushed Zander from her mind and smiled at her host.

"Please come in and have a seat, Miss…?"

"Britta," she said and cleared her throat. "Britta Baumhauer."

"Delighted to meet you officially, Miss Baumhauer. You may call me Andrew. My Hungarian name does not flow easily on the English tongue."

"You're Hungarian," Britta noted. Zander was also from Hungary. She put the realization away before she could begin to think too much. "I'm glad you speak English. German is really hard for me to understand."

Andrew nodded sympathetically and showed her a seat on his worn but clean sofa.

"Tell me, are you going to attend all of my shows, Fraulien? Are you addicted to magic," he asked, his eyes flashing, "or to the magier?"

Britta blushed and didn't answer. He continued.

"I find you distracting," Andrew said regarding her with his gaze. "Someone somewhere is missing you. If you were mine, I'd never let you out of my sight."

"Oh?" The compliment spoken so unabashedly stunned her and she stumbled to reply. *Why* had she come to his trailer?

"I apologize for my provocative manner. I never went to finishing school." Andrew smiled kindly and flashed very white teeth.

"I'm sorry for distracting you. I just can't figure out how you do the tricks. The things that flew into your hand…"

"I will tell you how it is done." He smiled then and inched closer to her. "You've earned it after paying the entry fee four times. Would you like to see? I will show you."

Britta nodded and Andrew held his hands up, fingers wiggling. He pointed one index finger toward her and just like that, her hair comb slipped out of her hair and her bangs fell down over her eyes with a feathery swish.

"Oh!" Britta gasped and her hands flew to tuck her long bangs behind her ears. "How did you...?"

"Like this." Andrew put one hand on his hip and pointed the fingers of his other hand like a gun toward Britta's blouse. "Bang," he whispered, breaking into a wide grin.

For a moment, Britta did not know what had happened, but then a breeze blew into her shirt and she looked down at her chest. The top button of her blouse was open and she could see the edge of her brassiere. Britta gasped again and buttoned it up quickly.

"It's real?"

"Yes, my lovely, very real. What else can I show you? Yes. I am certain that I might reveal everything to someone with eyes as blue as yours."

"Wow," Britta whispered and sat up from her perch on the old couch. Of course, she'd seen Zander move objects in a similar fashion, but he was different. He was *Zander*. Suddenly, Britta *did* want to know more of the Magier's secrets. "That's telekinesis. And it's real!"

"Oh, yes, *Fraulein*. May I?"

Andrew held out his hand, palm up, as if asking for Britta to take it. Without thinking, she did just that, and placed her fingers in his outstretched hand. Closing his fingers around hers, he slowly brought her hand to his face. He paused only moments before bringing it to his lips, briefly kissing the top of her hand.

"Uh...thank you," Britta said awkward and embarrassed.

"No, thank *you*," Andrew said and lowered her hand without releasing it. He leaned forward and placed his left hand on the couch next to Britta's thigh. "Britta Baumhauer, answer me this. Where is your husband? Why are you all alone?"

Britta's eyes widened and she cleared her throat. Where was Zander? No, he wasn't her husband, but he would be the closest man to fit the bill. Did she even know where he was? Britta's mind raced as she stared into the magier's bright eyes.

"You don't know where he is?" Andrew asked, his voice soft and velvety.

Britta made a small noise in her throat. Her head was growing fuzzy and she blushed. The magier was bewitching her with his gaze, another magician's trick that was as real as the rest.

"Yes, you caught me," Andrew cooed, his winning smile in place. "I am hypnotizing you, Britta. You intrigue me. You are very different from any other woman I have ever met. I want to figure you out and I am fairly certain that I could get to the bottom of it if I could convince you to open up to me…"

"You're reading my mind?" Britta asked weakly.

"Yes," Andrew whispered, eyes searching her face as surely as his mind did its work in her head.

"Are you going to take advantage of me?"

"I don't think so. Am I doing that now? Do you want to leave? You can go, you know. I am not holding you here against your will. Do you think that is what I am doing?"

"No. I don't want to leave. But my head…I feel like I am going to pass out."

"No, you're not. That sensation accompanies this trick. This *mind trick*. Just tell me about yourself. Your mind will clear as soon as you stop resisting."

Britta blinked her eyes and each time they reopened, she dove deeper into the magician's gaze. Finally after trying to figure out why the sensation was so familiar, Britta gave up and sank into the back of the couch, a sleepy smile on her face.

"Okay, Andrew. You've been very cooperative with me, telling me your secrets and all. What do you want to know?"

Andrew slipped off the low stool on which he'd been sitting and sank into the couch next to his guest, his leg touching hers on the dusty furniture. "Why are you alone, Britta? A smart man would never let you out of his sight."

"Zander trusts me," she smiled drunkenly.

"But how can he trust the rest of mankind? You need to be protected, Britta. You need to be guarded and escorted everywhere like a queen. Yet you stumble into my tent night after night, all alone, with a sadness in your heart." Andrew lifted his hand to Britta's long pony tail and tugged at the band until her locks fell free. "A woman like you should smile inside and out. Britta, what makes you so sad?"

"Do you think you could make me smile, Andrew?" Britta asked, not planning what she would say, but not sorry she asked such an odd question.

"Oh, yes. I know I could. I just have to figure out what it is that you want the most. I assume you have all of the comforts of life—a nice home, fancy clothing, priceless jewelry, and expensive perfume. But still, there is deep sadness in your heart and a stifling longing in your eyes." Andrew took the ends of Britta's waist-length hair in his hand and ran it through his fingers as he spoke.

Hot tears welling up in Britta's eyes and she swallowed them back as well as she could. The magier was right. She should be protected, guarded, and worshipped. Where was Zander? She was being hypnotized in a strange man's trailer.

No matter what was going on at the moment, Britta locked on the obvious: Zander was not there for her, and he hardly ever was. This stranger, Andrew the Magician, had hit the nail on the head. She was under-appreciated and overlooked by the man she loved. But Andrew was giving her his undivided attention. He thought she was worth his time.

"I fell in love with a man who has no use for me," Britta admitted through clenched teeth. "That's the sum of it, Andrew. I can't change him and he has barely tried to change me. You're seeing right through me. I *am* sad. And I'm lonely, too." Britta wiped away the tears that moistened her cheeks.

"Britta, you can cry on my shoulder. Go ahead..." Andrew released the ends of her hair and used the same hand to caress the top of her head.

"No, Andrew, I'm tired of shedding tears for him. I'm tired of waiting for him to rescue me. I'm tired of waiting for him to *notice* me. I don't care if I never see him again." Now more angry than sad, Britta raised her head and caught her host's eye. "I'm going to leave him. I don't need his money. He's not my sugar daddy."

"Sugar daddy? I'm not sure what that is, but are you serious about this? *Can* you leave him? I sense a hesitation in you, as if you doubt yourself on this. Yet, I also see that you do not fear him."

"No, he's harmless," Britta mumbled, then remembered Zander's true nature and corrected herself. "At least to me."

At that, Andrew did a curious thing. He stood to his feet, stared at her a moment longer, and then walked into the tiny kitchen nook.

"What's wrong?" Britta didn't rise, but she leaned forward over her legs. The dizziness had passed. "Are you okay, Andrew?"

"Britta..." Andrew spoke softly, his back to her.

Intrigued by his tone, Britta came to her feet and took a step toward him. "What? What's going on?"

"Granted, I only just met you, but..." Andrew tilted his head to the side, his voice carrying a mysterious tone. "There are some interesting images in your head. Some very interesting images."

Britta tried to recall what she had been thinking of. She'd been answering his questions. Did he really see images in her mind? Could he pick up such things in detail? Like Zander had proven to her in the past? Britta stood dumbfounded and waited for Andrew to finish his thought. She couldn't fathom what he was hinting at so she stayed mum.

"You are playing coy with me, Britta."

Andrew turned to face her and didn't step forward to close the gap between them. Britta noted wonder in his eyes that had not been there earlier, and a crooked grin had found the edges of his mouth.

A knowing grin.

"What? What?"

"This man, this Zander," Andrew drew out his words intentionally and watched her eyes. "He is not even *human.*"

"Oh, my God!" Britta gasped and covered her mouth with her hands. Somehow he had seen the truth. He knew that Zander was a vampire! "Oh, my God!" was all she could say and she repeated it again as she waited to see what the magician's reaction would be.

"Yes…you read like a fine novel, Britta Baumhauer. In full color, too. Oh, how you have treated that man. Oh, how you have tortured him…"

Andrew leaned back on the sink ledge behind him and crossed his arms at his chest. What was he thinking? From his mysterious smile, Britta just couldn't fathom. She tried to clear her mind, but the longer she stood there, the more images came to her mind concerning Zander and every single time they fought or cuddled or…

"I'd like you to stop that now, Andrew. Please, get out of my head!" Britta reflexively put both hands to her throat and then lifted a shaky finger towards the door. "Or I'll leave! I will, I promise!"

Immediately, the man mentally disentangled himself from her mind. Britta fell back onto the couch, blinking and rubbing her face. What now? What could she say to defend herself? To protect Zander's secret? What had she done?

"Now it is I who want to find this Zander character," Andrew said, still boring Britta with his hard gaze.

Britta swallowed hard and met his eye. "Aren't you afraid? I mean, if you saw what I think you saw?"

Andrew shrugged and shook his head. "Why should I fear him? I've not threatened him. I cannot fear my own brother."

Britta's eyes grew wide and she covered her mouth. *Of course! His supernatural abilities, his hypnotizing gaze, everything about him gave him away…and I didn't see it!* Britta couldn't think of anything proper to say.

She watched Andrew from her little nest on the sofa and hoped he would stay on his side of the trailer.

And that he would not try to bite her neck.

"I am no longer in your head, my dear, but will you still answer some polite questions for me? Concerning your vampire friend? I have been walking this planet for almost three hundred and fifty years and I have never met another of my kind."

Andrew leaned against the sink again, purposefully keeping his distance. "To think there's another vampire out there; he'd be watching us..." Andrew bent at the waist and peered out the kitchen window into the night. "I have always known they were out there," he said, his tone wistful. "I knew I could not be the only one. Especially since I was abandoned very early on by my master."

"Your master? Andrew, I don't know very much about Zander's past. I mean, I have some history with him, but I'm afraid he doesn't confide in me." Britta spoke quickly, deep down wondering if she was in danger of being attacked, even though her host was maintaining his distance to assuage her fear.

"Tell me how you met, Britta Baumhauer," Andrew said, his voice plaintive and his eyes soft.

Britta did not reply, but pressed her lips together. What was she supposed to do now? And where was Zander? He never allowed her to be so near disaster since they met. She'd come to rely on his telepathic monitoring.

Andrew sighed and stood up off the sink counter. "Are you going to tell me, Britta?" he asked and took two steps toward the couch.

"Stop. Don't threaten me, Andrew. Zander knows where I am and he'll come if he senses I am in danger. You don't want to be on his bad side." Not even sure if her threat held water, Britta barked out the first thing that came to her mind. She still had not called to Zander in her heart, and she was going to avoid it at all costs. She was actually still entranced with the magier.

Even if he was a vampire.

Maybe *because* he was a vampire.

"Oh?" Andrew crossed the short distance between them and held out his hand. "What if I were to kiss you? Would he know about that? Do you think he is watching you right now?"

Britta looked at Andrew's outstretched hand and then back to his handsome face. His feathery hair hung down over his forehead and framed his cheeks as he leaned toward her. *Was* Zander spying on her?

Would he instantly appear if another man, er, another vampire should kiss her? Never having been in such a position, she had no way of knowing.

"Does he kiss you, Britta?" Andrew asked, his English more accented as the moment heated the room. "When was the last time you were really kissed? Can you remember?"

Britta bit her lip subconsciously and considered his questions. No, Zander would not kiss her. He pecked her cheek often enough, but he would never kiss her. Not like a man kisses a woman.

But this *magier* would.

This vampire magician did not fear his nature. He was willing to give her a bit of the attention she lacked at home. What harm could come from it? Andrew wouldn't hurt her.

Britta hung on to that last comforting thought and reached for his hand. Andrew enfolded her into his arms. He smelled of sawdust and soap and Britta hung in his embrace for several long moments, her face tucked into the rough material of his costume. He murmured something to her she didn't understand and stroked her hair. When he mumbled the same words again, this time closer to her ear, Britta peeked out of the embrace.

"What did you say? I only speak English," she whispered, her face inches from his cheek.

"Maybe I was speaking to your lover. Maybe if he's listening, he heard me…" Andrew whispered, his soft breath landing on Britta's upturned face. "I said, 'I am about to kiss your bride, and I dare you to try to stop me.'"

"That's not too bright," Britta whispered back, now certain that Zander was going to appear magically at any moment. But she did not turn away from the magician's gaze. When he leaned forward to touch his lips to hers, she did not move back. *It's been so long,* she thought to herself, flushing.

"So far, so good, young Britta. Do you think it is safe? Are we likely to consummate this kiss?" Andrew asked telepathically, causing Britta to startle. *"Your lover speaks to you this way, no?"*

Britta nodded, wide-eyed.

"Then, here we go. And to hell with anyone who tries to stop us…"

Andrew's lips touched Britta's tenderly and soon, she fell wholeheartedly into his kiss. Wrapped in his arms, she could almost pretend it *was* Zander holding her, loving her, worshipping her the way she had always dreamed he would.

But it wasn't.

Zander wouldn't or couldn't love her this way. He had made that clear at the beginning. And why? Even as this 300-year-old vampire kissed her more gently than she had ever known, she remembered why Zander would never love her this way. It was because of the blood. Because of *her* blood and his desire for it.

So why can this vampire kiss me? He is not taking my blood...

Before she could dream up an answer for herself, Andrew pulled away and put his hands on either side of her face. Britta was light-headed and dizzy, but this time it was strictly sexual and perfectly natural.

"He did not come, young Britta. Did I not kiss you passionately enough to arouse his jealousy?" Andrew spoke softly and held Britta's gaze.

"Perhaps he doesn't get jealous," she whispered, disappointed and sad that she was probably right. Maybe Zander only showed up when she was in danger, and a kiss was not likely to hurt her. At least not a normal human kiss.

"I would be insanely jealous and covetous of a woman like you, Britta." Andrew's hands cupped her cheeks and his thumb traced her bottom lip. "Not much of a lover is he, this Zander?"

"He protects me," Britta whispered, wondering what it was she wanted from this man; this friendly and adoring vampire.

"He withholds everything from you, doesn't he Britta? Withholds love, affection, intimacy?"

Andrew knew it all from her eyes and Britta did not attempt to answer his rhetorical questions.

"You wonder why, don't you? And you wonder why he won't take that which he desires the most, don't you? From thousands of other people he has taken this one thing. But not from you. He flatly refuses you. You wonder why he won't take your *blood.*"

Britta blinked back a tear and swallowed hard. The man was right; Zander was stingy with everything that mattered. All things pertaining to love, he held back completely. Britta nodded her head slightly, and her fists gathered the cloth on the front of Andrew's costume. The ache in her spirit grew and her resolve to resist the magier and leave his caravan had all but dissolved.

Andrew placed a lingering kiss on her forehead and Britta thought she might die.

♦

"I could, Britta. I could take your blood. And I would be very gentle." Andrew smiled despite himself. The thought of sinking his aching teeth into the flawless skin of another vampire's beauty was almost too delightful to suppress. There was no doubt in his mind that her blood would go down his throat like the food of the gods.

But he wouldn't steal it.

He would wait for her to offer it to him. And by the look in her eyes, she was about to do just that.

"What do you say, Britta? Do you trust me?"

Britta inhaled sharply, remembering to breathe, and then nodded her head ever so slightly.

"But he might come. He still might come," Britta said under her breath.

Andrew could see that she was hoping he'd come as much as she hoped he wouldn't. It didn't matter. He had accepted the bait and was already moving her into position. He loosed the top button of her blouse with nimble fingers and ran his thumb underneath the fabric to her shoulder. After catching her gaze once more to reassure her, he used that thumb to tug her blouse downward to bare her shoulder.

Britta's hand instinctively went to her bosom, and Andrew shook his head. "Shhh, turn like this darling…" He spun her gently until her back was to him and he wrapped his left arm about her waist. His right hand busied itself with tucking her hair over her left shoulder, before snugging her in tight against him with both arms.

"Try to be still," he said, and then switched to telepathy as he opened his mouth over her throat. *This may sting a bit…*"

Andrew waited for the woman's heartbeat to return to a normal rhythm before doing the deed. She would quite likely be terrified once he latched on to her flesh. When she was ready, he prepared to use his sharp incisors to pierce her skin. He had plenty of practice on other voluntary donors to not puncture the victim, so much as to simply make a horizontal laceration. The cut would bleed freely enough, and then heal fairly quickly once the donor was on his or her way. As he predicted, the woman was startled by the sharp pain, but she relaxed almost immediately.

He held her tightly about the waist for her own benefit. The poor woman had spent so much time in the presence of an untouchable immortal that she had quite worked the experience up in her mind. She had a notion that it was a sign of a vampire's love to consume her blood.

As insane as that sounded, Andrew was happy to oblige. After all, her blood was right now coursing out of her body and into his own. It *was* an intimate exchange of sorts, and he was never one to turn down a free meal.

Andrew drank his fill and soon, the woman slipped into unconsciousness. She was safe, her heart beating strong and even in her chest. He reached into his back pocket for his handkerchief, easily holding all of her weight now in one arm, and he pressed the cloth firmly against her new wound.

Lifting her off the ground, he carried her to his lumpy bed in the corner. Her eyes fluttered open and she looked like she might speak. Andrew beat her to the punch.

"You'll be fine here, my darling. Shhh… You can sleep here. No harm will come to you. I will watch over you until you awake." Andrew tucked the quilt under her side and then carefully lifted her head to free her long hair to lie on the pillow above her. She puzzled him as her weak smile grew a fraction and she parted her lips again as if to speak. No words came so Andrew clicked off the lamp above the bed and made as if to stand up and move to the couch. Then she whispered his name very softly.

"Shhh… do not worry. You are going to be fine…"

He heard his name again, very soft, but definitely there. Andrew leaned down until his face was only inches from hers and she mustered up the strength to speak one more time.

"Andrew," Britta said, and closed her eyes. *"Andrew…he's coming. He saw. He knows. He's coming…"*

Andrew stayed put a moment and the woman on his bed fell off into a deep sleep. When he stood and crossed the room to the couch, he was thinking about her last words.

He's coming.

Andrew stood where he was a long time and let those few words tumble around in his mind. He wondered two things: Was he really coming? And if he was…what happens next?

◆

Zander was well hidden in the shadows of the woods that surrounded the magier's small caravan, but hidden only from mortal eyes. He did not doubt that the supernatural senses of Britta's new pal had already picked him up.

Zander chose to wait.

He leaned casually against a slender birch, arms crossed about his chest, eyes facing the silver-and-rust structure that the traveling *vampyr* called home. Zander's full-length dark gray trench coat blocked the cold wind that whipped about him, but he didn't notice. His mind was preoccupied with Britta.

His Britta. What had she done? And why had she done it? What were the odds that his lovesick companion would innocently run into another of his kind when he was conveniently otherwise occupied? And how was it that he did not know of this man's existence? This puzzled Zander the most. He had always prided himself in knowing that he was the only one of his kind. How could this wild one survive alone? And how long had he been alive, existing unrecognized among the mortals, and out of reach of Zander's psychic senses?

Zander scoffed. None of that mattered now.

Britta mattered.

Zander was tragically disappointed in her. He struggled daily to avoid tarnishing her spirit and soul, and she could not or would not recognize the validity of such a mission.

Now, he didn't want to face the possibility that he might lose her. He didn't want to hear the magician claim his woman so cavalierly when he had not suffered alongside her as Zander had. She was difficult to live with, and difficult to deal with, but she held his heart in her hand. She always had. What if she decided to stay with this carnival vampire? Would he allow it? He had the power to force his will, but the last century, he'd found a better way. His number-one priority was inner peace; Zander wanted peace, and allowing the world to make its own choices, had been the answer he sought.

What would Britta choose?

Zander sighed quietly and refocused his eyes on the door of the trailer.

The magier was in there, with his Britta, thinking God knows what. Zander concentrated on his unknown brother and willed him to come out.

Standing up off the tree, he uncrossed his arms and put his hands into his coat pockets. His mind mercifully clear, finally, he decided that he would face the matter as it came. Without planning or plotting to bring about an ending *he* desired. After all, Zander didn't know how he wanted it to end. Bottom line? It wasn't he who strayed.

The trailer door came open then, and a man's form filled the negative space. Zander concentrated on his thoughts. The magier was younger than Zander, or at least, had been when he had been transformed. He was dark-skinned, much like the Gypsies of the Balkans, and his overall expression was one of amusement, as if the man had not seen very much heartache or despair in his long life. Zander also saw in those short seconds, that the man was a playboy and charlatan, but he was no monster. The carnival kept him occupied, and he had developed quite a system of drawing blood from the mortals around him that left them weak and confused, but in no way sure of what had transpired. Taking it all in, Zander stood tall, his expression determined, and waited for the magier to make the first move.

◆

Andrew stood at the door of his trailer, fingers on the handle, unsure of what to do. The woman's lover was there, in the dark, under the trees, waiting for him to make the first move. He knew all of this intuitively, and absently he realized that it felt good to have his intuition switched-on again after so long. Since the other vampire's arrival, Andrew had felt more alive than he had in centuries. His eyesight was sharper, his hearing more acute, and his body…oh, his flesh fairly hummed with excitement.

Andrew glanced backward at the woman sleeping across the room. Her breathing was gentle and rhythmical, as it should be. He hadn't harmed her at all. Surely the being outside would know that. He would not have any reason to be *angry*. Maybe the vampire out there would thank him. After all these months beside that beautiful creature and he never laid a hand on her? Maybe he'd done the guy a favor.

Andrew chuckled. He'd never know *what* the guy thought if he didn't do something. Taking a deep breath, he scaled the two metal steps down to the ground. The woman's lover stood twenty meters away beneath white-barked trees, hidden from the light of the full moon. But Andrew hadn't needed any light. He saw the man clearly and he managed a half-smile and nodded. It was a gesture that he hoped conveyed confidence, but also an invitation to come closer. When the man did not move for several seconds, Andrew took two steps from the trailer and then motioned with his right arm toward his door.

Won't you come in? he thought, a little laugh in his heart. He wanted to remain jovial, after all, he had not approached this mad woman for affection. She had practically seduced him. Andrew remained optimistic and waited for the stranger to approach.

After a few more seconds, the man moved toward him. When he left the woods and entered the clearing, Andrew stood to the side of his door, and with the flair of a showman, lifted his arm to welcome the visitor inside.

"Please come in. I have been expecting you." Andrew hoped he sounded brave because to his own ears he sounded childish and afraid. But the man was coming anyway, and when he reached within six feet, he stopped and greeted him face-to-face.

In once brief glance into his eyes, Andrew gleaned a plethora of information from the man's mind. The first thing that he knew when looking into Zander's dark eyes was that he was powerful, and he knew it. This vampire had seen and done more in his lifetime than Andrew could even imagine, and much of it was bloody and abhorrent to the man who had executed the deeds. Zander carried within him an equally great regret. Andrew didn't know how to receive all that he'd discerned, so he decided to play it cool, and with a lot of respect. He waited for the man to enter and then followed him in, a small smile on his face that he hoped masked his anxiety.

Zander first stepped over to where Britta lay sleeping on the mussed bed. Andrew locked the door and stayed put, waiting patiently for his turn at the visitor's attention. Zander was taller than he, and had to stoop to avoid the low ceiling.

Andrew pulled out a chair near where he stood and motioned for his guest to sit on the edge of the bed. "Won't you have a seat, Herr? I realize this is a rather small caravan for such a tall man." Andrew hated the sound of his voice suddenly, but his visitor did as he asked and sat next to the sleeping Britta.

The silence lingered as Andrew wondered who would begin the conversation. Finally, Zander sighed with what sounded like impatience.

Andrew said the first words he could think of. "That's some overcoat you have there, Sir."

The vampire's eyes flashed with irritation as he opened his mouth to speak. "What is your name?"

"My apologies, Herr Zander, my name is Androni Miklos. I go by Andrew the Great." Andrew smiled at the last, but his guest relayed no reaction. "You are Herr Zander, and this is your Britta, no?"

His guest glanced back at the woman briefly and turned again, his face softening.

"Can you own the wind, Androni?" Zander asked in a smile that came across as a grimace. "Let me rephrase. No, I cannot say she *belongs* to me, but I have been responsible for her for some time."

"Oh. Odd way of putting things, eh?" Not really a question, Andrew shifted in his chair and watched the other man's face. Obviously, Zander was disturbed to find his woman as he did, but was he angry with Andrew? He tried a new tact. "She is headstrong."

Zander laughed aloud, his voice booming in the small space. "I won't keep you, Andrew the Great. I can see that everything is under control," his guest said chuckling and stood.

"Wait. You're not leaving?" Almost in a panic, Andrew stood as well. He was not ready to end his new acquaintanceship. "Aren't you going to take her with you?" Was the man going to leave her with him? Andrew hadn't planned on that contingency. Not that it would be a problem...

"Androni, you seem like a nice fellow, and I'm sorry we are meeting under these circumstances, but I will let you in on a little secret concerning Miss Britta Baumhauer."

"Yes?"

"She is incorrigible. I will be completely honest with you because I can see that you are man without guile." Zander paused as his compliment sunk in, and then continued with a wry smile. "I came because she called. She called me before you even kissed her. But I simply couldn't drop everything this time to save her. I wouldn't. She tests me constantly, and this time..."

"You wanted to see if she'd go through with it?" Andrew spoke softly hoping he did not insult his guest.

"Well, yes," Zander admitted.

"You're not *angry* with Andrew?"

Zander smiled and shook his head. "Androni, young man, you have no idea..." Zander stepped up to him and clapped him on the shoulder. "Perhaps she will have learned a lesson. Maybe she'll have it out of her system. At any rate, no, I'm not angry with you. Disappointed in her, but not angry with you. I thought you handled yourself fairly well under the circumstances. A lesser man, mortal or immortal, could have made this her *last* error in judgment."

"I am a gentleman, after all." Andrew flashed his teeth in a wider smile and was silent a moment, wondering what it would take to get the man to stay. His mere supernatural presence was intoxicating. "So, you're leaving her with me?"

Zander paused, reading Andrew's eyes. "I'm not able to take her home this moment. I ask you to allow her to remain here until morning. I will send a car to pick her up around 9 a.m. Then she can decide if she will come home."

"That simple then? You want her to choose?" Andrew shrugged as he spoke. He had no qualms about keeping her around. "What do you think she'll decide?"

"She'll come home with me. I will ask you to keep her safe until the car arrives to take her away."

"Of course. But Herr," Andrew glanced at her sleeping form and then back to the doctor, "how can I find you? I have never seen another of my kind since the beginning. My Master deserted me after only two years and I have never been happier than I am right now in your shadow." Andrew watched his guest's face and the empathy he read encouraged him. "I want to know you, and anything I have is yours. Everything I have, I give to you. What do you say?"

Thoughts of traveling alongside such a powerful vampire tickled his mind, but the man's face remained rigid. He was considering Andrew's offer, but it was taking too long. Andrew fell to his knees perhaps for the first time in his life, desperate for the man to accept. Taking Zander's right hand in both of his, he began to beg the man to agree to his wishes.

"Please, Herr. *Kérlek, vigyél magaddal,*" Andrew said in his first tongue. "I will not be in the way. I only want to learn from you."

After several seconds, his guest rolled his eyes. "I'm returning to the States. You may follow me there if you wish it."

"*Csodálatos!*" Andrew whooped and regained his feet, slamming his palms against the metal ceiling of his trailer. He'd found the most agreeable sensation in his flesh in centuries and the source of such glee had agreed to keep him around.

Zander put a finger to his lips. "Tomorrow, when the car comes for Britta, you may come as well."

"I have one more week of performances. I do not think I can leave before I have collected my wages." Andrew grimaced as he spoke the truth, but he had never been wealthy, and facts were facts when it came to travel and lodging.

Zander reached for his wallet and turned out every last bill. "Take this. It will get you wherever you want to go. If you get in my car

---

[4] "Wonderful!"

tomorrow, my driver will offer two destinations. Either my house in the country, or he will bring you to the airport. Do you have a passport?"

"I do." Andrew absently counted the first few bills, but when he reached one thousand American dollars, he stopped and pocketed the cash with a whistle.

"Good."

"You won't regret it. I have a lot to offer. A lot more than I can tell you about in this short time…"

"Good enough." Zander clapped him on the back and Andrew leaned toward the door.

"No, leave the door closed. Your celebratory racket must have half the camp out of bed. I will depart from here."

"Pardon me?"

Zander put his finger to his temple and then pointed loosely to Britta's sleeping form. "If you need to reach me, she knows how."

He winked once to Andrew and disappeared. Andrew gasped. He'd not seen the like since he and his own master parted company centuries ago.

Oh, what wonderful things this vampire could teach a willing student! And what a marvelous magician he would be if he could disappear, too!

Andrew began packing his things, and soon, the caravan was filled with the sound of singing.

Britta slept on; feckless temptress that she was.

Magier was inspired by the characters of Ellen C. Maze vampire series, The Corescu Chronicles.
www.ellencmaze.com

The Bonus

A Note from the Feckless Editor:

Angela Dolbear's, The Garden Key, *is easily my favorite novels. Delightful and insightful, this book entices the reader with comical, real-life dialogue, and ticklish emotions. You will laugh, and as you near the end, cry because it is nearly over. The following is a novel excerpt chosen for this publication because of the fecklessness of the roommate, Maggie, and the anti-feckless behavior of our heroine, Madeleine. Ya'll enjoy! I know I did!*

Signed, Ellen C. Maze, Editor

"The Garden Key... a book about lust, redemption and really good cheeseburgers"

Madeleine Winger's thoughts consume her. This college coed's mental object of affection is a gorgeous dark-haired, green-eyed musician. She doesn't know his name, and she has never spoken to him, but she can't stop her heart and mind from their unending crush on him. She proclaims herself a "lust-o-holic." But Maddy knows all too well that she must learn the *real* way to have a relationship this time, not the must-jump-into-bed-with-him-so-he'll-like-you, kind of way.

Peter, Maddy's "Adonis," is different from any other guy she has dated in the past. With Peter's fresh recommitment to his faith, Maddy would be the first woman he has dated in a year. It is a tale of pure sweetness and beauty as two people learn to love each other under the hand of the Almighty.

Maddy is also coping with her dorm roommate's drama, as well as her plastic surgery obsessed bleach blonde mother, who is persistently critical of Maddy's dyed-black hair and Gothic style.

Can Peter and Maddy wrestle with their desires and keep their thoughts in check and their hands off of each other? Their tale of relationship trials and triumphs will make you laugh out loud and you'll probably cry too, so keep a tissue or two handy.

THE GARDEN KEY, the prelude novel to MIND OVER MADELEINE, is a tale of lust, redemption and really good cheeseburgers that illuminates the urgent need for faith in our lives, especially when it comes to relationships.

www.Angela Dolbear.com *Cloud Pillar Publishing*

Hunk

By Angela Dolbear

I'M NOT LOOKING OVER THERE AGAIN. I'M NOT.

I wish I hadn't seen him walk in. Now I'm all distracted. I'm supposed to be in a state of worship, but instead I'm fighting with lust. I feel like standing up and saying, "Hi, my name is Madeleine, and I'm a lust-o-holic."

Oh, Lord, please help me to stop lusting over this guy. In the name of Jesus I pray, Amen.

"Maddy!" Maggie, my roommate and partner in crime, hisses through clenched teeth. Madeleine!" She jams the offering basket into my elbow, snagging the sleeve of my new crocheted cardigan. I quickly untangled the black thread and pass the basket to the woman sitting next to me.

LUST, you say? Yes, lust. In church no less. How can this be? A fine upstanding Christian young lady about to start her last year of college at a fine upstanding Christian university struggles with one of the most base and primal aspects of the human condition.

I just can't seem to get him out of my head. I do okay for a little while, then something will happen, some situation will come up, and then let the daydreams begin. This whole elaborate scene starts playing in my head like some cheesy chick flick…what I'm wearing, more importantly, what he's wearing, which is usually a black t-shirt that fits snuggly across his broad shoulders, paired with faded worn-in Levi's 501's jeans that look as if they were tailor-made for him. And I even write elaborate dialogue in these daydreams. He usually says something witty that makes me laugh, which is strange, since, well, I've never actually spoken to him.

"So, ya'll get much out of the message today?" Maggie asks, as we cross the crowded church parking lot toward my car.

"Yeah, it was pretty good," I mumble, as we climb into my car.

"Uh huh. I saw you eye-ballin' him. I can't believe you still have a thing for that guy," Maggie says into the mirror while she expertly outlines and paints her matte blood-red lips. She double checks her artistry in the mirror that is clipped on to the passenger's side visor, which she installed in my car during our freshman year. "Hon, I don't know why you just don't go up to him and just say 'hi.'"

"Oh, I don't know. Maybe because I lack the sexual fortitude that others around me exude." *Yikes.* I didn't mean that to sound as biting as it came out, but we've had this discussion too many times in the past for it to not irritate me.

"And just what is that supposed to mean?" she says as she feigns a hurt look.

"Oh, come on Mag, you know I can't," I say glancing at her. "I'd probably trip or fall, or both, and a long dribble of unintelligible gibberish would ooze from my mouth."

I make a quick left turn out of the church parking lot, and into traffic. Maggie shrugs and goes back to her make-up application, digging in her purse for various tubes and compacts.

"He's just a guy," she says into the mirror, while blotting her chin with a powder puff.

With her Dallas drawl, she makes it sound so simple. Like he's just some *gah*, and not my mysterious Adonis. Adonis. A pagan god for my pagan thoughts.

"Just walk up to him and introduce yourself, and let him do the rest," she says, and zips up her make-up bag. "Let him do all the talking. Just smile, look him in the eyes, and touch your hair a lot. Guys love that."

I stifle an outburst of laughter at the mental image of myself doing something like that with my extreme lack of feminine smoothness. Of course Maggie would think talking to guys is simple. Guys always look up when Maggie saunters into a room. I don't know whether it's her big platinum blonde hair styled very closely to the classic Marilyn Monroe coif, or her delicate cheekbones, dark brown exotic eyes and porcelain skin, all of which she inherited from her half-Japanese mother. Or maybe it's just the plain fact that she seems to put "it" out there, and guys take notice.

Maggie describes herself as hip-heavy, "a gal built for comfort and not speed," she once told me. She has three inches and a good fifteen pounds on me and my five-foot, two-inch petite frame. But she wears it so well that it seems like there's always some guy checking her out, wherever we go.

"Hon, it's not that hard," Maggie continues. "Guys only want one thing. And if they think there's even the teeniest chance they might get it, well, then you've got'em hooked."

"Oh, nice advice. From a pastor's daughter no less."

Maggie shoots me a look that would harm, followed with a quick icy pageant smile/tilted-head combo.

"Besides, I'm not sure those kinds of tactics would work on a guy like him," I say.

"Not coming from the Queen of Darkness, they won't," she quips.

I return her icy pageant smile which quickly morphs into a squinty-eyed sneer.

"Maddy, if you are serious about gettin' this guy, you are gonna have to stop dressin' like you raid the closets of the Addams Family on a daily basis. And honestly, did you buy stock in black eyeliner or somethin'?" Maggie asks.

"Have you been conspiring with my mother?"

"Look, I'm just sayin'. Hon, you need to put your curves to work for you. Shoot, if I had your thirty-four-D's and itty-bitty waist, I'd make sure they were prominently displayed instead of hidin' 'em under some big ol' sweater like you always do. Guys are more attracted to girls with those 'personality traits,' if you know what I mean." Maggie gives me a wicked smile.

"Well, that may be true, but I'm not going to change just to attract some guy. Been there. Done that."

"Even for Mr. Mysterious, with the cute butt?"

"How do you know what his posterior looks like?" I glance at her.

"Oh, Hon, Maggie the Cat knows all when it comes to the opposite sex," she says as a knowing grin slides across her face. "Besides, don't play innocent with me. I know your eyes have strayed on more than one occasion. I bet you could even tell me what those little measurement numbers are on the leather tag on the back of his jeans."

I try not to blush. She's right. I do know. After three years of rooming with her at Biola University in La Mirada, California, she knows me all too well.

I haven't always been this way. I was never really into the whole boy-crazy thing. They just weren't my fixation. Not that my world didn't flip upside down for a short period of time whenever a member of the opposite sex would show any inkling of interest in me, especially if he was remotely appealing, and moderately attractive. But my world just didn't revolve around guys like Maggie's world does. That is, until about a year ago.

Oh, Lord, please help me to stop this lust nonsense. He's just a guy. A guy I've never even met. In Jesus' name I ask, Amen.

As I finish my silent prayer, I back my car into the driveway of my mother and stepfather's mini-estate in the swanky part of Chino Hills.

"Anybody home?" My voice echoes off the marble floors and twenty-foot high glass windows in the foyer. No answer. *Thank You, Jesus!* My mother isn't home yet. Maggie and I run upstairs to my room to retrieve the stuff we packed to take to school. Maggie drove in from Texas and stayed the weekend with me, so she could get back to her school-time job at the Victoria's Secret in the Brea Mall before school starts next week, and to keep me company, which I'm grateful for.

I don't mind being home alone most of the time. I enjoy the peace and quiet, and the time to think and dream (yeah, mostly about *him*, I'll confess) without my mother interrupting me with her constant barrage of criticism and general acrimony.

My mother and my stepfather, Dr. Bill, cosmetic surgeon extraordinaire, spend most of the summer traveling through Europe. Usually, they return to the States for a brief stay at the Simpson House in Santa Barbara, California, where my mother recovers in peace and luxury from her latest procedures. Dr. Bill would have undoubtedly not only performed these procedures, but would also stay there with her to oversee her recovery as well.

This summer, they plan to come home directly from Europe. My mother said she had a little more "shopping" to do there and then they would be home, which I'm guessing is code for the fact that she had minor procedures done this time, and doesn't need the extended recovery time in Santa Barbara. It's always fun to see my mother after one of her "vacations" to guess what has been lifted, augmented, and/or completely reconstructed. Someday, I think I will pass her on the street and totally not recognize her.

We load up the backseat and trunk of my Toyota Corolla with Maggie's dorm room stuff she stored at my house for the summer, as well as the boxes filled with my own dorm-life essentials. I carefully place my cherished two-cup coffee maker on the floor behind my seat. We manage to pack up my car and get back on the road before Dr. Frankenstein and his bride return home.

As we drive out of my parents' cul-de-sac, my mind slips into autopilot and instantly starts replaying everything I saw about him in church today. All his movements. The way he walks, the way he runs his hand through the front of his wavy black hair when his head is down and he is reading his Bible. How the back of his long hair fans out across his broad muscular shoulders…*ugh! Stop thinking this junk already! Oh, Lord help me…*

Okay, lust isn't the only thing that is wrong with me, but it seems to be the sin of the day, or year, at least. So what else can I tell you that is wrong with me? Let's see, first off, I'm not your average everyday church girl. I don't have a tapestry cover for my Bible. I'm not what you would characterize as sweet or nice (but I'm working on it). I even tried the "Christian Girl" character on for size for a little while, but it didn't fit. I felt like I was living a lie all the time.

I don't wear white lacy stuff or pastel colors, or stylish matching outfits like Maggie. I think she and I are polar opposites when it comes to fashion. I don't want to get into judging or stereotyping other people, because I don't like it when people do that to me, but God made me different.

I wear black. All black, all the time. I love my new Doc Marten nine-lace-hole black patent leather boots, which Maggie and my mother both detest. I like things that are gothic, dark and edgy, and a little quirky. I like my waist-length coarse mousy brown hair dyed black, much to the dismay of my bleached-blonde mother. And I like tall, black-haired, beefy-built musicians with eyes the color of light green jade. Well, one in particular.

He shops at the music and video store where I work and goes to the same church as me, which I think is peculiarly awesome. He always comes into the store alone. Come to think of it, whenever I see him in the store or at church, he's alone.

I deduced he is a musician since he always buys two packs of GHS Boomers electric guitar strings. Eleven gauge, not the nines the wannabes usually buy. He typically wears a black t-shirt, either plain or with a logo from the latest Grunge band. Oh, and the Levi's. If he ever gets a new pair, that will be a sad day. I know, I know. I shouldn't be talking, or thinking like this. I definitely need help.

So does a person ever stop being an objectified figment of the imagination, and just become a person? It stinks that I have built this guy up in my mind so much, I think that if I ever actually speak to him, I will suddenly be stricken mute or I will completely pass out, and it will probably be on a day that I'm wearing a skirt that will slide up to display a regrettably placed hole in my opaque black tights.

As we turn onto the main outlet street, Maggie and I pull up next to a mini truck with two high school-aged looking guys inside in the second left turn lane on Chino Hills Parkway. They instantly start pointing at us and hooting like a couple of deranged owls. When the traffic light turns green, I burn rubber turning left onto Highway 142, and ignore the infantile cat calls coming from the truck.

"Did you at least get his name this summer?" Maggie asks, craning her neck to smile back at the boys.

"I told you, I haven't spoken to him yet."

"I know *that*. There are others ways to find stuff out, you know."

"Like what?" I dare to ask.

"Like does he ever pay with a credit card or a check? Checks are the best because most of the time you can get the guy's address and phone number." She has picked up a remarkable number of guys working at Victoria's Secret. Go figure.

"No, I don't know," I say. "I've never helped him check out at the cash register."

"Maddy! Why not? That's the perfect opportunity to start a conversation. I bet you purposely let someone else help him, don't you? So you don't have to talk to him."

I feel my lips tighten. I can't speak because what she said is true.

"Yeah, I thought so. You are so hopeless," she hisses, rolling her eyes.

Sometimes I think if I looked more like Maggie or my mother, I would possess the courage to go up and talk to him. It brings to mind a topic of conversion I've had with my mother, once or twice, maybe three or four times now. It usually begins with her addressing me by my full name, which is never good.

"Madeleine Marie Winger, why do you constantly dress like you are in mourning? There are other colors besides black, more *attractive* colors." Sometimes she adds under her breath, which she thinks I can't hear, "you certainly didn't get your fashion sense from me."

Thank God! Most of my mother's skin-tight clothing could be found in the closet of any trend-conscious fifteen-year-old girl. I think she hoped that when I gave my life to Jesus at nineteen, I would start dressing "better," maybe more like her. *Gag.*

"You know, you're not in high school anymore, Madeleine. If you want to attract a nice college boy, you need to start acting and dressing like the college student you are," my mother adamantly informs me.

My mind quickly flashed to visions of pleated plaid skirts and corduroy jackets with contrasting elbow patches. Weird and definitely not me.

"Mom, I'm not going to college just to find a husband, okay? My goal in life is not to get hitched to some guy just because he looks good on paper."

Instantly, I winced at my own remarks, wishing I had not said them. I know. I should be more respectful of my mother, and not give into my sarcastic fleshly tendencies. I'm working on it. One more topic for prayer.

But man, my mother. Doting wife for fifteen years of esteemed plastic surgeon, Dr. Bill Cutter. When she first started dating Dr. Bill, I *so* wanted to call him "Mr. Bill," after the little clay-mation character on my favorite old episodes of *Saturday Night Live*. I was six years old and wished I could have a Mr. Sluggo of my own to deliver me from my mother's new man. I could just hear Dr. Bill exclaiming "Ohhhh noooo," as my Mr. Sluggo pummeled him into a shapeless heap of clay. Yes!

But my mother insisted I address him properly, since doctors deserve respect. That's when I knew. Her persistent defense of him meant that Dr. Bill was here to stay. He was a doctor and she was going to marry him. He would be her new "Wallet," in that he would be able to support her comfortably *and* perform her upkeep at the same time. How convenient.

But Dr. Bill turned out to be a good guy. He treats us both really well, and he's good for my mother. Much better than my real father, I would venture to guess. How she ever ended up with my father, a part-time musician, and full-time off-shore oil rig worker, is beyond me. She skirts the issue whenever I bring it up. She seems miles away from her old life now.

I slow my car as we near the notoriously dangerous S-curves of Highway 142, also known on our local news as "Carbon Canyon Road," since sections of the canyon tend to burn up every year during the fire season in early Fall.

Maggie stares out the window at the passing hills covered with the dry brown brush of August and the groves of old Eucalyptus trees. With a heavy sigh, she studies her long French-manicured fingernails. She's quiet, and seems consumed by her thoughts. Her rare moments of silence usually mean she's frustrated with me.

"Look, I hate that I'm totally infatuated with a guy I've never met," I say, to try to clear the air. "I don't know anything about him or his character. I really don't want to have these intense feelings for him. Besides, I'm not even sure I want a boyfriend right now. I've got enough stuff to think about. Like, what am I going to do after graduation? *Agh!* Why can't I stop daydreaming about him? This sucks."

"I know sweetie," Maggie consoles me. "But I think I know what's really going on in that dyed-black head of yours. You're scared."

"Ding, ding, ding! Tell the lady what's she's won, Bob!"

"What's there to be so afraid of? Of meeting some guy you've had a crush on since Noah went into the ark? You might really hit it off with him. Or not. Maddy, you'll never know unless you *at least* talk to him. Come on, what've you got to lose?"

"A lot." I glance stone-faced at her. Maggie likes to fish for some juicy (gory, more like) details of stuff I did in my life before I asked Christ into my heart. Most of the time I don't like to talk about my B.C. days, unless it's for a good reason.

I pull into the alleyway next to the parking lot of Alpha Chi, the all female dormitory at Biola where we live. Our room is on First Odd, the ground floor hall of rooms on one side of the building. We start unloading our stuff into our room through the emergency exit door, which is left open only during moving days for easy access to the subterranean floor of the dormitory.

The old building smell is strong after being closed up all summer, but the scent is familiar, and not totally unpleasant. We're about to begin our senior year, class of 1998. My last year of college. Holy mackerel.

By the time I make the long hike from the campus bookstore to my dorm room, it feels like my back pack straps have worn trenches into my shoulders, matching the troughs long since dug from my bra straps. I had to buy eleven books for one of my upper division Communication major classes. Eleven. For one class. They're all paperback books, but still. I drop my backpack with a thud on the floor next to my desk. Vile country music fills my ears.

Uh oh. Maggie is lying on her bed with her arm strewn across her face. I know this posture. It usually means some massive drama has transpired in my absence. Something in the universe has gone terribly awry, all while I was at the campus bookstore.

"You okay?" I dare to ask.

"Kill me now! I'm gonna be writin' papers this semester 'til my fingers are worn to the bone!" Maggie flings her arm down to her side.

Phew, just a case of "Syllabus Shock." It usually strikes every semester after the first week of classes. You'd think we would get used to hearing about all the projects and papers we will be required to complete over the semester, but it's still an overwhelming amount of information to receive in one week.

"Anyone call?" I ask while stacking my new books on the shelf above my desk.

"Hmmm…yes. Adonis called for you. He wants you to meet him in the Garden of Eden at midnight. Oh, and he said don't wear anything black. Unless of course, it's a black lace push-up bra with matching black panties!" Maggie gives me another one of her infamous evil smiles.

"Ha, ha. You're sooo funny. I'm astounded by your rapier wit." I hate it when she teases me about him.

"Hey, do you have to work tonight?" Maggie asks, ignoring my sarcasm. "I've been jonesin' for some Del Taco."

Del Taco is classic Southern California Mexican fast food-style cuisine, ideal for college students on a budget. The menu is very similar to Taco Bell, but a little more like real Mexican food. We reserve trips to In-N-Out Burger, the ultimate in SoCal eats, for special occasions. Not that In-N-Out is expensive, it's just special. They make the best burgers ever, especially if you order your Double Double "Animal Style," which means extra everything. *Mmmm.*

"I'm off tonight, but I should go pick-up my paycheck," I tell her.

"Great! It's a date. My treat. Let's blow this joint." Maggie jumps off her bed and begins fixing her face in her vanity table mirror, while I grab my keys and purse.

After a quick bite to eat, we get back in my car and travel the brightly lit streets of Whittier to the local Music Plus. The store is not crowded, but then it usually isn't, not like the Music Plus in Chino where I transferred from when I started going to Biola.

The glass front and sides of the store gleam in the street lights and bright signs from the surrounding buildings. As we walk in the store, Maggie and I are warmly greeted by my co-workers on duty.

"Hey Maddy, I thought you were off tonight?" our resident metal-head Jaime says. He always seems to know my schedule.

"I am. Just picking up my check."

"Cool. You ladies got plans tonight? I'm off at ten."

"Oh, gee Jaime…we've really got to get back to school. Early class in the morning." I grab Maggie by the arm with a squeeze.

She has already slipped into her "Marilyn" posture for Jaime, complete with her index fingernail hanging on her lower lip, and batting her long, mascara encrusted eyelashes at him. I try to pull her toward the backroom door. But as I turn, I stop dead in my tracks. *No, no, no! Not with Maggie here! Oh, Lord, please help!*

There he is. *My crush.* Across the store, standing in the "M" section of the rock CD bins. His head is down and his hair is covering his face as he searches through the discs, but I know it's him. I'd know that lovely mane of black wavy hair anywhere. I turn away quickly. Maybe Maggie won't notice him. Play it cool. Yeah right!

Good. Maggie is still flirting with Jaime, with her chest thrust forward. I focus on the front door. *Keep your eyes straight ahead…don't look over there.* I pull her toward the front door, and quickly wave to my co-workers as we escape out the front door.

"That was quick. I didn't even see you go into the backroom…Hey! Wait a minute!"

Maggie steps back from my car, closes the passenger door, and stands with her hands on her hips. In plain view through the plate glass windows, you can see him inside the store standing in the aisle between the rows of CD bins.

"Maggie, please! Let's go!" I beg her.

"Not a chance, Sugar-pants! It's fate, or kismet, or whatever. A divine appointment."

"Please, Maggie, no! Get in the car! Let's go! I look completely awful right now!" I say, hoping to appeal to her deep-seeded sense of vanity so she will let us go.

"Madeleine, darlin', this is your golden opportunity."

"Come on, Maggie! I'll let you dress me and do my make-up for a day. A whole week! Can we please just go?"

I look Maggie straight in the eye. I feel like I'm going to be sick from the waves of panic crashing down on me. Maggie considers my outfit and appearance consisting of an oversized faded black t-shirt, old black jeans, ailing black Converse Chuck Taylor high-tops, my long hair scraped back in a ponytail, and no hint of make-up. She looks back at the window, and then back at me. With a heavy sigh, she opens the car door and climbs inside.

"Alright, but this is the last time. If we see him at church on Sunday, you *will* go up and talk to him. Or else I will!"

"Hey Maddy, you forgot your check," Jaime calls as he walks toward my car. He is grinning like the Cheshire Cat in Alice of Wonderland. He kind of looks like it, too.

"Oh, thanks, Jaime. I guess I have a lot on my mind." He hands the envelope to Maggie through the open window, and leans down on the car door. His long bleached blond hair falls forward and brushes the top of the open window. I have visions of him and Maggie wearing rubber gloves and sharing a bottle of peroxide.

"You ladies got any plans Saturday night? My band's playing at the Whiskey in Hollywood." He reaches into the inside pocket of his standard issue black Music Plus vest and pulls out two tickets. He hands the tickets to Maggie.

"Well bless your heart, aren't you sweet! Madeleine and I would love to come see your little band play." Maggie is such a bad liar, and I don't think Jaime picks up on her Southern sarcasm either.

I look up at the window, just in time to see a guy with sandy brown shoulder-length curly hair walk up to my Adonis, and say something to him that makes him laugh. Oh, be still my beating heart. What a sweet smile!

"Hey, Jaime, do you know that guy in the store there?" Maggie asks, as she notices me staring at him.

"Which one?" Jaime seems a little dejected.

"The tall one, with the black hair."

"No, not really. But I know his band practices at the same rehearsal room building in La Habra, as my band does. I've seen him there a couple of times. I think he's a guitar player. I've only heard his band play a little. They suck." Jaime says that about all other hard rock bands except his.

"Okay, thanks, Jaime. We've really got to run. I'll see you later." I turn the key in the ignition and release the parking brake.

"Okay. Hey, I'll see you tomorrow. You close, right?" He backs away from my car, and walks back toward the store, waving and smiling.

I give a quick wave, and pull out into traffic. So, I wonder who that was with him tonight. Like I said, I've never seen him with anyone before.

"See how much information you can get if you only ask?" Maggie looks pleased with herself. "Now you know where his band practices."

"Yeah," I mumble. I'm still reeling from the close encounter. Okay. So I will admit it. I'm a little scared to meet this guy. Maybe more than a little scared. Scared, for a lot of reasons.

"So, now we need to come up with a plan." Maggie looks intently ahead.

"Like what? I just happen to show up at some rehearsal studio, when I'm not even in a band?"

Maggie gets a devious look in her eye. "I know! You could—"

"No way! I'm not going to use Jaime."

"Hon, why not? You know he has a major crush on you?"

"Maggie, that is so wrong."

"Oh, come on. It's not like he wouldn't do it to you."

"That doesn't matter. I don't do things like that." I shoot Maggie a serious look. "Besides, if it's meant to happen that I'm supposed to meet this guy, then it will happen."

"What if you miss that opportunity? Like what if it was supposed to 'happen' tonight?"

"It's not time yet, Maggie."

"How do *you* know?"

"I just know."

"Hon, don't you think it's already some kinda providence that this guy goes to the same church as you way out in Chino Hills, and shops in the music store where you work, way out here in Whittier?"

"Yeah, maybe, but I'm not ready for it, okay? So please just drop it, okay?"

"Ready for what? You talk like you're gonna marry this guy!"

Maggie is really starting to irritate me. *Breathe in, breathe out.* "Look, if I do meet him, I'm not ready for any of the potential outcomes, okay?" I try to keep my voice calm. "If I meet him, and he rejects me, I will be devastated."

"Oh, hon, he won't," Maggie tries to reassure me.

"And if I meet him, and we hit it off, and we start dating, I'm afraid of what could happen, you know, being alone with him."

"He's a big strappin' guy, but he doesn't seem the rapist type to me." I'm not sure if Maggie is serious or she's trying to make a joke.

"Maggie. It's not *him* that I'm worried about…

The Feckless Authors

(In Alphabetical Order)

Angela Dolbear   www.AngelaDolbear.com

ANGELA DOLBEAR is honored to serve the Body of Christ as a worship leader and women's ministry leader. She is the author of three other novels, and a study guide for the young adult/new adult series, THE GARDEN KEY TALES, which has inspired many to a closer walk with Christ.

She loves mid-century style, cosmetics, fashion, and all things girly. She also loves her energetic and sweet Lab, Abby, and her awesome husband Tim, who is an excellent care-giver in her battle with scleroderma (and he is cute, and a really good cook. "God is good!" -- AD).

Social Media:
www.AngelaDolbear.com
Instagram: authorangeladolbear
Facebook: Angela Dolbear Author

Bibliography
• The Garden Key (second edition, 2011)
• The Garden Key Reflective Study Guide (2014 Cloud Pillar Publishing)
• Mind Over Madeleine (2014 Cloud Pillar Publishing)
• Fish Out of Water (2016 Cloud Pillar Publishing)
• A Tormentor's Tale (2019 Cloud Pillar Publishing)
• "Expiration Date" (2014 short fiction, Cloud Pillar Publishing)
• "Invisible" (2013 short fiction, Cloud Pillar Publishing)
• The Garden Key Audiobook (Angela Dolbear, Narrator 2014 Cloud Pillar Publishing)
• "Audio First Aid – Trouble Shooting Audio Disaster on the Fly," with Tim Dolbear, Professional Sound Magazine
• CONNECTIONS, Biola University Alumni Magazine, various articles.

Feckless Tales: Hunk (The Garden Key excerpt)

Kat Heckenbach grew up in the small town of Riverview, Florida, where she spent most of her time either drawing or sitting in her "reading tree" with her nose buried in a fantasy novel...except for the hours pretending her back yard was an enchanted forest that could only be reached through the secret passage in her closet. She never gave up on the idea that maybe she really was magic, mistakenly placed in a world not her own. As the years passed, and no elves or fairies carted her away, she realized she was just going to have to create the life of her fantasies. She shares that life with her husband and two homeschooling kids.

A graduate of the University of Tampa, *Magna Cum Laude*, B.S. in Biology, she spent several years teaching, but never in a traditional class-room—everything from Art to Algebra II. Her writing spans the gamut from inspirational personal essays to dark and disturbing fantasy and horror, with over forty short fiction and nonfiction credits to her name. Enter her world at www.kat-findingangel.blogspot.com, where you will find links to more of her stories and artwork, including her illustrations for www.splashdownbooks.com.

Bibliography of short stories:

- "Like Stink on a Dog"—*Daikaijuzine*, February 2011
- "Serpent Uncoiled"—*A Flame in the Dark*, June 2010
- "Dude"—*ResAliens*, April 2010
- "The Gift"—*Digital Dragon Magazine*, November 2009
- "Willing Blood"—*The Absent Willow Review*, July 2009 (Editor's Choice winnner)
- "Clay's Fire"—*The Four Horsemen*, print anthology by Pill Hill Press
- "The Guitar"—*While the Morning Stars Sing*, print anthology by ResAliens

Feckless Tale: *Delete*

Krisi Keley   www.onthesoulofavampire.com

Krisi Keley is a writer and artist with a degree in Catholic theology and education in foreign and classical languages.

Her first novel, *On the Soul of a Vampire*, is Book I in a planned trilogy which examines ideas about good and evil, the nature of the soul, and the unconditional love of God through new theories on the immortal creature of the night.

Krisi lives in Chester County, PA, with her family and eight dogs, currently at work on Books II & III in her trilogy.

Bibliography:

- *On the Soul of a Vampire* (2010)
- *Pro Luce Habere Volume I (On the Soul series Book 2)* (2011)

Feckless Tale: *Valéry*

Other Interests:

Krisi is an accomplished fine artist. Find her art online at www.zazzle.com/kkeleyart

225

Elizabeth E. Little · www.evershadeseries.webs.com

Elizabeth E. Little lives in Central Alabama—a world apart from the realm of shadow and magic that permeates her novels. Her first novel, *Reign of Shadow,* is her escape from reality. With poems published in various hardcover collections, she is working on additional fantasy novels.

Elizabeth is an accomplished professional artist and graphic designer. Currently employed by traditional publisher Little Roni Publishers LLC out of Clanton, AL, she has more than 400 world-wide-distributed book covers to her credit.

Feckless Tales: *Pink-slip, Lab-Rat,* & *Friends*

Have a peek at Elizabeth's terrific artwork under the pseudonym, Hyliian, at www.hyliian.deviantart.com

In 2009, Ellen's first novel, *Rabbit: Chasing Beth Rider*, introduced a peculiar idea to the reading public: redemption from abomination. This message, expertly woven deep within the fabric of her contemporary vampire tales, caused a hunger and a thirst for more. On multiple occasions, Rabbit reaches #1 in several categories on Amazon.com. Ellen invites all *Feckless* readers to taste her Rabbit series, in print and eBook, wherever books are sold.

Pictorial Bibliography

Feckless Tales: *Vegas, Comeback, Victory, Gloves, Tzadik, Runaway, Canaan, 88, Bully,* & *Magier*

▶ Stu Loudon

Stu Loudon has, despite his best efforts, always been considered somewhat 'different' by those around him. Stu lives with his wife and children in Brisbane, Australia where he works as a lawyer. His passion is for seeing people express and celebrate their divinely created individuality and creativity. Stu is also living proof that, despite the rumours, lawyers CAN go outside into the sunlight.
Email: authorstuloudon@gmail.com

Feckless tale: *Thirst*

▶ Kevin R. Maze

Kevin R. Maze has written short stories ("The Wake" appeared in the Winter 1995, No.2 Edition of the literary magazine *Melting Trees Review*) and was a regular columnist for www.critics.com ("Movie Previews"). In 2009, Kevin completed a screenplay with independent filmmaker, writer/director Ron DeSoto (*Plague*). *Wisp: A Small Town Nightmare,* is his first novel, available on Amazon.com.

Feckless Tales: *dtour, Regeneration,* & *Excursion*

Pete has tried his hand in many facets of writing: from short stories, poetry, newspaper articles, church plays, a screen play, to Christian Rock Lyrics. In 2010 he published his first novel.

Whisper a Scream is his first Christian Horror Novel of a trilogy. It tells the story of Solomon Noche, who discovers a cult sacrificing children to a demon in a small town in the hills of Kentucky. It deals with demons, deception, lucid dreams, time travel, and deliverance through Christ.

Whisper from the Woods is book II due out in the spring of 2011. In *Whisper from the Woods*, Noche discovers a serial killer named Silencer (who believes it's his divine destiny to eradicate sin one 'chosen' at a time) has been dumping bodies in the woods behind his home. As he is thrust into a horror adventure through his nightmares, backwards riddles, and a cryptic journal he realizes that the last person he must save is the killer himself.

Pete currently lives in Kentucky with his wife, Tammi, and their four children. He has a BA in Psych from Oral Roberts University and a MA in Counseling from Eastern Kentucky University. He is a Licensed Professional Clinical Counselor in the state of Kentucky.

Bibliography:

- *Screaming Archangel* – Screaming Archangel (Christian Rock CD- lyricist, 2004)
- *Whisper A Scream* (Green Hat Publishers, 2010)
- *"vociferate"* a short story (Digital Dragon Magazine, October 2010)
- *Whisper from The Woods* (Green Hat Publishers, spring 2011)

Feckless Tales: *Shocked & Quack*

Rabbit: Chasing Beth Rider

by Ellen C. Maze

#1 Customer-Ranked in Horror & Occult on Amazon Kindle.

Whoever thought writing a bestseller could be so dangerous?

Author Beth Rider's second vampire novel has hit number one and she is flying high on her new-found fame. But at a fated book signing that runs late into the night, Beth is confronted by an evil she'd only experienced in nightmares…

Praise for *Rabbit: Chasing Beth Rider*

"Maze's storytelling is fast and fun, overflowing with ideas and spiritual insight." ~ Eric Wilson, author of *Fireproof*, and *Valley of Bones (The Jerusalem Undead Trilogy)*

"Riveting and eye-opening…a powerful testament to the often overlooked spiritual strength that lies within us all." ~ *Apex reviews*

"What a great book! It kept me on the edge of my seat, waiting for what was going to happen next. With all the strange powers at work in this world, this book reveals the greatest Power of all." ~ Rabbi John Giddens, *www.ChavurahShalom.org*